MAUREEN JOHNSON

Suite Scarlett

HOT
KEY
BOOKS

First published in Great Britain in 2013 by Hot Key Books
Northburgh House, 10 Northburgh Street, London EC1V 0AT
First published in US in 2008 by Point, an imprint of Scholastic Inc.

A CIP catalogue record for this book is available from the British Library.

ISBN: 978-1-4714-0202-9

1

This book is typeset in 10.5 Berling LT Std using Atomik ePublisher

Printed and bound by Clays Ltd, St Ives Plc

Hot Key Books supports the Forest Stewardship Council (FSC),
the leading international forest certification organisation, and is
committed to printing only on Greenpeace-approved FSC-certified paper.

www.hotkeybooks.com

Hot Key Books is part of the Bonnier Publishing Group
www.bonnierpublishing.com

This book is dedicated to anyone who has ever played a dead body on stage or screen. It takes a big actor to lie on the ground and keep quiet. Droop on, my lifeless friends.

Acknowledgments

Write a book, and you end up with a lot of people to thank. I wish I could list them all, but I don't want this to get so long that you end up thinking this is the first chapter. Just know that there were other people who deserved thanks. Shafted, angry people.

Thanks to my agent, Kate Schafer, my editor, Abigail McAden. I am pretty sure that without these two, I would be in a ditch somewhere, mumbling incomprehensible things about cheese and the Swedish economy. Because of them, this book is in your hands. (Or your hand, singular, if you are one of those read-while-you-eat people. Or stashed in your bag, if you are stealing this book. Or in your robotic claw, if I am addressing Our New Robot Overlords.) Anyway, thank them. And if you don't like this book, please blame them and pretend that I had nothing to do with it.

Thank you to everyone at Scholastic who made me feel welcome and let me play with the Pensieve in the lobby. Special thanks to Morgan Matson, who ran all around New York to fetch the manuscript from many unlikely locations. Also to David Levithan, who is as fine a dancer as he is a writer/editor/teacher/social coordinator/astronaut(?).

John Green, E. Lockhart, and I spent many, many cold New York winter mornings together while the first draft of this book was being written. We shared many hot drinks and a cold or two. Scott "I killed Zane" Westerfeld and Justine Larbalestier fed me many excellent meals and while giving me the most useful notes in the world. Libba Bray made guacamole. Cassandra Clare and I spent an unforgettable night of squalor together that changed us both. Holly and Theo Black bought me a weapon. Collectively, the N.B.s, (you know who you are) provided better advice than the Brain Trust.

Special thanks to the people at the Dreampower Pet Rescue Ranch who found Dizzy and Jake on a bitter Denver night. And to Oscar Gingersnort, who fed and watered me. Oh, and he helped put me out when I accidentally set myself on fire during the final draft, but that is a different story, and not the one you are about to read . . .

ACT I

The Hopewell has been a family-run institution on the Upper East Side for over seventy-five years. It is a jewel box of a hotel, just a slender five stories in the East Sixties, just blocks from Central Park. Furnished in 1929 at the very height of Art Deco style by one of the top designers of the age, J. Allen Raumenberg, it remains a bastion of classic Jazz Age New York glamour. You can practically see the flappers walking across the herringbone lobby floor.

Each guest room is individually named and decorated with the original furnishings, and though time has taken a bit of a toll, they are still a marvel. Of special note is the Empire Suite, the last and most magnificent of Raumenberg's creations. The silver-blue wallpaper is prewar Parisian and is perfectly lit by the delicate, plum-colored crystal Viennese light fixtures and dramatically cone-shaped, rose-colored wall scones. The rosewood furniture was made in Virginia to his specifications, as was the hand-sewing of all the silver and rose-pink silk accompaniments.

The crowning glory, however, is the gigantic round mirror that sits above the dressing table—a sliver of the top smoked out, to look like a moon just on the verge of being full. There is something magical about this room. It has a spirit of romance and possibility that none of the major hotel chains can ever evoke.

Make sure to start each morning with the hotel's signature toasted cherry bread, decadent spiced hot chocolate, and the delicate sweet almond biscuits made by the brilliant in-house baker and chef.

What is most unusual about the Hopewell, though, is the total involvement of the large Martin family who own and run the hotel. Though the service is occasionally patchy, the personal touch makes all the difference....

—THE "WHADDYA SAY WE DO NEW YORK?" GUIDEBOOK, 8TH EDITION

A PARTY BEST AVOIDED

On the morning of the tenth of June, Scarlett Martin woke up to the sound of loud impromptu rap penetrating her thin bedroom wall from the direction of the bathroom next door. Scarlett had been trying to ignore this noise for fifteen minutes by incorporating it into her dream, but it was a difficult thing to weave the constantly repeated phrase, "I got a butt-butt, I got a mud hut" into a dream about trying to hide a bunch of rabbits in her T-shirt drawer.

She blinked, groaned the tiniest groan, and opened one eye.

It was hot. Very hot. The little window unit air conditioner in the Orchid Suite, the room she shared with her older sister Lola, hadn't really functioned correctly in years. Sometimes it left her shivering, and sometimes, like this morning, it did nothing at all except move the hot sheets of air around and give the humidity a nice fluffing up.

Hot weather made Scarlett's blonde, curly hair into a big fright wig. What in winter were chin-length ringlets became insane, puffed-up worm creatures as soon as June arrived. One of these sprung into action and jabbed Scarlett's eye as soon as she opened it. She pulled herself upright in bed and opened the sheer purple curtain next to her bed.

It was a well-known fact that you could *almost* see the Chrysler Building from the Hopewell Hotel, if the other buildings hadn't been there. Still, she could see into the apartment buildings that backed up to the hotel, and that was always interesting. In a city with so many different types of people and so much competition, mornings were an even playing field where no one looked good or knew where anything was. There was the woman who changed her outfit four times each morning and practiced different poses in the mirror. Two windows over, the obsessive-compulsive guy was cleaning all the burners on his stove. A flight down, there was Anything for Breakfast guy who would (as his name implied) eat anything for breakfast. Today he was pouring melted ice cream over cereal.

Another neighbor, a woman of about seventy, was completely nude on the rooftop patio of the adjacent apartment building. She was reading *The New York Times* and carefully balancing a cup of coffee by squeezing it between her thighs, which was a completely unacceptable sight at this time in the morning. Or really, any time.

Scarlett reeled backward onto her bed. The rap got louder as the shower that had been running underneath it was turned off. The lyric had moved on to, "Got shoe and socko, get me a taco..."

"Tell me when you're done in there!" she yelled to the wall. "And shut up!"

The response came in the form of a cheery rhythm beat

against the wall. The rapping continued, but it was quieter.

Scarlett had almost nodded back off when her door flew open and her older brother, Spencer, leapt into her room triumphantly, arms raised above his head, like he'd just won the marathon. His wet hair was standing on end in a post-toweling shake, and his brown eyes were glistening manically.

"I...am...finished!" he announced.

Spencer rarely got to sleep past five in the morning because of his job doing the breakfast shift at The Waldorf-Astoria. Scarlett, who got up at normal-person hours, never saw him in his work clothes—the black pants and stiff white dress shirt that enlonged and slenderized his already very long and slender frame. As he stood over her bed, dripping water from his still-wet head onto her, he looked about eleven feet tall and dangerously awake. Any more than four hours of sleep was too much for him.

"Wake up, wake up," he said, giving her a friendly poke on the top of the head with each word. "Wake up, wake up, wake up, wake up, wake up....Is this annoying? It *looks* kind of annoying, but only you can judge."

"I already saw Naked Lady on the roof," Scarlett protested, swatting at his hand and pulling up the sheet to protect herself. "I'm damaged. Stop tormenting me."

Spencer paused his poking and went to the window. He looked out for a moment as he fastened his cuff buttons, a thoughtful expression on his face.

"I don't know if you noticed where she's holding that mug," he said, "but I'm kind of worried that she might burn herself on the..."

Scarlett squealed and rolled over, stuffing her face into her pillow. When she looked up again, Spencer was leaning against her bureau, loosely looping a black tie around his neck.

"I switched shifts to be here this morning," he said. "I'm doing the host stand for lunch, which is really, really boring. See the lengths I go to for you? Am I your favorite brother?"

"Favorite and only."

"Words that warm my heart. Now, come on." He shook her blanketed foot as he left the room. "We do not get the *waffles* until you rise. So rise! Rise! Rise, sister!" He continued yelling the words, "Rise, rise!" all the way down the hall.

Scarlett slipped out of bed, grabbed her shower basket, and walked to the door. The long cuffs of her blue-and-white striped pajamas scuffed under her feet, getting trapped under her heels and making her stumble. It was even hotter in the fifth-floor hallway, which didn't even have a dysfunctional air conditioner to cool it.

As soon as she stepped out of her room, Scarlett had her second sibling encounter of the day. Her little sister, Marlene, had also just stepped out into the hall, answering the call of the waffle. Marlene took one look at Scarlett, squinting at her through her light hazel eyes that often had a truly disturbing golden appearance. The bathroom would only fit one. Scarlett was just about to open her mouth to begin the negotiation process when Marlene bolted for it, slamming the door shut behind her. Scarlett heard the faint scrape of the lock, and a single, sharp laugh of triumph, not unlike the sound of an angry Canadian goose.

It was 8:03 in the morning. And it was Scarlett's fifteenth birthday.

At 8:15, unshowered, one curl still poking her eye, Scarlett got into the ancient Art Deco elevator. She pulled the gate shut, the outer doors closed, and the elevator made its impossibly slow way down. She leaned against the massive silver sunburst on the back wall—one of J. Allen Raumenberg's (and Scarlett's) favorite touches. The elevator stopped just once to pick up one of their four current guests, a man named Mr. Hamoto who spoke no English at all.

All of their current guests were Japanese, from the same company. Mr. Hamoto nodded briskly, but looked a bit harried. He stared impatiently as the elevator creaked its way down to the lobby, then he almost sliced open his finger trying to get the outer gate open. Scarlett had to politely step in and release the catch. There was an art to it, and if you didn't know it, you could be trapped in the elevator for a while.

She walked through the empty lobby and slid back the doors of the dining room. This was the largest room in the Hopewell—its own little wing, with a high ceiling and a dozen tall, thin windows facing both the street and the building next door. Fifty years ago, this room was packed every morning with guests enjoying a hearty breakfast off prim bone-china plates, served up with silver cutlery and coffee pots emblazoned with the HH monogram. The china had long been chipped and retired. A drug-addled waiter stole the silver in the seventies. The floor was subsiding, the chairs no longer completely matched, and the chandelier was missing pieces.

Still, it was a happy room. It had been designed to amplify the best qualities of each part of the day. In the afternoon, it caught the breeze. In the evening, its diamond-cut top windowpanes caught the sunset and refracted it into a dozen colors. On sunny mornings like this one, it was drenched with light. In the sunniest corner, four tables had been pushed together to create one long family-sized table. There were balloons taped to the backs of the chairs, and blue and yellow streamers fanned down from the ceiling creating a colorful canopy. Scarlett recognized both the streamers and the balloons from Lola's high school graduation party four days earlier. Someone had gone to some effort.

Spencer was already seated, fork in hand.

"I did this," he said, pointing at one of the linen napkins. They had been folded into decorative cone shapes, and each had a single yellow tulip tucked inside.

"No, you didn't," Marlene said sourly, coming in behind Scarlett. "Lola did."

This, Scarlett already knew; she could recognize Lola's handiwork. Spencer had been joking, but jokes were not Marlene's strong point.

"Come," Spencer said, patting the seat next to him. "Sitteth next to me, so that I may chooseth the second-best waffle after you."

Martin family birthday breakfasts followed a strict tradition. First, there were Belgian waffles, made by Belinda, the beloved Hopewell Hotel cook. These were served up with an array of toppings: chocolate syrup, fresh lemon whipped cream, stewed strawberries, and powdered vanilla sugar. The air should have been thick with wafflely perfume. Instead, there was an acrid, confusing smell, undercut by a light touch of smoke.

Scarlett looked to Spencer, and he met her gaze with a raised eyebrow. He smelled it, too.

"That's not right," he said.

The kitchen door swung open, and Lola emerged. She was immaculately dressed in her "beauty scrubs," lean black pants, a slim black T-shirt, and low heels. Her white-blonde, stick-straight hair was wound into a knot.

Lola always looked good. This was just one of the laws of Scarlett's universe. Like Spencer, she was thinner and taller than average. She had tiny, sharp eyes and thin lips, both of which managed to convey fullness. She was universally regarded as beautiful, in an easily-bruised and delicate kind of way. Painters would want to capture her beauty on canvas. Doctors would want to give her a blood transfusion. Such was Lola's appeal.

"Happy birthday!" she said with a smile. "This is really hot. Don't touch it for a minute."

She set down a small jug of chocolate syrup wrapped in a towel. The syrup, usually a gooey pot of chocolaty perfection, looked a bit more like something you might get if you melted down a tire with a pound of butter. Before Scarlett could ask why they were having buttery stewed tire for breakfast, her dad came bursting out with a large plate of waffles.

Scarlett's dad was frequently the most dressed-down of them all. He had an affection for a thrift shop in the village where NYU students tended to shop, so his wardrobe consisted of a lot of vintage T-shirts and hoodies, well-worn jeans, and incredibly strange shoes. (Today, he was wearing his threadbare "My name is Mr. Pineapple" shirt.) People sometimes thought he was their older, blonder brother or cousin. Guests rarely ever thought he was in any way in charge of the hotel, much less its official owner.

"Belinda isn't here today," he said, settling down a plate of deflated, undercooked waffles, topped by a few deeply charred ones. "We did our best."

Truthfully, this was a disappointment. Birthday breakfasts were sacred events, but Scarlett wasn't about to scream in protest. Marlene, however, was more than prepared to do so.

"We can't eat *those*," she said.

"They're not that bad," her dad lied, picking through them. "This one looks okay."

He found one in the middle that looked like it had hit the waffle iron at exactly the right time, purely out of luck. He stabbed it with a fork and lifted it toward Marlene's plate. As usual, Marlene was the center of everything, even on Scarlett's birthday.

Lola was fidgeting with the syrup, even though she was one of the least fidgety people Scarlett knew. Spencer gave Scarlett a long sideways glance. Something was very much not right here.

Her mom followed a moment later, bearing the rest of the breakfast on a tray. There was something vaguely French about their mother—her pale skin and dark eyes and hair, the natural grace and poise (those went right to Lola when traits were being handed out). Like Scarlett, she had a head of thick curls. Unlike Scarlett, hers didn't look like they had been styled in space, where gravity is not a factor.

Her skills with food were not very French, though. It was clear that the whipped cream had come right from a tub in the freezer (and was, in fact, still in the shape of the upturned tub and glistening with ice crystals). The strawberries were raw and unevenly cut, instead of the warm, thick, stewlike version that made Scarlett's heart flutter. The sugar was just a bowl of sugar—not powdered, and not vanilla.

"I guess you heard," she said, giving Scarlett a birthday hug. "We did what we could. I hope it's okay. And, hey—presents!"

There was no choice but to accept the situation gracefully, so Scarlett smiled and thanked everyone. Given the choice between burned and slightly undercooked, she went with the latter and was presented with a floppy, vaguely wafflelike object. Spencer took three charred ones. Lola settled for a spoonful of strawberries. Her dad tried to tough out a plate of whatever was left, but her mom just stirred her coffee nervously. The eating part of the breakfast—usually the longest and most festive—was wrapped up with considerable speed and a lot of untouched food.

"Present time!" her dad announced.

These birthday events were probably the most organized and ritualized things the Martins did. Gifts always followed the same pattern—siblings presented first, oldest to youngest. Then there was the presentation from their parents. This year, however, was special, and Scarlett knew exactly what they would be giving her.

Spencer produced a slightly bent-up envelope from somewhere behind him.

"I know what you like," he said. "Happy birthday."

Inside was a handwritten coupon for a piggyback ride around Central Park. Being seriously broke, he was not above giving the gift of manual labor. Also, he was the closest thing she had to a pony.

Lola came next. She passed forward a brown-and-white striped Henri Bendel box. That was where she worked, and therefore, very likely to be where the gift came from (as opposed to just being a really nice box with crap inside). Her parents and Spencer provided an appreciative chorus of *oohs* and *ahhs*. Inside, there were three very small objects, each wrapped in thick, strong paper that was hard to tear. The first object was a tiny bottle of some kind of blue liquid that Lola promised would "balance" her complexion, which was probably a good thing, even though she had no idea what that meant. The second was a mysterious white tube that was promised to bring further balancing. The third was a distinctive shape—a small rectangular box. A lipstick box.

"It's Chanel," Lola said, even though Scarlett could clearly read the word Chanel on the side. The lipstick it contained was a very dramatic shade of red. It looked like it may have been used once before. The tip was just very, very slightly flattened. Lola sometimes got samples. It was still a really good gift. Lola chose things very carefully, and even if Scarlett didn't quite understand them, they were undoubtedly *right*.

"I think that's a good shade for you," Lola said. "You can handle strong color."

The next came from Marlene, who was picking at her waffle unhappily. It was a coupon for a free dish of ice cream at a store a few blocks away. This shocked Scarlett at first. Marlene

12

tended to have a lot of these kinds of things, but she didn't share them. Then Scarlett noticed that it was expired. That made a lot more sense.

It was time for the gift that everyone had been waiting for. There was a box on the table, which was passed down, hand to hand, until it reached Scarlett. She already knew what was inside, but it didn't make it any less exciting. There were many layers of cardboard protection and plastic bagging to get through, but finally, she could see it, tiny and silvery.

"I hope that's the one you wanted," her dad said.

It was. She was the last person in her entire school to get a cell phone. Literally. She nodded happily. It was nice to join the rest of the planet.

"And here's the other part," her mother said. "Following tradition..."

She passed a jewelry box down the length of the table. Seeing a box like that, most people would have expected a necklace or a bracelet, but Scarlett knew that was not what was inside.

When it reached her, she creaked the box open to reveal a key ring with a silver S dangling from it, along with a single key. A tiny piece of paper, the size of a Chinese fortune cookie fortune, rested at the bottom. It read: EMPIRE SUITE.

"It's yours now," her father said. "Take good care of it."

At age fifteen, each Martin was "given" a room in the hotel to care for. This was not an ancient tradition—it had started with Spencer four years earlier. He had gotten the rough-and-ready Sterling Suite. Lola had the attractive but small Metro Suite. The Empire Suite was something else entirely—the showpiece, and the most expensive of the hotel's twenty-one guest rooms. It was rarely occupied, except for the occasional honeymoon couple or the lost businessman who couldn't get a room at the W.

So this was either an honor or a "we don't actually want you to have to deal with any guests" gesture.

Before Scarlett could even react, her mother was on her feet, sweeping away the grim remnants of breakfast. Spencer was still shoving waffle embers into his mouth when his plate vanished from underneath him.

"We're just going to go over some of the new cleaning routines," her dad said. "Marlene, if you want to go..."

It would hardly have been possible for Marlene to leave the room more quickly, at least without the aid of some kind of an engine. It was instantly clear to Scarlett that whatever was about to happen had nothing to do with cleaning. That was just the only topic that could instantly drive Marlene away.

"We all need to have a little talk," her father said, getting up and sliding the dining room doors tightly shut.

SINK, SANK, SUNK

Perhaps it sounds like a wonderful thing to be born and raised in a small hotel in New York City. Lots of things sound fun until they are subjected to closer inspection. If you lived on a cruise ship, for example, you would have to do the Macarena every night of your life. Think about that.

There are always tourists in New York. They come in droves in the fall and winter, cruising in through the tunnels in massive out-of-town coaches. Between Thanksgiving and New Year's, the city's population seems to double. There are no tables in restaurants, no seats on the subway, no room on the sidewalks, no beds in the hotels.

But by summer, most of them have gone. The city boils. The subways swelter. Epic thunderstorms break out. Stores have sales to get rid of unwanted goods. Theaters close. Even many of the inhabitants leave. Certainly, most of Scarlett's friends had. Dakota was at a language immersion program in France. Tabitha was doing volunteer work for the environment in Brazil. Chloe was teaching tennis at a camp in Vermont. Hunter was with his father, helping him run a film festival in

San Diego. Mira had gone to India with her grandparents to sweep temples. Josh was doing some kind of unspecified "summer session" in England.

Every single one of them was off doing something to beef up their college applications—and set them apart from everyone else. Even Rachel, who was the only other person she knew who had to work, was doing it at a gourmet beachside delivery shop in the Hamptons. They were off being developed, molded into perfect applicants.

Only Scarlett was in the city for the summer, not doing anything to improve herself. It wasn't laziness or lack of ability. She was more than willing and able. The question was entirely one of funding. Hotels make money—but they also bleed it. Especially hotels with fragile decorations and plumbing from 1929 that sit empty much of the time.

This was all part of the reason that Scarlett knew that this "little talk" probably wasn't going to end up being a discussion about going to Paris or bringing a live koala into the lobby to give hugs to all the guests.

"Scarlett," her father said, sitting back down, "you're old enough now to be included in these discussions. I'm really sorry we had to do this today—now—but there's no other time."

Scarlett looked at Spencer nervously, and he tapped his foot against hers reassuringly. His expression, however, was anything but relaxed. He shifted his jaw back and forth, and kept puffing air into and hollowing out his taut cheeks.

"As you may have guessed," her mother began, looking to Scarlett first, "things have gotten a little tight recently. I'm afraid Belinda didn't call out today. We had to let her go."

Scarlett was too shocked to speak, but Spencer let out a low groan. Belinda was the last regular staff member. The others had gone over the course of the last two years. Marco, who handled all the facilities and repairs. Debbie and Monique, the cleaners. Angelica, the part-time front desk person. And now Belinda...the last remaining draw to the hotel. She of the spicy hot chocolate and cherry bread that people raved about.

"We'll get by," her father said, "just like we always have. But we have to get serious about a few things. We're going to be counting on all of you. Lola, as you two probably know, is taking a year off to work at Bendel's and to help us out here, especially with Marlene. And we're really grateful for that."

Lola looked down modestly.

"Scarlett," he said, looking a bit nervous now, "we have a big favor to ask of you. We know you plan on looking for a summer job..."

It wasn't just a plan—it was a desperate need. A job meant money for clothes, for movies, for basically anything above and beyond eating lunch and getting her Metrocard for the subway. It was the money everyone else in her school just got handed to them in the form of a credit card.

"...but we're going to need some of your time. Possibly a lot of your time...looking after the front desk, answering the phone, cleaning up. Things like that. We'll try to up your allowance a little when you go back to school to make up for it."

It didn't seem like something that could really be argued. The reality of life without Belinda, with no staff at all, was simply too stark.

"It doesn't sound like I have much of a choice," she said.

Spencer and Lola were both giving her looks of pure sympathy. But the meeting was far from over. Everyone turned to Spencer. He drew in his cheeks completely and looked as innocent as you could with a sucked-in face.

"Spencer," her mother began slowly, "last year, when you graduated from high school, we all made an agreement. You had one year after graduation to get things together. One year to get a paying acting job in TV, or film, or commercials, or Broadway. Something that pays."

"I've been to more callbacks than anyone I know," Spencer said. "It's a tough business."

"And we're proud of you," she replied. "We know how good you are. But the year is going to be up in three days. You promised that if you didn't have acting work, you would accept the offer to the culinary academy. You got a year's deferment, but in order to get the scholarship, you have to agree by then."

"Three days," Spencer said, exhaling slowly.

There was a moment of heavy silence, during which the fumes from the waffles got slightly more intense.

"Having dumped all of that on you," her mother said, obviously feeling guilty, "we'll clear up the kitchen, and you guys can talk this out a little. We just needed to put it all in front of you, and this was the only time we could do it. And, Scarlett, we'll talk tomorrow about the specifics. Enjoy today."

"Enjoy today?" Scarlett repeated, when they were gone.

"Yeah," Spencer said, shaking his head. "Bad close. Very bad. No points for style. Really, it sucked through and through. In fact, I think that was the most suck ever compacted into ten minutes. You couldn't cram any more in."

Scarlett noticed a black car stopping in front of the building. She couldn't see it very clearly through the window at that distance, but she knew who was in it. So, apparently, did Spencer.

"I stand corrected...." he said, eyeing the car.

"I have to go," Lola said apologetically. "I had no idea about all of...this...until this morning when I came down to decorate. I have to go to a breakfast with Chip before work."

Spencer examined the contents of the now cold-and-gluey syrup, sticking his finger in the jug and pulling out the thick film. He seemed to consider dropping this in his mouth for a moment, then decided against it and scraped the tarlike substance off with the butter knife.

"*A* breakfast?" he said mildly. "Didn't you just have a breakfast?"

"It's for his dad's investment partner's birthday," Lola answered. "They're having a little breakfast thing at their club before they go out on the boat for the day. I'm not going to eat—I just have to put in an appearance before I go to work."

Spencer had never quite forgiven Lola for dating Chip, Durban School's senior class secretary, Gothamfrat.com's #98 on the "New York's 100 Top Prep School Scenesters" list. Spencer took a lot of glee from the fact that Chip only made ninety-eight, considering that someone at Durban wrote the list in the first place. That had been his nickname ever since.

"One doesn't want to be late for one's appearance at the club," Spencer said. "One doesn't want to start talk. Give

Number Ninety-eight my love and kisses."

Lola gracefully ignored this little needling by stacking all the used silverware on her plate.

"It's free makeover day at the store today," she went on. "It's going to be tragic. Every tourist in New York is going to be there. I'll try to get back as soon as I can, and we can talk. And, Scarlett...happy birthday. It'll be okay."

She hurried out, her heels just barely clicking against the herringbone floor. She slid the doors shut behind her gently, leaving Spencer and Scarlett alone with the remains of the party. Spencer got up and watched as Chip greeted Lola outside the car.

"I don't get it," he said. "She never even smiles around him. Back when I had girlfriends, I looked happier than that, didn't I?"

Spencer had never been short of company in high school. He had been quite the ladies' man. That had dried up in the last year, along with his work prospects.

"I have *literally* been more passionate with a fake streetlight," he said.

"You were in *Singin' in the Rain*," Scarlett pointed out.

"That didn't make it any less real. The worst part was—that streetlight didn't even call me the next day."

Scarlett couldn't even bring herself to smile at the joke. Instead, she pulled down a balloon and pressed her face into it, letting herself sink into a world colored in cheerful, rubbery yellow. She bounced her chin against the balloon a few times and let it fall to the floor, where it promptly popped on a small piece of splinter that was coming up from one of the boards.

That was her summer in a nutshell. Boom.

"I needed a job," she said. "Everyone else at school just gets cash to spend. Now I'm just going to be stuck here every day, doing the wash and getting evil looks from Marlene."

Spencer turned from his spying. He had too much respect for her to deny that she had a point.

"I'm sorry this is how your birthday turned out," he said. "But all jobs suck. You might as well have a sucky job that you don't have to get up early to go to. Plus, they can't fire you."

"I guess," she said glumly. "But what about you? We only have three days."

"I'll do...something. I'm going to call every single person I know in the entire world. Maybe somewhere out there...maybe something will come up."

Scarlett slumped further in her chair and stared up at the chandelier. From this angle, she could see the thick membrane of spiderwebs that seemed to hold it together.

"Look," Spencer said, stepping away from the window, "it'll be..."

Just as he moved, his foot seemed to get stuck. He tripped hugely, taking flight before landing face-flat on the floor with a loud, painful smack. Even though he had been doing that trick her entire life, it never failed to get her. The painful smack was his hand slyly hitting the floor to sell the gag. She laughed out loud despite herself.

"Just checking," he said, looking up from the floor. "I was kind of worried your face would stick like that."

He reached for the little table to pull himself up, then

jerked and almost fell over again. For a second, Scarlett thought he was doing another gag. Then she saw that no, the table leg had just given. He caught it before it tipped and propped it back up with a whack to hold it in place.

"No matter what," he said, "promise me one thing. No matter what happens here, no matter how broke we get, promise me you'll never do that."

He pointed in the direction of where the long-gone Mercedes had been.

"Get in Chip's car?" Scarlett asked.

"Date a bank account instead of a person," he said. "Or anybody I don't like."

He looked at his watch, which was currently being held together by electrical tape.

"I have to go, too," he said, picking up his backpack from the floor under his chair. "We'll talk later. Don't worry. We'll figure it out."

He ruffled her curls as he passed. He was the only person allowed to do that.

Scarlett picked up the Empire Suite key from the table. This was her fifteenth birthday. No job. No prospects. No exciting, life-changing project. Just an empty hotel room, some leftover balloons, and a bunch of people telling her how it was going to be fine, and obviously lying.

"I need a plan," she said to it. "Something needs to give. What do I do?"

The key did not answer, because keys generally do not speak. This was probably a good thing, because if it *had* replied, Scarlett's problems would have taken on a new level of complexity.

THE GOOD SHIP REALITY HAS DOCKED

Generally speaking, New York City is a good place to spend your birthday. You can go to a show, you can shop, you can eat and see the sights. There is very little you *can't* do in New York, if you set your mind to it.

The problem, however, is if you are alone and broke. If you have about sixteen dollars left to your name, with no prospect of getting many more...if your friends have scattered around the globe, your older sister is working a ten-hour shift, your younger sister probably wouldn't put you out if you were on fire, and your brother, who would normally have spent the day with you, is out trying to save his career...it's not all it could be. Especially if you live there, and have therefore seen all the sights, because the "sights" are really just the "things on your street."

If you add to that the fear that your family is on the verge of total financial collapse, you have the makings of a birthday that is memorable for all the wrong reasons. You should probably go back to bed.

Scarlett tried to make the most of her day. She wandered around some stores and went to Central Park. She'd even gotten away with using the expired ice-cream coupon, which felt like a minor victory. When it got too hot and walking around got tiring, she went home and sat on her bed with her computer.

Her computer was one of the things in life that made her very happy, despite the fact that it was old and very slow. It was a hand-me-down from Chloe, who got new computers and phones on a regular basis. Aside from Marlene, Scarlett was the only Martin with a personal computer; everyone else shared the one at the front desk.

This was especially useful since Scarlett liked to write—and you didn't need money to do that. She could be one of those people who published a book at age fifteen and went on to worldwide fame and fortune and didn't have to scam ice-cream places with expired coupons.

That sounded very appealing, so she spent several hours trying to string together some meaningful sentences. She tried to write about what she knew—but what she knew didn't seem very interesting. No one was going to want to read about getting stuck in the elevator or missing subway trains or having furniture break underneath you.

Lola came home at a little after eight, and went immediately to take a post free-makeover-day bubble bath. The tiles, massive clawfoot tub, sloped high ceiling, and skylight in the bathroom next to the Orchid Suite created a perfect echo chamber, enough noise to easily penetrate the thin walls—so Scarlett never got to miss a thing in terms of the bathroom activities. It was just one of those little bonuses that life had thrown her way.

Scarlett's writing process was therefore interrupted by Lola and Chip's phone conversation. Tonight's was all about shirts. Granted, she was only hearing Lola's end of it, but this was still pretty clear. Spencer was right—their conversations weren't exactly romantic. This one certainly wasn't. Who made the highest count cotton dress shirts? Was tawny rose just pink, was pink what he really wanted, and if so, was it *this* pink? Was it better just to get shirts made? If so, by whom?

So very, very boring. Everything was boring.

Scarlett listened to the distant droning on about shirts and stared at the screen. Nothing was coming to her now—nothing but thoughts about shirts. She put on her headphones to block it out.

A few minutes later, Lola returned to their room, wrapped in her silky, pink knee-length robe. She sat down on her bed primly, knees tucked together, and stared at her dresser. She cocked her head slightly, following its angle. One of the legs had come off years ago and been replaced by one that was a centimeter or two too short.

She let out a light, airy sigh. Lola was often like this when she finished talking to Chip. Not exactly sad, but not brimming with excitement, either. Tonight, she seemed a bit more pensive than usual. She picked up her brush and stroked her hair slowly.

"Problem?" Scarlett asked.

"Something's come up tomorrow," Lola said. "I have to go somewhere with Chip. But I'm supposed to be taking Marlene to an event in the morning."

"Oh," Scarlett said sympathetically. Marlene was strictly Lola's job, because Marlene pretty much refused to go anywhere with anyone else.

"I was wondering if you could do it, since you're not...well, working. And it won't take long."

"Me?" Scarlett gasped.

"Well..."

"Don't you, um, have work?"

"I took off," Lola said. "Or, I will in the morning. I'll call in sick. She really likes going places with you. She just doesn't know how to show it."

Scarlett leveled a look at her sister that could have penetrated a cement barricade.

"It's really not that bad," Lola said. "Honest. I won't forget this. I will owe you, and you know I'm good for it."

Lola was actually good for these kinds of things. She very much operated on the system of doing and returning favors. Her credit was impeccable. That wasn't the problem. The problem was Marlene would burst a blood vessel. She would scream and howl and make all their lives a misery.

Before Scarlett could point out this incredibly obvious fact, there was a rapid knock on the door. After a short decency pause, Spencer let himself in without preamble. He went airborne and landed hard on Scarlett's bed, causing her frail computer to bounce. She grabbed and stabilized it before it exploded into its component parts.

"I have news," he said. "Remember how I told you that I was going to call everyone I knew? It turns out that one of my friends from school knows these people who are doing *Hamlet*.

26

One of their cast members just got cast in a touring company of *Mamma Mia*, like, yesterday. So he's leaving, and they called me to come in and read for the part."

"Spence," Scarlett said. "That's amazing! You're going to be Hamlet!"

"Well, not Hamlet. I'm up for Guildenstern, one of Hamlet's guys—and also one of what the script calls *two clowns*, who are actually unfunny gravediggers. Here's the thing, though. This isn't just a straight-up *Hamlet*, it's kind of like a carnival. It's the happy *Hamlet*. Until everyone dies, including the guy I would play. But until we bite it, we basically run around like idiots through the whole show."

"So it's perfect for you," Lola said earnestly.

"Pre*cisely*," Spencer replied. "The list of stuff they wanted is pretty much the entire bottom of my resume...lots of fistfights and falling."

"Which you do," Scarlett said happily. "Better than anyone. It's the perfect part!"

Spencer scratched under his chin thoughtfully for a moment.

"Which is good, right?" Scarlett said.

He scratched some more.

"There's kind of a catch," he said.

"Catch?"

"It's with this group called First National Bang Theater Company, and this show is their Shakespeare in the Parking Garage production. Technically..."

He held up one finger at this.

"...technically, it's on Broadway. Just, really far down Broadway."

Lola sighed.

"You mean it's on the *street* called Broadway, right?" Scarlett said.

"Right. But no one ever said what that meant, specifically. So I can say the theater is *on Broadway*, which it is, and no one can call me a liar."

"Spence," Lola said. "That's not Broadway. That's not what they meant in your deal."

"Does it pay at least?" Lola asked.

"Subway fare counts, right?"

Lola played with the belt on her robe and said nothing.

"I *need* this play," he said. "Agents will come to this. Casting directors will come."

"You want to do *Hamlet* in a parking garage instead of going to school?" Lola said. "Spence, you know that scholarship offer is about to expire. Can't you figure out a way to do both? It's full tuition. And we need a cook."

"I know what it is," Spencer replied, squaring off to Lola. "But in exchange for the money, they farm me out to restaurants for forty hours a week. That's on top of full-time classes. How am I supposed to act when I'm working eighty hours a week? For *two years*. Also, even if I did it, I really don't want to work in *this* place my whole life."

He held up his hands as if to say, "You see my problem."

"I guess," Lola said, without much conviction. "But it still couldn't hurt, Spence. I mean, you'd be a trained chef with lots of experience, and you could always fall back on that."

"Well," he said, "I realize not all of us date millionaires. They're pretty good to fall back on, too. All that nice, soft cash."

28

He propelled himself off Scarlett's bed before Lola could reply.

"Anyway. Gots to go. Have to prepare."

He patted Lola's head as he bolted out the door. Lola carefully pulled the loose strands of her long blonde hair from her brush and thoughtfully wound them around her finger.

"I know you think I'm being hard on him," she said quietly. "But I think at some point, you have to get practical."

"Define practical," Scarlett said. "Because it sounds like you're saying he should give up. Spencer is a good actor."

"I know that," she said. "I know it's hard for him. I get it. And I know that's why he makes fun of Chip because he's well-off."

"He's rich," Scarlett corrected her.

Lola cocked her head to the side noncommittally. She never said that Chip was rich. The word seemed vulgar to her. It was always *well-off* or *comfortable*, but the real word was *rich*. The pink diamond stud earrings that sparkled demurely when she tucked her hair behind her ears, the stack of stubs of opera and ballet tickets...these were all reminders that while Lola was still a Martin, she spent some of her time in a very different world.

"There's nothing wrong with what Chip is," Lola said. "Having money doesn't make him a bad person. Spencer is hung up on this idea of being a poor actor."

"I don't think he wants to be poor. He wants to work."

"Nobody wants to be poor. But you need to use some sense if you want to avoid ending up that way. Look at us. Look at where we live."

"You make it sound like we live in a burned-up car under a bridge," Scarlett said. "We live in a hotel, in the middle of Manhattan."

"Exactly. This place is worth millions. We should be rich, too. But we're not. I'm pretty sure we barely own this place anymore. We can live in it, but if we left it, we'd have nothing but debt. This place owns *us*."

There was a slight edge creeping into Lola's usually calm voice that unsettled Scarlett.

"It's not that bad," Scarlett said.

"Not that bad? Scarlett, where are your friends this summer, while you're here?"

This was a bit of a low blow.

"All I'm saying," Lola went on, returning to her reasonable tone, "is that we all have to face the fact that we live here, and that things are like they are. Mom and Dad break their backs to keep things going. They do every job now. He's had a year to try. And if there is a scholarship offer, he should take it."

Scarlett's eyes automatically turned to the graduation cap that sat on the top of Lola's dresser.

"What about you?" she asked.

"Don't worry about me," Lola said, getting up and opening her armoire. "I have my year now to figure out what I want to do next. I have my job, which I love. And in the meantime, I have somewhere I have to be tomorrow. So, is it a deal? Because if it is, I have something special for you to wear."

She lifted out a plastic garment bag attached to a thickly padded hanger. She hung this on the edge of the door and unzipped it, revealing a sleekly-cut black summer dress—light enough for day, dressy enough for night. The perfect dress. It was Dior. Chip had purchased it for Lola two months before for some event that required a designer label. This was Lola's biggest gun—the most valuable thing she owned, aside from the pink diamonds.

"This must be important," Scarlett said.

"It would mean a lot to me."

"Where exactly would I be taking her?"

"Somewhere fun!"

"Seriously, Lola. Where am I taking her?"

"To the set of *Good Morning, New York*!" Lola said. "You don't have to do a thing. Just sit in the audience while they stand around doing something for a segment on healthy cooking. I promise you. It'll take two hours. That's all."

She waggled the dress and smiled her sweetest smile.

"That won't fit me." Scarlett said skeptically. Lola was taller, but Scarlett was far curvier.

"Of course it will!" Lola said, refusing to be daunted. "We're almost the same size. In fact, this will look *better* on you than me. You can fill it out in the right places."

It was clear that Lola was determined to make this work.

"Why not?" Scarlett said, turning back to the futile effort struggling along on her screen. "Might as well start the summer on a high note."

THE GOOD BURN

When Scarlett woke the next morning, Lola was already awake and out of the room. Scarlett found that her hair had grown during the night, like a mushroom, and her curls clung to her eyelashes. She grabbed her shower basket and stumbled out into the hall, half-blinded.

The bathroom door opened just a sliver, and the smell of burning hair slithered through the crack. Spencer was long gone, and Lola's blonde locks were so fragile that she never used any heating devices on them. That left one person.

"Marlene?" she asked the crack. "Are you on fire?"

The door was *foomped* shut as hard as it could be, which wasn't very hard. The door was a little crooked and didn't shut completely.

"Just tell me if there are actual flames coming off your head," Scarlett said, patiently leaning against the wall.

"Shut up."

Scarlett nodded. Marlene couldn't be on fire and telling her off at the same time. Well, maybe she could...but she couldn't be a complete fireball, and that was what mattered.

"I'm going to need the shower, too," she said.

"I'm busy."

It didn't sound like Marlene knew about the switch yet. She wouldn't have been talking to Scarlett at all if that were the case.

"Can I just..."

Foomp. The door stuck shut this time. Marlene must have hit it hard.

It was a complicated thing having a cancer survivor for a little sister.

There was a time—thought it seemed like a *long* time ago—when Scarlett remembered liking being an older sister. She took Marlene on the carousel in Central Park. She took her for ice cream down the block (as long as Spencer or Lola walked with them long enough to help them cross Second Avenue). And then, one day when Scarlett was eleven and Marlene was seven, Marlene got cranky. A few days later, they first saw the little bluish lump on Marlene's neck. A week later, it hadn't gone away, and it was joined by another bluish lump under her arm. She went to the doctor's office one afternoon and didn't come home that night.

That was the beginning of it all. The disease entered all of their lives.

Marlene was in and out of the hospital for seven months. What leukemia really was...what it really meant...Scarlett didn't really get the details. She understood more from watching how the rest of the family reacted. Her parents stopped paying as much attention to the hotel. They did what they needed to, but they reserved most of their energy for the hospital. They closed doors more often, physically huddled together more.

Lola, at thirteen, was already very responsible, very popular, very perfect. She could easily have become a queen of her class, but she softened her ambitions to spend as much time with Marlene as she could. She started doing things around the hotel without being asked.

Spencer, at fifteen, still messed around—but Scarlett noticed that he started to make much more deliberate efforts not to get hurt. He went to the hospital regularly to entertain Marlene, covered up his excesses carefully (and there were plenty), and picked up all the slack when it came to Scarlett. While everyone else was busy, they cemented their already strong bond.

And so, the pairs were set, and they had never altered. It was Lola and Marlene, Spencer and Scarlett from then on.

The Powerkids were Marlene's "class"—part of a charity surrounding the group of kids in her unit. Even though she had been in remission for two years, the Powerkids were still the center of her life. The Powerkids gave Marlene a social calendar that easily rivaled Lola's. She went to basketball games at Madison Square Garden and baseball games at Yankee Stadium. She saw the Rockettes every Christmas. She went on special tours of the Bronx Zoo where they let you feed the monkeys. She had met the mayor, at least a dozen major league sports players, and a handful of TV stars. She had also gotten to switch on the lights on top of the Empire State Building one night.

It had definitely crossed Scarlett's mind once or twice that having cancer was a serious boost to your social life.

She went back to the Orchid Suite and sat on her bed. A

fat pigeon landed with a heavy thump on the outside of the window air conditioner and stared in at Scarlett. It shook out some feathers and squatted there, apparently finding her an engrossing sight.

Lola entered, smiling brightly and carrying a steaming mug of coffee, which she handed to Scarlett. Lola was already dressed in a pretty white sundress, imprinted faintly with white dots. Her fair hair was wound into a loose knot on the back of her head, and her pink diamond earrings flashed warmly.

"She won't let me shower," Scarlett said.

Lola looked at the dress hanging from the wardrobe door worriedly, then fished around in the Drawer of Mysteries—the massive, slightly unstable top drawer of her dresser in which she kept special samples of expensive products and magical clothes-fixing devices. She removed a small baby-blue package of what appeared to be wipes of some kind.

"These are amazing," Lola said, delicately drawing a wipe from the pack. "They have verbena, Turkish sea salt, vitamin A, sage, and ginger."

"Do I eat it?" Scarlett asked, taking the wipe by the corner as it was offered. "Sounds healthy."

"It's about twenty times better for you than soap," Lola said with a smile. "They're a hundred and fifty dollars a pack and very, very effective. I only have them because the company rep likes me."

Lola resealed the pack with the same kind of care that doctors use when packing up organs for emergency transport. Then she left for a few moments to let Scarlett rub herself down in spicy-herby-salty goodness. At first, it was freezing cold. Then her skin tingled wherever the rub had touched. Actually, it almost burned—but it was a strange cold-burn. The wipes clearly did *something*. She wrapped her pajama top around herself and stood there shivering in the heat.

"Feel clean?" Lola asked, as she came back in.

"Clean, and kind of rashy."

"That's the ginger," Lola said. "It's stimulating your pores."

"Is that a good thing?"

Lola's smile said that it was impossible for pore stimulation not to be a good thing.

"Now," she said. "I just need to get you some things. Drink your coffee."

Scarlett sat and sipped while Lola dug around in the next drawer, the one filled with perfectly folded panties, spooned together bras, floral sachets, and tiny packets of special detergents for the most delicate materials.

"Here we go," she said, lifting a complicated adjustable bra from her drawer. It looked like something that had been removed from a parachute, all clamps and straps and impossible-to-disengage safety features. She helped fasten Scarlett into it, then removed the dress from its padded hanger and handed it over.

"What is this thing you're going to?" Scarlett asked.

"A clambake."

Scarlett stopped with the dress halfway down her face.

"You're leaving me with Marlene for a clambake?"

Lola pulled the dress down and shifted it into place. It strained a bit over her hips, but it eventually gave.

36

"This looks great on you," she said soothingly. "It's a little long, but I can fix that by tying this a little tighter."

The dress tied at the back of the neck. Lola adjusted it carefully. It was only when everything was moored in place that Scarlett was allowed to put on deodorant.

"Clambake," Scarlett muttered. "Chip and the clambake. It sounds like a mismatched partner cop comedy."

"See? You haven't lost your sense of humor."

"I haven't gone anywhere yet."

"Come on." Lola steered Scarlett in front of the mirror. "Let me fix your hair."

For a non-curly-haired person, Lola could handle Scarlett's anarchist hair with surprising skill. More products were pulled from the magic drawer. A curl was pulled out here, scrunched up there. Two types of fine mist were sprayed, and a small amount of a light-as-air waxy substance was snapped over the tips.

"Perfect," Lola said. "Why don't you try out the makeup I got you yesterday? That red lipstick would be fabulous with this. I'm going to go tell Marlene what's going on."

Scarlett twisted up the lipstick as Lola went next door. She heard the whole conversation through the wall.

"Guess what!" Lola said. "Scarlett's going to take you today!"

This had exactly the effect that Scarlett had predicted.

"*Why?*"

"Because I have to go somewhere with Chip."

"*Where?*"

Marlene had a journalist's instinct for questioning.

"Just somewhere."

"I want you to take me," Marlene said. "It's *TV*."

Scarlett resented the implication that she was somehow less worthy to sit in a studio audience than (the admittedly photogenic) Lola, but she was used to this kind of thing from Marlene. She twisted the lipstick open and carefully tapped it against her lower lip. The color was strong.

"Come on," Lola said coaxingly. "It'll be just as good."

"No, it won't."

"My little sister loves me so much," Scarlett said quietly to the mirror. "I am her *favorite*."

There were general moans of protest now. A low whine. These were coupled with soothing words from Lola as she tried to tame Marlene into submission. Scarlett rolled her eyes. Only Marlene could throw a temper tantrum about who was going to take her on one of her countless interesting trips.

"It's a favor," Scarlett heard Lola say. "Just for me. I'll tell you what. You go with Scarlett today and, later this week, I'll bring you into the store and get you a makeover. Deal?"

There was a pause and a banging around of what Scarlett assumed was the curling iron. Hopefully Marlene wasn't trying to scorch a hole in the wall with it to stare at her through. It wouldn't have surprised her, though.

"Fine," Marlene finally said. "I have to finish my *hair*."

Lola returned, a mask of placid innocence on her face.

"She's trying to look like you," Lola said, smoothing down her dress. "You should be flattered."

"Somehow, I don't think that's what she's doing."

"That lipstick is perfect," Lola said, deftly switching subjects. "Told you. You really need to go for bolder colors. You have the skin and the hair for it. Some people spend thousands of dollars a year and fry their hair to a crisp trying to get your shade of blonde or those kind of curls."

Lola was always sincere. That's why it was hard to deny her anything.

"Speaking of frying hair, you should probably keep an eye on her," Scarlett said, running the lipstick over her bottom lip one more time. "I'll be ready in a few minutes."

Scarlett was poking around in her closet for some shoes when her phone rattled on the dresser. It was the front desk.

"Get down here now," her mother whispered urgently. "Now—*now*. Whatever you're doing, drop it."

There was something in her voice that told Scarlett this was no drill. She shoved on a pair of flip-flops and ran.

A GUEST ARRIVES

There was no one behind the desk when Scarlett answered the emergency call—and no one had put out the WE'VE JUST STEPPED AWAY. PLEASE RING THE BELL FOR SERVICE! sign.

"Mom?" Scarlett said, hoisting herself up and looking over the desk.

Her mother was not crouching underneath.

Scarlett looked around in bafflement, then went behind the desk and sat down.

A tall woman suddenly stepped from behind the archway leading to the dining room. She had short, deep brown hair, cut through with an even darker streak, like a chipmunk. She wore skinny jeans on the bottom and a pink kimonolike shirt on top. Scarlett had seen lots of similar items in Chinatown, but there was something about the way the material hugged her form so gracefully, how the pink was soft and muted instead of super shiny...something told her that this was the real deal. Silk. Thick silk. Many worms had given all they had to make that shirt.

The woman was standing with her fisted hands planted on her hips. Something about her stance suggested that at any moment she might raise her arms above her head and superhero it right through the ceiling and every consecutive floor until she hit the sky.

Both Scarlett and the woman stared a bit on seeing each other.

"Did you just call me mom?" the woman said.

"Not you," Scarlett said quickly. "My mom...is here."

"Your mother is here?" the woman said, looking around.

"Not right now."

"But she's staying here?"

"No."

"Should you be behind that desk?" the woman asked.

"Do you need help?" Scarlett replied.

"Do you *work* here?"

"I live here," Scarlett said. "I can help you."

"Oh, so your mother is..." Scarlett could see the woman putting two and two together and slowly, ever so slowly, pulling a four into focus. "Who said child labor was dead? I'm being helped. But thank you. Someone, probably your mother, is getting me an espresso as we speak, an espresso that will hopefully prevent me from falling over. I've just gotten off the plane from Thailand. Twenty-nine hours. Have you ever been on a plane for twenty-nine hours? I haven't sat still that long since I did a marathon meditation for two days when I was on the ashram. My ass could take it then. I don't want to sit down again for a week, at least. I'll admit it. I have jet lag."

The majority of that was delivered in one long breath. She swiveled her torso, cracking her back loudly, then strode over to the desk and peered at the framed pictures that hung behind it, showing all the successive generations of Martins posed in front of the hotel. The last picture had been taken four years ago. Scarlett loved the way her braces caught the sun in it. Eleven had been a rough year, for many reasons.

"God!" the woman said. "How many of you are there?"

"You mean my brothers and sisters? Four."

"Four!" The woman laughed again. It was a strangely animated laugh, like someone had attached her chin to a string and was jerking it toward the sky. "You don't see that much in the city. I guess your parents aren't fans of birth control."

Scarlett had had this exact thought many times herself, but she didn't really like hearing this stranger saying it out loud. Nor did she like strangers hanging over her, practically staring down her cleavage. But it wasn't the cleavage, or lack thereof, that the woman seemed most interested in.

"That's Dior, isn't it?" she asked, pinching the strap and feeling the material.

The woman was close enough for Scarlett to smell—she carried a faint fragrance of incense, and a light perfume that had an expensive feel inside of Scarlett's nose.

"Yes," Scarlett admitted.

The woman leaned over farther and stared at the picture again.

"Interesting group," she said. "All the girls are blonde, like your dad. And your brother is brunette, like your mother. Good-looking guy, your brother. How old is he?"

"In the picture or now?" Scarlett asked.

"I'm only interested in now," the woman said with a smile.

"Nineteen."

"Older sister as well? She's stunning. How old is she?"

"Eighteen."

Her interest seemed to end with Spencer and Lola. She tapped a fingernail against her front teeth.

"It's not exactly what I pictured," she said, turning to look around the lobby.

Scarlett didn't know what to say. The hotel was what it was. Not the best. Far from the worst.

Her mother entered from the kitchen, bearing a white mug on a saucer, with a tiny pile of orange rind clustered around it. The woman eagerly accepted this, pinching up all of the orange and dropping it into the cup.

"Four shots of espresso," her mother said.

The woman nodded and sucked this back like it was nothing at all.

"This is my daughter Scarlett," her mother explained.

"We've met," the woman said. "Nice name. And nice dress. I'm more of a Vivienne Westwood woman myself. But really, I like small, up-and-coming designers, right out of design school. You get all the freshest ideas for a song."

Scarlett's mother's face had slipped into that half-paralyzed mask it got when a seriously paying customer was around.

"This is Mrs. Amberson," she said to Scarlett. "She'll be here *all summer*."

"All summer?" Scarlett repeated.

"All summer," Mrs. Amberson said.

"All summer," her mother said again. "In the Empire Suite."

"The Empire Suite?" Scarlett said.

"This is adorable," Mrs. Amberson cut in. "Do you often

43

sing in rounds? Makes sense. You look a bit like the Von Trapps."

It took Scarlett a minute to realize that she was talking about *The Sound of Music*. Actually, yes. Maybe they were a little Von Trapp like. Many, blonde, repetitive. Also, running for the hills sounded like a pretty good plan.

"Will your husband be joining you at some point?" her mom asked, sitting back down in front of the computer.

"Oh, no," Mrs. Amberson said. "My husband is more of a concept than a person."

She let that mysterious sentence linger in the air for a moment.

"Oh...fine," Scarlett's mom replied. "Just checking. And just so you know, we have a policy here at the Hopewell. As a family, we personally take care of some of the rooms."

"So I read." Mrs. Amberson pulled a *Whaddya Say We Do New York?* guidebook from her voluminous bag. She flipped the book open to the correct page with one shake of her hand. It looked like it had been turned to that page a number of times; the spine had cracked there as a kind of permanent bookmark. "The Empire Suite comes highly recommended. How fortunate that someone just canceled and it was free."

The size of the lie almost caused Scarlett to burst out laughing. But that would only result in her mother having to kill her in front of the new guest, so she played with the stapler instead.

"It is," her mother said, forging on. "Scarlett is taking care of your room. She'll be able to give you a hand with day-to-day matters, errands, things like that."

Mrs. Amberson looked Scarlett up and down like she was sizing her up for a harness.

"I could really use something like that," she said. "I'll bear it in mind."

"Why don't you let me get you another coffee?" her mother said. "Scarlett, if you'll just..."

She grabbed the desk pad and scrawled the words: GET UP THERE AND AIR THE ROOM OUT!!!!!!!!!!!

Scarlett felt her eyes widen. She was supposed to be taking Marlene out—possibly screaming and wrapped in a sack—in five minutes.

"I..."

Her mother turned and leaned over the desk.

Scarlett's mother did not have a severe face. In fact, she just looked like an older, female Spencer, which was usually not intimidating at all. But like Spencer, she could occasionally muster a truly dangerous look. Spencer reserved his for the stage, but her mother kept it for moments just like this.

"I'm just going to go upstairs for a minute and open the windows," Scarlett said.

"Good," Mrs. Amberson replied. "I assume that someone will come for the..."

She waved at her bags.

"Oh, of course," Scarlett's mother replied. "I'll have someone bring them right up."

She said this breezily, as if there were dozens of staff members lingering discretely in the shadows, waiting to do these kinds of tasks. The illusion that this was a *real* hotel had to be kept alive.

Instead of staying where she was, Mrs. Amberson followed along right behind Scarlett.

"I'll just go up with her," she said. "Too much coffee unbalances me."

Scarlett opened the gate to the elevator and they climbed in together, then she pulled the gate shut, hard. It made a terrible squeaking noise in protest.

"That's charming," Mrs. Amberson said, nodding at the gate. Whether that was sincere or sarcastic, Scarlett wasn't sure.

Standing side by side, Mrs. Amberson towered over Scarlett by several inches. Scarlett was fairly tall herself, so she suspected heels. She looked down to see that Mrs. Amberson was wearing tiger-print ballet flats. She caught Scarlett looking and turned her gaze to Scarlett's flip-flops.

"So," Mrs. Amberson said, removing a very old and expensive-looking red cigarette case from her purse, "Dior, huh?"

"It's my sister's," Scarlett said quickly.

"Your sister has good taste. Expensive taste. I take it this elevator is original, mechanics and all?"

"Um...yeah."

"Very authentic."

Again, Scarlett had no idea what that remark was meant to mean. After about six days, the elevator triumphantly reached the fourth floor, and Scarlett sprang the gate. The Empire Suite was a long room at the front of the building, with three tall windows facing out to the street. The key stuck in the lock a little, but Scarlett got it open after a moment or two of jiggling.

It had been at least four months since anyone had occupied the room. It was painfully hot and still. Most normal hotels had AC running constantly, and the steady stream of guests meant that the rooms were regularly freshened. This room hadn't been dusted since Monique left weeks before. The room was neat, but had that odd feeling that empty, expectant rooms tended to get—almost like they were angry that they'd been neglected. A superfine layer of dust had accumulated. That was her problem now. Hopefully Mrs. Amberson wouldn't run out and down the street to somewhere better.

"I may need to...wake it up a little," she said.

"Wake it up," Mrs. Amberson said. "I like that. Very evocative."

Mrs. Amberson stripped off the pink kimono, revealing a tight, short-sleeved tunic top, like something a dancer might wear. She tapped the cigarette case on her forearm and walked around the room, pausing to admire the dressing table and its moony mirror. This was the highlight of the room, in Scarlett's opinion. Along with the gorgeous mirror, the table had a dozen small drawers that presumably used to hold all of the little things necessary for a woman in the twenties—lipsticks, bracelets, small bottles of illegal booze.

"Well," she said, apparently satisfied. "This is the good kind of authentic. I can smoke on the balcony, right? Don't worry. I won't burn the curtains."

She was already climbing over the desk, out of the window, and onto the tiny, sheltered ledge outside. It was really for flower boxes. It definitely didn't qualify as a balcony.

"That's not really for people," Scarlett said. "I don't know if that'll..."

"I don't weigh much. And it's only four stories. I'll take my chances."

She sat against the short wrought-iron rail, sticking her arm through the bars, away from the window. She kept the curtain tucked back with her leg.

"You don't smoke, do you?"

"No," Scarlett said.

"Good," she said through pursed lips as she lit her cigarette. "You should never start. Smoking kills. Oh, that's good...."

That last remark was addressed to the trail of smoke leaving her lips.

"Twenty-nine hours," she said. "No smoking on the plane. No smoking in the airport. No smoking in the cab."

Mrs. Amberson regarded her through the filmy veil that she breathed into the air. Scarlett felt the minutes ticking away. It was one kind of scary thing taking Marlene someplace. It was another, much more scary thing to take her there late.

"Is there anything you need?" she finally asked. "If not, I'll..."

"It's been a while since I've been in New York City," Mrs. Amberson said.

She went back to smoking for a few more moments and, once again, Scarlett was left waiting for some kind of a sign of release. It was like Mrs. Amberson had her held there with a phantom leash.

"If you want anything..." Scarlett tried again.

"I undoubtedly will," Mrs. Amberson said. "I'll need to think about it."

"I'll leave my cell phone number," Scarlett said quickly.

She scrawled it down on the hotel notepad on the dressing table.

"Here it is!" she said, pointing at it as she backed out of the room. "Call me anytime! I'll just let you get settled, check on your bags..."

Mrs. Amberson didn't answer. She just made an *mmmmm* noise, which Scarlett decided to interpret as a dismissal.

"Do you mind if I call you O'Hara?" Mrs. Amberson asked, just as Scarlett reached the door. "Like Scarlett O'Hara?"

"Whatever you want!" Scarlett said, as she backed out of the room.

"We're going to be great friends, O'Hara," Mrs. Amberson added. "I can feel it, and I'm always right about these things."

THE STAR

Back on the fifth floor, Lola and Marlene were standing in the hall side by side in a frozen tableau, like something from a horror movie. Marlene's face was palpably red.

"Where did you go?" Lola asked under her breath.

"I have a guest," Scarlett explained. "She just arrived."

"I got Chip to come by with the car to get you over there on time."

"Oh, good," Scarlett said flatly.

Lola plastered a happy smile on her face and turned to Marlene.

"Ready to go?" she asked.

"We're *late*," Marlene said. "It's ruined!"

"We're not late! And I told you, the car is coming!"

"Why can't you take me?" Marlene said, slumping against the wall.

Scarlett felt the dangerous look coming into her own eye, but Lola touched her lightly on the elbow in reassurance.

"We talked about this," Lola said reasonably. "You're doing me a big favor, and I won't forget that. You're going to *love* your makeover."

Marlene considered this by rolling along the wall and burying her face into the wallpaper, like she was trying to stencil it with an imprint of her scowl.

"And Chip said that he really, really wanted you to come out on his boat," Lola added, in what sounded like a touch of desperation. "Remember the boat? How they have the little kitchen downstairs with the champagne glasses? I can do the makeover and then we can go on the boat. It doesn't get much more glamorous than that."

Marlene rolled toward them, the scowl still very much present.

"I don't want stupid lipstick like that," Marlene said, looking at Scarlett. Scarlett involuntarily balled her fists into the Dior dress. It just wasn't worth it. It really wasn't.

"You know I make everyone up differently," Lola said. "That color is for Scarlett. But you look better in lighter colors. I have a new apricot gloss set aside for you. It's my favorite."

Marlene seemed slightly placated by the fact that she was getting Lola's favorite color, as opposed to whatever Scarlett was wearing. Scarlett touched her lips. Was it too dark? Did she look like a clown? No. Lola didn't make mistakes like that.

"We *will* be late if we don't hurry," Lola said, extending her hand. "And remember, when we see Mom, don't say anything, okay? You're in on my secret. I need you to keep it."

Marlene accepted the hand and walked with Lola, brushing past Scarlett without a word.

"You know what?" Scarlett said, as they got to the elevator. "I'll take the stairs. It'll look more...convincing. See you down there."

Lola threw her a look over Marlene's head that might have meant, "I'm sorry" or "Please don't sweat too much in my dress" or both.

The Mercedes was waiting silently outside the hotel. Chip, Number Ninety-eight himself, was sitting in the backseat. He had a copy of *The Wall Street Journal* on his lap, which Scarlett found hilarious. Chip had never struck her as a reader. In fact, when she called up a mental picture of how he spent his free time (which she sometimes did), she always pictured him playing with an Etch-A-Sketch and not quite getting how it worked. She was never sure why, but it seemed to fit.

It was hard for Scarlett to tell if Chip was actually handsome, or if his pricey haircuts, regulation rich boy tan, lacrosse body, and sublime dental work caused the illusion of handsomeness. He had golden-reddish hair, much like Marlene, really huge eyebrows (which Spencer suspected he got waxed into shape), and big pouty lips.

Lola managed to lean in first and gave him a little kiss before Marlene squeezed into the car. She loved Chip. Sometimes she seemed to love him more than Lola did.

"There might not be enough room back here for all four of us," Chip said, nodding a greeting at Scarlett. "Someone should ride up front."

He didn't say, "*You* should ride up front." Not directly. But it was understood, since Lola and Marlene were already in the back. As she got in, she glanced up and saw Mrs. Amberson looking down at them curiously from her perch on the not-a-balcony. She raised her cigarette. Scarlett gave a half-hearted wave and got into the car.

"We're making a stop first," Chip called up to the driver. "Rockefeller Center."

The car glided into action at his command.

"You will never believe this," Chip said to Lola. "My parents are sending me to this class called Steering Wealth in a few weeks. It's for people who, you know, are going to inherit stuff and have to know how to do stuff with it. Hedge funds and stuff. I have to go all the way to Boston to sit around in some hotel for three days."

Lola tutted in sympathy. Scarlett made a fake crying face. Out of the corner of her eye, she noticed the driver crack a small smile.

"You have to come up with me."

"Boston?" Lola said. "I have work...."

"You have to. We'll stay with my friend Greg and go sailing."

"Chip, seriously. I can't take off three whole days. I'm running out of excuses."

"I'll be fun," Chip said. "And I'm not going to make it if you don't come. You'll like Boston. You have to get used to coming up there anyway when I move in the fall."

Chip hadn't gotten into Harvard. All they knew was that he was going to school "in the Boston area." She and Spencer had a lot of very amusing theories on what this actually meant, several of which involved crayons.

"I guess you're right," Lola said. She didn't say it with much conviction.

"Can I come?" Marlene asked.

"You want to go in my place?" Chip asked her.

Marlene laughed like she had never, ever in her life heard

anything as deliciously entertaining as that. It was appalling.

The driver took the car along Central Park South, past the big hotels. Or, as some may have put it, the *real* hotels.

"Is the corner of Sixth okay?" Chip said. "Can you just walk down? We kind of have to get moving."

"It's fine," Scarlett said. "It's just a few blocks."

The car came to a graceful stop between two horse-drawn carriages at the park entrance.

"When you get home," Lola said in a low voice, "just say that we met up on the street and you walked Marlene the rest of the way home, okay? I really owe you."

She adjusted Marlene's wonky, slightly crispy curls and gave her a hug. Once the car slid away, Marlene's smile was replaced with a look of barely contained rage.

"Why did you *do* that?" she snapped.

"Do what?" Scarlett replied.

"The car! I wanted to go down to the building! They would have taken us if you didn't say something!"

Now Scarlett saw the error of her ways. Marlene wanted her friends to see her get out of the chauffeur-driven car.

"They had to go," Scarlett said. "You wouldn't want Chip and Lola to be late, would you?"

Marlene's reply was to bolt from the curb and cross the street on her own, before the light had changed. Scarlett had to run after her. They barely missed getting clipped by a bus. Marlene kept ten paces ahead of Scarlett. Scarlett tried to speed up for a while, but then just gave up after the second block and let Marlene get ahead and slip out of sight. She finally caught up to her in the frigid lobby of 30 Rock. The building had a heavy glamour, with its black and gold walls and floor, the massive murals of planes flying and people building, the army of NBC pages scurrying around. Marlene had already latched on to a few of her Powerkids friends, and Scarlett was more or less forgotten.

One thing about disease: It didn't care how much money your family had, or what neighborhood you came from. The Powerkids were a mix of Connecticut and New Jersey suburbanites; residents of Harlem, Chinatown, the East and West Villages, and the Upper East and West Sides; Staten and Long Islanders; people from every corner of Brooklyn and the Bronx. These were the people Marlene had lived with for her hospital stay. This was her element.

The studio of *Good Morning, New York* was much smaller than it appeared on TV. To watch the show, you would think they had hundreds of people in the audience. In reality, there were some risers and room for maybe two or three dozen. It was only half full. It was also completely freezing. There were countless cables dangling from the ceiling, and shockingly bright lights.

The famous chef was also shorter than he looked on TV, and he was wearing a lot of makeup. It seemed to take the crew forever to set up the kitchen. Bowls of vegetables were being set out on the counter. The Powerkids were not particularly impressed. They were used to better entertainment than this. To entertain herself, Scarlett started playing with her phone, plugging in every number in the little book she kept in her purse, even really irrelevant ones, like people at school she barely knew outside of Biology study group and Dakota's housekeeper.

A stage wrangler with a headset came out and addressed the group.

"Okay," she said. "We're going to film the cooking segment now. We're going to need one or two of you to help in the demonstration and chop up some vegetables."

The bored Powerkids suddenly came to life, and every hand went up. Scarlett was barely aware of it, and didn't even notice when the woman said, "And how about you, in the back?"

Someone elbowed Scarlett softly in the neck and she looked up.

"Me?" she asked.

"Yes. Let's get a bunch of different ages down here and mix it up a little."

"But I'm..."

The woman couldn't hear her, and was waving her down impatiently.

"Don't worry!" said the chef. "I only bite my food!"

An obligatory laugh.

Marlene was not happy about this at all. She gazed at Scarlett in deadly reproach as she made her way down. She tried to throw Marlene a "I didn't mean to do this" look, but the wrangler was already positioning her by a chopping board and a massive knife.

"You're the oldest," the chef said. "So we'll have you do the more serious chopping, okay? What's your name?"

Scarlett said her name was Scarlett.

The chef's makeup was touched up, and there was a general scrambling and shifting around of dishes. They seemed more important than the two Powerkids and Scarlett, who were shoved into a few different positions before the whole thing was settled.

"We go live in one minute," the wrangler said. "Don't worry. You'll be told what to do. Just be natural and have fun."

She barked this out in the least fun-sounding way possible.

"Live?" Scarlett said, looking at the cameras and the lights.

The word live had never been mentioned before this. There was a lightness in her head, like all of her ability to think floating off of her brain like steam. The wrangler began counting down the minute as the cameras were shifted foward.

And then, there was a loud, horrible noise. Scarlett looked down and saw, to her horror, that her tiny phone clutched in her hand was ringing. The number was an extension of the Hopewell.

"Maybe you should answer that," the chef said, good-naturedly.

In the shadows, behind the lights, Scarlett could see the wrangler shaking her head and raising her hands in frustration. Scarlett glanced down at the phone fearfully. The camera swung toward the chef, who was still cheerfully goading her to answer. The wrangler came forward to signal to Scarlett to make it stop. She had to do something, so Scarlett flicked it open and slapped it to her ear.

"Why don't you answer your phone?" Mrs. Amberson asked.

"*I'm in a TV studio,*" Scarlett whispered.

"A television studio? Why are you in a television studio?" Mrs. Amberson's voice was clearly audible to all around.

"Tell her we're cooking up some healthy quesadillas with the Powerkids!" the chef called over his shoulder. "She should come on down!"

Another obligatory laugh from the audience.

"Who was that? Where are you?"

"Good Morning."

"Good morning to you, too, O'Hara. But that doesn't answer the question."

"It's a show. For quesadillas."

"What?"

The wrangler held up ten fingers, nine...

"Do you need something?" Scarlett whispered urgently.

"I need white plum tea. Whole leaf. Loose. Organic. Also, I want to talk to you. Can you meet me for lunch?"

"When?"

"Let's say twelve-thirty. Where did you say you were?"

"Rockefeller Center."

The wrangler was down to four fingers.

"Of course you are," Mrs. Amberson said. "Well, meet me in the lobby of the Algonquin Hotel then."

Scarlett snapped the phone shut without a good-bye and dropped it to the floor, where it clacked loudly. She didn't care if it shattered. The camera swung over to her as the chef passed over to her side of the counter.

"That your boyfriend?" he asked.

"Um..."

"Hey! It's a party down here! Everybody should come!"

"And two, one...We're live."

A blinding red light came out of the camera, causing her to reel backward.

The chef and the host started talking. Their cheerfulness

was even more excessive in person than it was on TV. The next five minutes passed in a haze. The Powerkids threw vegetables into a pan. At some point, there was tofu and an avocado.

Scarlett looked down and realized that a cucumber had been placed in front of her by a slinking crew member and that she had grabbed it unconsciously and was grasping it for dear life. Then she realized that it probably didn't look good to be seen squeezing cucumbers on live TV.

When she was called upon to slice this, she found herself relaxing a little. The chef came over and helped her. It was all over much quicker than it had taken to start, and lights were being shut off. As they were filtered out of the room, Marlene kept ahead. Scarlett had to hurry ahead and catch her by the shoulder.

"I didn't do it on purpose," she said.

Marlene shrugged her shoulder away.

"I didn't," she said again. "Come on. You saw what happened."

"So why didn't you say no?"

"I tried to."

"No, you didn't."

Well, that was true, actually. She didn't. In her head she was trying to say no. But in truth, she had just done as she was told.

"You've been on TV before," Scarlett said. "You did that telethon."

"When I was *nine*."

This was a stupid conversation to be having, especially in the sleek black hallway of Rockefeller Center, in full view of people from the show and the other Powerkids. It was stupid under any circumstances.

"I have to meet my guest for lunch," she said. "So I have to take you right back."

"I'm supposed to have lunch with *them*."

"I don't have any choice, Marlene. It's my job. Let me take you home...."

"I'm coming," Marlene said. She was just doing it to be difficult—and frankly, her technique was working. But Mrs. Amberson was going to have to meet Marlene sooner or later.

More to the point...Marlene was going to have to meet Mrs. Amberson. And that, frankly, was kind of an amusing prospect.

LUNCH DATE

The Algonquin Hotel was one of the most pedigreed establishments in the entire city, famous for its literary connections in the twenties and thirties. Mrs. Amberson was settled on a small sofa in its dark paneled and richly appointed lobby. Where the Hopewell had sparkle (or used to have sparkle), the Algonquin had a deep, cultivated charm. And...guests.

"It's this or a short hospital stay," she said, greeting Scarlett with a raised glass of a deep red liquid with a celery stalk sticking out of the top. "Bloody Marys are one of the truly medicinal cocktails. The only way I can beat this jet lag is by staying up all day, and this is going to keep me alive. And who is this?"

This was directed at Marlene, who was stalking along behind Scarlett like a wet cat.

"My sister Marlene. We were at an event this morning for her group."

Marlene dropped into a plush chair at the farthest end of the little table.

"Group?" Mrs. Amberson said, pulling out the celery and taking a big bite out of the stalk.

"Powerkids," Scarlett said, sitting down a little closer. "It's a cancer survivor thing."

This was usually the place where people would go into a long, "You had cancer? What a brave little girl you are! How terrible, at your age. You know, they say that children who have been ill..." Blah, blah, blah. It was always the same, and Marlene never listened to a word of it. Mrs. Amberson, however, didn't say a thing. She just cocked an eyebrow at Marlene and jabbed her celery stick back into the glass. It was a strangely satisfying reaction for Scarlett, who was equally sick of hearing the speech.

"I'm hungry," Marlene said.

Mrs. Amberson smiled lightly and passed Marlene the menu.

"Help yourself," she said.

This, Scarlett had not expected. The Alonguin was a nice place, which meant it was also an expensive place.

"I...um...I only have eight dollars on me," Scarlett said. That was half of her current fortune.

"It's on me," Mrs. Amberson said. "Get what you like, Marlene. You, too, O'Hara."

The menu was surprisingly heavy, bound in very thick pieces of leather. The food on it was fairly normal—just some sandwiches and snacks—all stupidly expensive, as she had figured. This was odd...being taken out to a place like this for lunch, by a guest, no less. She was supposed to be doing things for Mrs. Amberson, not the other way around. She quickly picked the cheapest thing and said water was fine. Marlene had no such compunctions. She ordered a plate of the house special miniburgers and a nonalcoholic pina colada with extra cherries.

"A girl who knows what she wants," Mrs. Amberson said.

"Can I go make a call while it's coming?" she asked.

Oh, yes. The fifteen-year-old rule did not apply to Marlene. She'd had her cell phone for years. The excuse was that she needed it to call home when she was in the hospital, which was a pretty good excuse, but still.

"Go right ahead," Mrs. Amberson said. "I have some things to discuss with your sister."

Marlene skulked over to an empty sofa on the other side of the room, far from them.

"I'm sorry," Scarlett said. "She's just a little..."

"You are an interesting bunch," Mrs. Amberson cut in. "And you don't have to apologize. I hope you don't mind that we're meeting at another hotel. No offense to yours, but this one has a pedigree and a fabulous bar."

"You said this was your first time in New York in a while?" Scarlett asked, out of a sense of obligation.

Mrs. Amberson smiled wryly. She reached for her cigarette case, then seemed to remember that she wasn't permitted to smoke inside. She dropped it back into her purse with disappointment.

"I used to live here," she said, "some time ago. Back during the glam and the disco and the punk. But I was mostly a Broadway girl."

"Broadway?" Scarlett repeated. "You should talk to my brother. He's an actor. He's trying to get on Broadway."

"Sweetheart," Mrs. Amberson said, "a quarter of the people in this town are trying to get on Broadway, another quarter have been."

It wasn't really clear what Scarlett was supposed to take from that remark—if it was meant to be reassuring, or insulting, or purely informational. Mrs. Amberson had a very disconcerting habit of making everything sound semi-insulting.

"School's out, right? So, what do you do? Do you have some kind of...*camp* or something?"

"No," Scarlett said. "Just work."

"Work?" she laughed. "Your family owns a hotel. And you're wearing a Dior dress, I might point out."

"The dress is my sister's," Scarlett said, unable to hide her annoyance. "It was a gift. We are the opposite of rich."

As soon as she said it, Scarlett bit her lip. Maybe it wasn't the best idea to advertise to the new guest that they weren't exactly the most successful family in the city. But Mrs. Amberson looked intrigued. She sat back and stirred her Bloody Mary until her celery cracked in half where she had chomped into it.

"Let me guess," she said. "Does the dress have anything to do with the owner of that car I saw you getting into this morning?"

"It's from my sister's boyfriend," Scarlett said. "That was his car."

"Ah." She stirred the Bloody Mary for a moment, looking very pleased with herself. "The opposite of rich is the best thing to be, anyway. There's nothing like working for what you want. It's the only way."

This seemed odd coming from a woman who was clearly of the rich persuasion. But maybe she had worked for it. Mrs. Amberson drummed her nails on her lap for a moment and gazed at Scarlett.

"So," she said, "what do you do with your time?"

That was a good question, one for which Scarlett didn't really have an answer. So she went with her most recent idea.

"I write."

"Write?" Mrs. Amberson said. "Very ambitious. I like it. And you're certainly in the right place. Why, this hotel...do you know what it's famous for?"

"The Algonquin Round Table," Scarlett said. "The group of writers who used to meet here."

To be fair, hotel lore was somewhat of a specialty in the Martin family, but Scarlett would have known that anyway.

"A reader," she said, impressed. "And who said the book is dead?"

Then she seemed to lose interest in the whole matter with a massive yawn. She fished around in her purse for a pen and a notebook, and spent a few minutes scrawling. Then she fished around some more, producing some strange multicolored bills.

"Baht, baht, baht...here we are."

Dollars followed. She pushed them toward Scarlett.

"Here's money for the check, and for that tea, when you get the chance. Keep the rest—I'll be sending you out on errands, I'm sure. That will cover them for a while. I'm going to yoga. See you later."

Mrs. Amberson downed the rest of her Bloody Mary and demolished the rest of her celery stick. Then she picked up a sleek little gym bag by her feet and was gone without another word.

Scarlett looked down and saw that she was holding what had to be about five hundred dollars.

"What was that all about?" she asked herself.

She was still sitting there holding the wad of cash when the waiter showed up with the massive plates, the water, and the decked-out fake pina colada, thick with a dozen cherries.

"Where did she go?" Marlene asked, coming back and snatching up the glass.

"To yoga."

Marlene seemed satisfied by this turn of events and gobbled down her miniburgers. She ordered a second colada. Scarlett nibbled at the snack plate she had gotten. It was a relief when her phone rang and Spencer's name appeared on the screen.

"I need you," he said when she answered.

"Stop it, Orlando. Stop calling me. If we get married, my name will be Scarlett Bloom, and that sounds like a rash."

"You can't see me right now," Spencer said, "but I actually just *peed* myself laughing. My shorts are soaked."

"You say that like it's uncommon."

"And the laughs keep coming. If you're done..."

"I am," Scarlett said.

"I actually do need you. It's *incredibly* important."

"Did you get the part?" Scarlett asked, sitting up and taking notice.

"You will only know the story if you come and meet me in the park at four. By the Mad Hatter statue."

THE SCENE PARTNER

For a day that started off with no real prospects, this was turning into a whirlwind.

First, there was a subway ride uptown to the hotel, dragging Marlene all the way. She rattled off the prearranged "I just ran into them on the street" story to her dad, which was accepted without comment. Marlene looked murderous, but she didn't contradict it. Scarlett changed her clothes and sailed through her chores—washing sheets, sweeping the lobby, breaking down the grocery delivery boxes for the recycling, wiping down the brass fixtures in the elevator, vacuuming the second floor hallway. She made it back into Lola's dress and to the park just in time.

A few minutes later, Spencer came barreling along, illegally cutting across some grass, on his scrappy, duct-taped-covered bike. He was glistening with sweat when he stepped off and dropped it on the lawn.

"Did you get it?" she asked.

He couldn't answer for a minute, because he had grabbed the water bottle off his bike and guzzled half of it back with such force that the other half ended up running over his chin.

"I just rode all the way up from the East Village in about ten minutes," he said, putting his head back and taking a deep breath. Then he wrapped her in a huge, sweaty hug, dripping water on her from his chin. This was answer enough.

"Where were you when I called?" he asked. "And why are you wearing that dress?"

"Lola lent it to me. And I was just having lunch at the Algonquin Hotel."

"Of course you were," Spencer said, releasing her and sinking to the ground. "I must have forgotten your normal Tuesday schedule. The other guy, my scene partner, is on his way up. I have to be off book in *two days*. You're going to help me learn my lines, right?"

"Don't I always?" she said.

"Yeah, but it's been a while. I thought maybe you changed your policy or something."

Spencer pulled out a copy of *Hamlet* from his messenger bag and started leafing through it.

"Take you me for a sponge, my lord?" he asked.

Scarlett turned.

"Take *you* me *for a sponge*, my lord?" he asked again.

"No," Scarlett said.

"That's one of Rosencrantz's lines. I don't know what this means. Maybe it makes sense if you read the play. Maybe he turns into a sponge."

"I think that's what *Hamlet's* about," she said. "People who turn into sponges. Oh...I have a guest. In my room."

"You met him? Her? It? Them?"

"Her. She took me out to lunch. She gave me this to run

her errands."

She flashed the cash quickly.

"Someone is actually using the family policy for good," he said approvingly. "See. Exciting things always happen to you. The best I ever got was that woman who kept having me come up to fix her TV. There was a lot of bending involved. I felt used and dirty."

"It's the price you pay for being one of those weedy but good-looking types," Scarlett said.

"Weedy? You hurt me. I prefer tall and scrawny. Unlike my partner, who's right behind you."

Scarlett turned. There were a lot of people wandering around...people with massive baby strollers, joggers, the lost, the tourists, the assorted insane. Cutting through them and walking directly for Scarlett and Spencer was a guy that Scarlett felt like she knew. He was just a hair shorter than Spencer, but fuller and more muscular where Spencer was, as she had just commented, weedy. He had sandy hair, loosely cut and slightly overgrown in a very appealing way. There was something almost uneven about his face—one side of his mouth kept creeping up in a smile where the other stayed flat. His clothes were nondescript, just a black T-shirt and a pair of green cargo shorts. He managed to look ordinary, but it was the most engrossing kind of ordinary that Scarlett had ever seen. Ordinary plus.

"Sorry," he said as he approached. "I had to take the subway. My scooter wouldn't start. Have you learned all your lines?"

His voice was deep and full, with a very slight Southern drawl softening the end of every word.

"I learned the whole play," Spencer said. "Backward. Meet my sister. She's here to help. Eric, this is Scarlett. Scarlett, this is Eric."

Eric smiled at her like he had known her forever. And it still felt that way. She had seen him. She knew him. He was pointing at her like he knew her as well.

"I *saw* you," Eric said. "Just recently. Today."

"Was it on TV?" Scarlett asked, feeling her face flush.

"Yes! When I was at the gym. You were on some morning show."

Spencer's head whipped in her direction. She held up her hands.

"It was an accident," she said. "I took Marlene to a taping. I was supposed to be in the audience, and I ended up making these...quesadillas."

"Oh," Spencer said with a nod. That wasn't like *really* being on TV. It wasn't like she had gotten a recurring role on a sitcom. He relaxed.

"I feel like I've seen you, too," she said.

Eric nodded.

"Was I doing this?" he asked.

He pulled off his backpack and took a running dive and rolled across the ground, doing three summersaults in a row, all the while clapping at himself like he was on fire.

Amazingly, this did ring a bell.

"It was the commercial," he explained, dusting himself off and walking back. "It got stuck in a lot of people's heads, but no one can really remember where they saw me."

"That's it!" Scarlett said. He had played a guy who accidentally set himself on fire cooking dinner, and then ended

70

up getting a pizza delivered while he was still smoking slightly. It had been on constantly around Christmas.

"We're both TV stars," he said.

Scarlett felt her chin go a little weak, like it was about to drip off her face.

"Let me see that again," Spencer said.

"What, the roll?"

Spencer nodded. Eric did it again, running and diving onto the ground, rolling three times, clapping feverishly. Spencer watched carefully, cocking his head to the side. Then he set his script down and recreated it perfectly, adding an extra roll.

"That was good," Eric said. "When I first tried it, they wanted me to do it like this..."

And then it really began—a showdown the likes of which Scarlett had never seen. She was used to Spencer doing this on his own, to entertain her, or whoever was around, or just for his own personal amusement. She wasn't aware that other people spent their time doing the same things, especially people like Eric.

Spencer started by fake-punching himself in the face, complete with an authentic punching noise and reaction (called the "nap," Scarlett had been told). He knocked himself completely to the ground. Eric was duly impressed by this, and did the same thing to himself, but in the stomach, throwing himself back very far. Spencer countered by pretending to trip and throwing himself over two separate benches—the second one, backward. Eric couldn't top that. They exchanged fake blows for a while, comparing the noises they made. Then, there were backflips.

After about an hour, it came down to the issue of who could walk on their hands the longest. In this, Spencer was slightly at a loss. He was fairly strong, but Eric had much bigger, stronger arms. Spencer went a lot of steps quickly before rolling over. Eric was slower, but unquestionably more powerful. He kept going for a full minute after Spencer.

"What did you think?" he asked, as he gracefully let himself down. He was out of breath and his face was deeply red. "Who wins?"

Spencer was back on his hands, trying again.

"You're good," she said.

"Yeah, but he's *really* good. He's got skills. Serious skills. He has to show me how to do that fall."

Spencer wandered off on his hands, mumbling his lines. He disappeared around the statue.

"But you won," she said. "Definitely. You stayed up longer."

He smiled that uneven smile.

"I'm *going* to do that fall," he said. "You watch. Give me a few days. You'll be around for a few days, right?"

"I don't know," she said. "I guess. If you guys need help."

"We need help," he said. "And I need a witness."

Even as it was happening, Scarlett knew she would remember this moment for a long time—this first exchange with Eric, the way he was looking down at her, tousled, slightly sweaty. Perfect.

Spencer reappeared, now on his feet. Then he collapsed on the grass.

"I'm done," he said. "Time to start with the lines."

Spencer had only mastered a few lines in the hour or so he

had the part, but he gamely tried to go though their scenes without the script, having Scarlett feed him the lines. Eric was incredibly patient, repeating his lines endlessly to give Spencer the chance to catch up. He had an amazing voice— serious and actory. With every word he said, Scarlett felt herself falling deeper into a soupy trance, which was barely broken when Spencer threw down his book and made an announcement.

"We gotta go," he said. "It's family night at the Hopewell."

Scarlett looked at her watch. They had been there for two and a half hours. It felt like ten minutes.

"What's the Hopewell?" Eric asked, packing his things away.

"We live in a hotel," Spencer explained. "It's called the Hopewell. Our family owns it."

This startled Eric.

"Wow. You *own a hotel*. You guys must be loaded...."

He shook his head.

"Sorry," he said. "That just came out. That was really rude."

"It's okay," Scarlett said quickly. "We get it all the time. And we're not. Really not."

"Really not," Spencer said with a deep nod. "Really, *really* not."

They walked east out of the park, crossing through the boutiques of Madison Avenue, the towering apartment buildings of Park Avenue. Eric walked with them toward the subway. He was very talkative and open. She learned he was eighteen and from a small town outside of Winston-Salem, North Carolina.

"Getting that commercial...that was a fluke," he said, jumping back as a cab cut in front of them. He clearly didn't quite know how to walk the streets yet. "My acting teacher in high school set up a weekend trip for some of us who seemed serious about performing. You know—get the New York experience for a day or two, go to some shows, look at the big buildings. They had us do a one-day audition workshop, and it just happened that the guy casting the commercial was there and thought I was funny."

"I can't *believe* that," Spencer said. "I live here! I go to auditions all the time. That's never happened to me."

"Just dumb luck," Eric said. "They would have taken you if you were there that day. You're a lot better than me."

Eric's generosity, his praise of Spencer's talent...these were very endearing qualities. Scarlett tried to tell herself that this was what she liked about him, and that it wasn't just his almost disturbing physical perfection.

"Anyway," he went on, "once I got that, I decided to make the big jump. I was going to go to state university, but I got enough cash from the job to go to NYU instead. I'm starting in September, but I decided to move up a little early and get used to living here. You go to school, Spence?"

"Not at the moment," Spencer replied. "Hopefully that will continue."

Eric looked at the regal buildings that lined the park along Fifth Avenue—the embassies, institutes, clubs. Scarlett could see that New York was still making a very big impression on him at every turn. Things she paid no attention to at all probably shocked and awed him. It made her feel very worldly, which was a new sensation.

"Well," Eric said, as they reached the subway. "It was good meeting you. Have a good dinner. Family night sounds nice. I kind of miss my folks."

And then...Scarlett heard herself speaking.

"Come with us," she said. "Have dinner."

Out of politeness, Spencer didn't make any weird faces or sudden moves, but he did slip a look in Scarlett's direction. Family night was not a "bring everyone you know over" kind of a thing. People had come in the past—Marlene occasionally dragged along a Powerkid, and Spencer had brought one or two of his high school girlfriends—but that was back when they had a cook.

"It's just one more person," Scarlett said. "There's always lots of food. Tons."

When he didn't reply for a moment, Scarlett thought he was trying to think of a polite way of backing out of this sudden invitation. But then he looked to them both, smiling broadly.

"I'm always up for free food," Eric said. "And I actually like going to family stuff. If it's okay..."

"Sure," Spencer said quickly. "Definitely. I warn you though...if you like food that tastes good, this may come as a bit of a shock. But there should be plenty of it."

"Lots is my favorite kind," Eric said. "Lead the way."

ONE BIG, HAPPY FAMILY

When they reached the hotel, Spencer took Eric upstairs to clean up a little before dinner. Scarlett ducked behind the front desk. Lola stashed a few quick-fix items in the back of one of the file cabinets—a mirror, some little papers that blotted oil from your face, a clear lip gloss. She fumbled around with these for a moment, then went into the dining room to prepare the way as best she could.

There was a pungent odor in the air that smelled vaguely like exhaust fumes. Marlene was making a half-hearted effort at setting the table by dumping silverware in the middle. Her dad brought a defeated-looking salad from the kitchen. He had decided to wear his hipster cowboy shirt. It was white-and-blue check with yellow roses embroidered on the collar. He'd bought it from the thrift store downtown and was exceedingly proud of it, not realizing that even the coolest NYU student would have a hard time pulling off that look. Spencer's code name for it was "The Texas Style Massacre."

Of course he was wearing it tonight. Of *course* he was.

"Someone else is coming," Scarlett said, trying not to sound too nervous. "A friend...of Spencer's. From out of town. From

North Carolina. His name is Eric. He doesn't have any family around, so…we brought him back. Is that okay? He's upstairs."

Marlene stopped shoving around the silverware and gazed at her. She was talking too much and too fast. If she did this all night, she would scare Eric away—that is, if he didn't take one look at her dad's shirt and leap right out the window.

"I guess it has to be if he's already here," her dad said. "I just hope we have enough. We have another guest for dinner."

"Who?"

In reply, a tall figure appeared in the doorway dressed in what looked like a blue silk karate outfit and little Japanese slippers.

"I'm not late, am I?" Mrs. Amberson said with a smile. "I lose track of time when I'm meditating."

Her face was tautly stretched into a smile that didn't seem entirely sane to Scarlett. It wobbled just a bit in the corners. Also, she was carrying what appeared to be a dead ferret in her right fist.

"No," Scarlett's dad said, obviously trying not to look at the dead animal. "Right on time. Please, sit down."

The addition of Mrs. Amberson and her dead ferret to this mix was not something Scarlett had anticipated. She sat down quickly to steady herself, and Mrs. Amberson planted herself right next to her, slinging the ferret around the back of her neck in a swoop that grazed Scarlett's ear.

"I hope you don't mind this," she said, flicking the thing with her finger. "It's a vintage fur collar I converted into a bead cushion imbued with essential revitalizing oils. I call him Charlie."

So the ferret had a name. Even better.

"Marlene and I have met," Mrs. Amberson said, preempting any introduction. "I'm very excited to meet the rest of the clan."

Spencer came through the doorway that very second, followed by Eric. Eric had changed into one of Spencer's T-shirts. Spencer was taller and more slender than he was, so the fabric gripped his body snugly, showing off the massive muscles in his arms. Scarlett felt herself rock forward in the chair.

Spencer sighed when he saw the cowboy shirt, but Eric didn't so much as raise an eyebrow. He shook her dad's hand as if nothing was amiss. The two of them sat down on the opposite side of the table. Mrs. Amberson shrugged her shoulders lightly, allowing Charlie the Dead Ferret to shift a little.

"Amy Amberson," she said, all smiles. "I'm the new guest. I'll be here all summer."

"All summer?" Spencer repeated.

"I think it's adorable how you all do that," she said. "Spencer...another wonderful name. All associated with classic films. There's Marlene Dietrich, who played Lola in *The Blue Angel*. Scarlett, of course, is Scarlett O'Hara from *Gone With the Wind*. And Spencer is Spencer Tracy, one of the great leading men of all time."

As she spoke, she was taking in Spencer and Eric with much too long and appreciative a look. It started on Eric and his tight shirt, but it landed and lingered on Spencer.

"I'd say you're more of a Cary Grant type," she added.

"Believe it or not," Scarlett's dad said, roughly shaking a can of grated cheese to dislodge the lump from the bottom, "we just liked the names. It wasn't intentional."

"We all know what we're doing," Mrs. Amberson said. "Whether we realize it or not."

"This is really nice of you," Eric said politely, filling the silence that came after that baffling remark. "Thanks for having me."

"Manners!" Mrs. Amberson said. "Nothing is more attractive than manners."

"I have manners, too," Spencer said. "Lots of them."

There was a crash from the kitchen that sounded like a small garden shed being pushed down a flight of stairs. Her dad set down the cheese and calmly excused himself.

"I hear you're an actor," Mrs. Amberson said to Spencer.

"You heard correctly," he answered, motioning to Eric. "We both are."

"I'm an actress as well. Or, at least I was. I'm always interested in mentoring young thespians."

A slightly vulpine smile crossed her lips.

It was obvious that Spencer had picked up on Mrs. Amberson's signals. There was a playful glimmer in his eyes. Even his posture changed in a moment—he got straighter and started twirling his fork between his fingers like a tiny baton.

"I've always wanted to be mentored," he said, slipping into a truly horrible grin.

Scarlett was trying to figure out how to get her knife under the table and stab Spencer in the knee without hitting Eric by accident, when, out of the corner of her eye, she saw the black Mercedes stop in front of the hotel.

"It's them," Marlene said, springing out of her chair. "Lola and Chip. I'm going to ask Chip to stay, too."

Spencer's smile fell away completely and he stopped the evil flirting game.

"Is that Lola?" Mrs. Amberson said, craning her neck to look at them out of the window. "My, my. She's stunning. You know who she reminds me of? The lead singer of ABBA. The blonde. I got stuck in a bathroom with her once, at Elaine's. I was trying to tell her a joke. It was right after "Dancing Queen" came out. The joke had something to do with a dancing queen, and I know it was good. But she's Swedish, and I was a little drunk, so I'm sure you can imagine how that went down."

She took a deep breath and rubbed her cheeks roughly to wake herself.

"The Swedes are a difficult people to know," she added thoughtfully.

Scarlett turned up her eyes slightly. She was sure that Eric would be staring at Lola out the window. All guys stared at Lola. It wasn't Lola's fault, and Scarlett didn't resent her for it. Really, it had never been a problem until today. To Scarlett's surprise, though, Eric wasn't paying Lola the slightest bit of attention. He was looking squarely at her, Scarlett Martin. And he was smiling.

From this close, she could see the color of his eyes perfectly. They were a misty, shifting blue marbled with gray, like smoke rising through an early morning sky. Something deep inside of her was switching on—something felt like it was *moving*. It felt like the same part of her brain and stomach that responded to steep elevator drops. She was falling....

In her panic, she forced herself to turn away, and found herself looking into another pair of eyes—this time, the two glassy ones of the ferrety creature on Mrs. Amberson's shoulder.

"I'm so sorry," Lola said, hustling into the dining room. Marlene had Chip by the hand and was dragging him along right behind her. "I forgot. I thought it was tomorrow...."

As soon as they came into the room, Eric shifted his attention away smoothly, but she could feel that she was still in his focus.

The kitchen door swung open and Scarlett's parents emerged with a lasagna that had a foul-smelling gray cloud hovering over it. If they were startled that yet another visitor had joined them, they didn't show it, possibly because they were concerned with the thing they had just dragged from the hellish depths of their temperamental industrial oven.

More introductions were made. Two more chairs were pulled up to the table. A pitcher of instant iced tea was passed, as was the droopy salad and a still partially frozen loaf of garlic bread. The lasagna hissed when it was touched by the metal spoon. Everyone ate in silence for a few moments, except for Mrs. Amberson, who was fine with a glass of water and a little of the bread. She graciously explained away her small appetite by saying that her stomach was still in a different time zone.

"What do you do, Chip?" she asked. "Are you a student?"

"I just graduated," he answered, cautiously picking at his food.

"High school?"

"Yeah," he said. "I went to Durban."

"Where is Durban, again?" Spencer asked, all innocence. "Is it on Ninety-eighth Street?"

"No," Chip said. "Seventy-third."

"You sure? I could have sworn it was on Ninety-eighth. Something's on Ninety-eighth. What could I be thinking of?"

Spencer flinched suddenly. Scarlett didn't see her do it, but Lola must have gotten to him somehow. She had to shove some of the lasagna into her mouth to keep from laughing, and almost screamed from the scorching pain. She accidentally elbowed Mrs. Amberson in a mad grab for her iced tea.

"And what about you three?" Mrs. Amberson asked, jostled back into the conversation.

"Lola, Spencer, and Scarlett got into specialized high schools," Scarlett's mother chimed in proudly, "Spencer went to the High School of Performing Arts, Lola just graduated from Beacon, and Scarlett goes to Frances Perkins."

"That's one thing that seems so weird about New York," Eric said. "There are so many kinds of high schools. In my town, there was just the one high school. That was it. One football team. One prom. Here, it seems like everyone does something special."

He looked at Scarlett again when he said *special*. She suddenly realized she was clutching the edge of the table with both hands, like a bar on a roller coaster ride. She quickly released her grip, praying that he hadn't noticed. Maybe he had, and he hadn't meant the good kind of special. Maybe he meant the kind of special associated with people who are only allowed to use plastic safety scissors.

"You in a show or something, Spence?" Chip asked. He

often tried to bond with Spencer, which was about as wise as a chicken trying to bond with a hungry alligator. But before Spencer could open his mouth, Eric answered.

"We're in a show together," he offered, happily spooning up a second huge helping. "We're in *Hamlet*. Spencer just joined the cast today."

It was like someone had made that needle-being-dragged-across-a-record screeching noise that they sometimes use in movie previews. Both of Scarlett's parents turned in unison.

"It just happened," Spencer said quickly. "Really. Today. About four hours ago."

Mrs. Amberson latched on to this at once.

"*Hamlet, Prince of Denmark!*" she exclaimed, unaware of the myriad expressions flying across the table, the drama that was silently being played out. She launched into a half-hour-long story about her friend getting mugged while he was on his way to perform in Shakespeare in the Park. She talked so long that dinner was finished when she concluded, and she had clearly exhausted herself. Marlene openly glared at her in boredom.

"If you'll excuse me," she finally said, "I need to head to bed. Thank you for a lovely evening, everyone."

Eric stood when she left, then made his own polite farewells.

"We'll walk you out," Spencer said, nodding at Scarlett.

"Make sure to come back," her dad said knowingly. "We should talk."

Out on the sidewalk, Eric remained blissfully unaware of the furor he had accidentally caused.

"I have to get going," he said. "Your family is...so different from my family."

"We know what that really means," Spencer said.

"No. They're great. I mean it. Thanks for bringing me along. See you tomorrow, Spence. And thanks for the invitation, Scarlett."

He reached out to shake her hand as well, holding it just a moment longer than necessary. His hand was strong, a little rough along the bottom of the palm. This beautiful creature had actually come into her life, had dinner at her house, touched her hand, and now he was leaving.

There was no time to revel in the moment, though.

"Can you help me think of a way to keep from ruining my life in the next fifteen minutes?" Spencer asked, spinning her around to face him. "I'd really appreciate it."

THE DAY OF RECKONING

"I had kind of been hoping to lay it on them myself later, when I had time to think of a clever story in which I became famous and highly-paid, but it looks like it's going to be now. Why did you invite him here?"

Spencer was about to lose it. He was pacing up and down the sidewalk in front of the door and rubbing his face so hard that it looked like he might be in danger of snapping off his own nose.

"What should I say?" he begged, his voice cracking a little. "It's not Broadway. It's not TV."

"It's Shakespeare," she offered weakly, knowing that that made no difference.

"Do I lie?" he asked, peeling his hand off his face. "I'm okay with lying, except...I'm going to get caught, when, you know, they actually come and see it's in a parking garage. Or when they ask me how much I'm going to make, and I say, 'Four dollars a day.' They won't be impressed. They will be the opposite of impressed. I have to make this work, Scarlett. Think."

Scarlett bit her finger and thought.

"Why?" he said. "Why are we not Chip? He doesn't have this problem."

"He's going to rich camp in Boston," Scarlett said, trying to cheer him with that morning's gossip. "He wants to drag Lola along because he can't hack it there by himself."

This did not have the desired effect.

"Great," he said, pressing the heels of his hands into his forehead. "That's just great. I can't think about Chip. I can't think about why Lola is with him, I can't think about any of it. How does that guy...live? How can he do so much nothing and get paid for it?"

"You're not thinking about this," Scarlett said.

"Yes, I am," Spencer said. "This is all I am going to think about all night. Why are all rich people so useless? And why are they all around us?"

"Because we live in New York?" Scarlett said. "Best city in the world? And we live in a hotel? Where they sometimes come and stay, and that's how we survive?"

"It's not fair," he said. "Why does Lola bring him here?"

"Because he's her boyfriend."

"You say that like it makes sense. Okay. Okay. Have to think."

He took a deep breath and sat down on the sidewalk.

"They liked Eric," he said. "That's good. That's something. They can see I'm in a show with someone who's polite. Not a complete freak. That always helps."

"Yeah..." she said. "And he's good. He's just like you. He does all those things you do. Mime, or..."

"I'm not a mime," Spencer quickly corrected her. "Or, just

86

the once. They made us do it for school. Never tell anyone I'm a mime. People punch mimes. It's just stage combat, physical comedy...basic actor stuff."

"Whatever it is," Scarlett amended, "you know you're incredible at it. Eric said so, too."

"Yeah, well, everyone does something. *He* got a commercial out of it, anyway."

The door swung open, and Marlene stood there, hands on hips.

"Are you getting a real job?" she asked.

"No comment," Spencer said.

Marlene didn't move.

"We're having a talk in private," Scarlett said.

"The street isn't private."

Now Marlene was a lawyer.

"Come on, Marlene," Spencer said gently, "give us a minute."

"But I want to hear."

"That's why private was invented," Scarlett said. "For times just like this."

Their privacy was further interrupted by the appearance of Chip and Lola. Spencer narrowed his eyes and looked like he was on the verge of coming out with something truly exceptional to say about his nemesis, when Lola cut in quietly.

"Mr. Kobayashi in the Sterling Suite needs his toilet unblocked," she said. "And then Mom and Dad want to meet you in the Jazz Suite."

It was very hard to make a good snap following that. Marlene giggled softly and went back inside.

"Thanks for passing the message," Spencer said.

Chip didn't linger. He gave them a nod of good-bye, and Lola walked him up the block.

"It's going to be so sad when he goes to Boston," Spencer said, watching them. "But it is exciting to know that, somewhere, there's a school with a major in Alphabet Studies."

"School," Scarlett said, suddenly. "That's it."

"What? What's it?"

"Eric goes to NYU, right? Are a lot of people in your cast from NYU?"

"NYU, Juilliard. I'm the only one who's not, I think. Why?"

"Clearly," she said, "this is a joint NYU–Juilliard production. Maybe not *officially*. Who would make you leave a production run by two of the top theater schools?"

Spencer struggled with the idea.

"Look," she said, "they just want you to have some kind of degree in something—some kind of security. It's kind of a showcase. Professors from these places will come to the show, right?"

"Probably," he said. "Maybe."

"This will give them hope. That's all they want. And you *do* get paid. Just try not to tell them how much."

"It's better than anything I could have come up with," he said. "I was just going to resort to crying a lot and banging my head against the wall. It'll take some work to sell it, though...."

He got up from the sidewalk and grasped her by the shoulders.

"This may be the last time I see you as an actor," he said. "Also, I'm about to become very, very unclean. I have a bad feeling."

Lola came up behind them and politely excused herself to get past.

"I'll meet you upstairs," she said to both of them. "And good luck."

"Luck?" Spencer repeated, stepping toward the door. "What's luck got to do with it? Skill, baby. Nothing but."

He did the walking into the door trick for good measure, probably just to amuse himself, and then headed off to meet his fate. Unlike Scarlett, who always smiled, the gag only seemed to perplex and sadden Lola.

"Is he ever going to stop doing that?" she asked.

"Hopefully not," Scarlett said.

It was a long, painful wait in the Orchid Suite.

Lola was on her bed, her foot balanced on a book, carefully removing her toenail polish. Scarlett went to her mirror and took one last look at herself in the dress. Maybe it was the Dior dress that had caused Eric to smile at her, the production staff to pull her down to the stage floor, Mrs. Amberson to invite her to lunch. Maybe that was all it took in life—some really good dresses.

"Sounds like everything went well this morning," Lola ventured carefully.

"Except for the part where Marlene wanted to kill me," Scarlett said, sitting up on her bureau. This probably wasn't a safe move, as it wobbled under her, but it kept her distracted from what was going on a few doors down.

"I think she's all right. And Mrs. Amberson bought lunch for the two of you. That was nice. She's very..."

Lola didn't know how to finish that. Come to think of it, neither did Scarlett.

"Spencer's friend is very cute," Lola said, carefully rubbing her toes clean with one of her special wipes. "I don't think I'll mind if he does this play if he keeps bringing home friends like that."

As soon as she thought of Eric, Scarlett was nauseous again. She beat her heels into the dresser handles, then let herself down heavily. She opened up her computer. Several e-mails had come in from her friends. Chloe met a guy she liked. Tabitha had been bitten by a weird spider and her eye was all puffy. Josh sent a single, very drunken line: I KAN SING IN WELSH!

Scarlett didn't have the energy to reply to anyone, so she tried to write for a bit. She ignored her disjointed notes from the night before and started with a clean page.

Write what comes into your head, she told herself.

What came into her head was a pair of eyes—that stunning marbled blue.

Eric. He was a subject she could get into. She described every part of him she could think of. The soft, low voice. The slight shadow of sandy stubble that framed an angled face. Thumbs casually hooked into pockets. A graceful shuffle from foot to foot as he spoke, his focus up and all around him...

She was absorbed in the task when there was a single knock, the door flew open, and Spencer strode in. Scarlett snapped the computer closed quickly.

"Well," he said, "it's done."

"Done," Scarlett said, "as in..."

"As in I told them, and they said they would think it over tonight and tell me tomorrow. So I have a whole night of it hanging over my head. Hooray!"

He collapsed to the floor in a dramatic heap. Lola leaned down and looked him in the face.

"What exactly did you say?" she asked.

"I *may* have said that it was an invitational audition for Juilliard," he said. "That may have come out of my mouth at some point. I also may have made something up about a possible scholarship to NYU. It's not that these things are true...but we don't know that they're not true, right?"

"If you say so," Lola said mildly.

Something odd passed between Lola and Spencer, a long moment of silence and staring—Lola from her high ground on the bed, and Spencer from his fainting pose on the floor. His face had become very serious.

"If you have a problem with me, you should just come out and say it."

"I still think you should consider the scholarship," Lola said. "But whatever you decide..."

"Thank you."

"Maybe you can let me make my own decisions, too," Lola added.

"I always do."

There was some unknown argument between Lola and Spencer that had hummed along in the background for as long as Scarlett could remember, some residual vibration from their own personal Big Bang. It was never clear what it was about, and it never came to any kind of a head. It simply surfaced now and again as static, unexplained and transient.

"I need to get out of here," he said, bouncing up and breaking the tension. "It's too hot to even breathe. I need to burn off some energy. Do you think I would *definitely* kill myself if I tried to do a fall down the Central Park steps, or just *probably* kill myself?"

"I'd go with the first one," Lola said, picking up the nail polish brush again.

"That's what I thought, too," Spencer said, disappointedly. "Think I'll just go curl into a ball."

"What's the problem with you two?" Scarlett said, when he was gone.

"There's no problem," Lola said. "We have different ways of looking at things. We always have."

"It's more than that," Scarlett said.

Lola replaced the nail polish brush and looked up at Scarlett.

"I'm afraid for him sometimes," she said.

Lola's plainspoken sincerity struck a chord. If she was being very truthful with herself, Scarlett was a little afraid, too. She never questioned Spencer's ability...just their general luck. She worried for them all. Every day something else seemed to chip off this quivering pile that was their lives. It could only be a matter of time before the whole structure came crumbling down. But unlike Lola, she could never say that out loud.

"Whatever the case," Lola went on, "it's his problem, Scarlett. It's good that you care so much, but you have to lead your own life. I mean, you have your own problems. And you have a guest to take care of."

Lola was right, but the reminder still wasn't very welcome. She did have problems, like the weeks of nothing that spread out in front of her, the lack of money, of general life. At least Spencer had a goal, even if it was kind of a hard one to reach.

Come to think of it, maybe she did have an unreachable goal of her own.

She opened her computer again, where her imaginary Eric was waiting for her, looking at her again like he had at the table. Something *had* happened there, something that wasn't imaginary. And if that had happened...well, anything could.

"Maybe this time," Scarlett said. "Maybe things will work out."

"Anything is possible," Lola replied. "But honestly, it would kind of take a miracle."

THE SHORT ARM OF THE LAW

The next morning, Mrs. Amberson was dressed in her yoga clothes and smoking on her ledge when Scarlett knocked on the door of the Empire Suite.

"Forget that for now," she said, as Scarlett set down a pile of fresh sheets and towels on the dressing table. "You and I are going somewhere!"

"We are?" Scarlett said, looking down at her T-shirt and wrinkled shorts.

"I need to get reacquainted with the city," she said. "It's been a good twen...*while* since I've lived here. Do you even know what New York was like in the seventies and eighties? This Disneyland that you live in is not the New York I had to deal with. You didn't ride the subway after ten at night unless you had a deep desire to get mugged at knifepoint. Times Square was porn central. It was a genuinely *frightening* place."

She said this with a great deal of affection. She sprang off the sill and over the desk, tossing her lit cigarette over her head, narrowly missing the rail and having it bounce back into her hair.

"We're going for a walk," she said. "It's time for me to rediscover New York."

It was a steamy, sticky morning, but this did not make Mrs. Amberson slow her pace at all. They headed west to Central Park, entering at the zoo gate, negotiating their way through the crush of double-wide strollers.

"I couldn't help but overhear you and your brother talking outside last night," she said. "It sounds like you're both in a bit of a pickle."

By "couldn't help it," Scarlett assumed that she meant, "I was hanging off my window ledge to make sure I caught every word."

"It'll work out," Scarlett said. "Spencer's really talented."

"I like your attitude. But he's not the only one with a problem, is he?"

She let that statement linger and took a deep drag of her cigarette, exhaling smoke for what seemed like ten minutes, like a machine about to explode.

"I lived in New York during a very important time," she finally went on. "I thought I came back to New York to revive my acting career, but I've realized what I should really be doing is writing my story. You said you were a writer. That's what made me think of it."

"You're going to write a book?" Scarlett asked. "Just like that?"

"That's right. And it's going to be amazing! That's why we're taking this little walk—to get the creative juices flowing."

Well, something got flowing, but mostly it was sweat. At least for Scarlett. Though her face glistened a little, Mrs. Amberson didn't sweat. It was unnatural. They marched down Sixth Avenue, pausing briefly at Radio City Music Hall.

"I was almost a Rockette," she said. "But I didn't make the height requirement. I was one inch too tall. One inch. I didn't think I'd ever get over it. I did eventually, but it took a while."

She got out another cigarette, struck her match on the building face, and waved Scarlett on. For an hour, Mrs. Amberson pointed out places where her friends had lived, restaurants that were no longer there, former clubs, sites of muggings and random acts of violence.

"Where are we going?" Scarlett finally asked, as they turned on to Ninth Avenue.

"To my roots," Mrs. Amberson said.

Five more blocks of marching. There were lots of apartment buildings here, but they weren't as pristine as some of the others they had passed. They finally stopped in front of a narrow gold-brick building, only a few stories high.

"It wasn't *like* this," she said.

"What wasn't like what?"

"I lived here," she said. "In 1978. It was the most frightening building you could imagine. I sat up there, on the fire escape, and watched a man run down the street firing a gun. I saw people get mugged, stabbed, beaten. My fire escape was more exciting than the news. I used to have to lock myself in at night with six locks."

A woman came out of the building walking a tiny dog on a pink leash.

"I'm going to be sick," Mrs. Amberson said, watching the pair walk off. "What's happened to this city?"

Mrs. Amberson tried the door, but it was firmly locked. She hit a few random buzzers, but no one answered.

"Come on," she said, turning back toward Ninth Avenue. "There's something else I want to see."

This stretch of Ninth Avenue was a mixture of restaurants and bars of every sort. Thai. Greek. Chinese. Italian. Ethiopian. There was a wine bar, a beer bar, a cupcake shop, a pet boutique, and a store full of upscale paints. In short, a happy little cosmos of urban needs were fulfilled in its short distance. In the middle of it all was a midsized fancy grocery store called Food Paradise, with a large display of exotic fruits, imported cheeses, and fine pastries in the window.

"Well, at least *that's* still here, sort of," she said. "But it wasn't a paradise."

She crossed the street midblock, dodging a cab, and went into the store.

"You should have seen the dump that was here in the seventies," she said, eying the olive bar. "It was truly disgusting. Moldy Wonderbread, roaches. Back then, I used to make ketchup soup."

She walked up and down every aisle, mumbling about what she saw there. All of the food, so nicely laid out, seemed to make her first sad, then annoyed, and finally, weirdly jubilant. Scarlett just got hungry.

"Let's go," Mrs. Amberson said abruptly. "I've had enough."

She took Scarlett's arm and wheeled to the door. A friendly-faced security guard cleared his throat and stepped in front of them.

"Just a minute, please," he said. "Please open your bag, miss."

Scarlett was surprised to find that this remark was addressed to her.

"What?" Scarlett replied. "Why?"

"Just please open it."

Mrs. Amberson stared up at the ceiling, and Scarlett got a very sick feeling in the pit of her stomach that she couldn't quite account for.

"Please open your bag, miss," the man repeated.

Scarlett pulled her bag from her shoulder warily. It was unzipped. It had been zipped before, she was sure of it. She held it open. To her amazement, there were three cans of tuna fish lying on top that had definitely not been there when she left the house.

"Those aren't mine," she said.

"I know that," he said. "All right. Step over to this office with me, please. Let's make this easy, okay?"

Scarlett felt her legs start to go soft and found herself reaching out to Mrs. Amberson's arm for support. It was amazingly muscular.

"Scarlett!" Mrs. Amberson said. "I thought we were past this!"

"What?" Scarlett replied, wheeling around.

"We have come way too far for this," Mrs. Amberson was rambling on.

"What are you talking about?"

Mrs. Amberson angled herself between Scarlett and the man.

"Listen," she said. "This is totally unacceptable, but please hear me out. I'm a volunteer with Teen Reach New York, which is a group that works with troubled teens."

The man crossed his arms over his chest. Scarlett's jaw dropped in shock.

"This is Scarlett," she continued. "We're transitioning her out of a very bad home environment. Scarlett used to have to steal to feed her brothers and sisters. I'm her one-on-one counselor—just a volunteer—and I take her out and help her develop new, socially acceptable habits. I've been trying to teach her how to buy nutritious meals on a budget. I was supposed to be watching, but she's fast....She's a good girl, though."

By now, other people were watching them. All activity in the three closest checkout lanes had stopped. Mrs. Amberson was shaking a little now, like she had truly been rattled by this whole event.

"Please," she said. "Arresting her won't do any good. We've done so much work to get her out of that part of the system. I'll..."

She looked around anxiously, then pointed to a wall of paper balloons, each one marking a one dollar donation to a local food bank.

"I'll pay for the tuna and I'll buy a hundred of those balloons," she said. She got out her wallet and pulled out a handful of twenties. "This is my money, and I will give the food bank a hundred dollars. Other people will benefit, along with Scarlett. And she'll never come back in the store again. Obviously, the counselors and the doctors have some more work to do. But please. The girl stole *tuna fish*. This is how she used to have to live. She's not one of these kids that steals for a thrill."

The man was clearly struggling with this one. He had what he clearly believed was a shoplifter...and one of them was a shoplifter...yet Mrs. Amberson's apparent anguish had moved him.

"She doesn't come back here," he said. "Ever."

"Understood," Mrs. Amberson said, shoving the money into his hand.

"You want to sign the balloons?" he asked.

"No. I think we'd better go. Thank you for your understanding."

She put her arm around Scarlett's shoulders and pulled her along, out into the blinding sun. She didn't stop until they were down the block and around the corner, where she threw up her hand for a cab, which she ushered Scarlett into.

"Sixty-ninth and Lexington," she told the driver. "Mind if I smoke?"

"No," he answered happily. "I will, too, then. No one ever lets me, you know?"

"Make my day."

They both lit up. Scarlett sat, still not recovered enough to speak.

"Did you hear that?" Mrs. Amberson said ecstatically. "Did you hear what just came out of my mouth? I haven't lost a thing. I am going to call my agent and tell him that he has to try to get me some kind of role as a child protection agent or something on Crime and Punishment. Someone who comes on and testifies and looks all shaken up but professional. Trouble is, I think my agent is dead. I guess I need a new one. . . ."

"You stole tuna fish," Scarlett finally managed. Her voice was loud enough to startle the driver and cause him to slide the panel behind his head shut. "You put it in my bag."

"What's even better," Mrs. Amberson said, "is that he didn't notice this. You covered so *well*!"

She reached into the waistband of her pants and pulled out a candy bar.

"I didn't cover anything," Scarlett said again, not bothering to lower her voice. "You almost got me arrested!"

Mrs. Amberson turned this time, but looked utterly unperturbed. She gazed at Scarlett through a thin veil of cigarette smoke.

"I would never have let that happen," she said. "He was only bluffing. Wasn't that *fun?*"

"I'm banned from the store! They think I'm a juvie tuna fish thief with a whole team of counselors and doctors!"

"You'll never go to that store. It's all the way across town. And they'll never remember you, I promise. They just say that."

"That is *not the point*!"

"You seem upset," Mrs. Amberson said mildly. "You're just full of adrenaline right now, and you're using that adrenaline as panic. Performers constantly go through this, and we turn our head rush into performance. We use it. We enjoy it. Now breathe through your nose and out of your mouth, a nice cleansing flow of air. The store got money to cover what was taken. You didn't get into any trouble. A very worthy organization got a hundred dollars to buy food for hungry people. Enjoy the moment!"

She was using a cooing, lulling voice that Scarlett felt was probably copied from one of her yoga instructors. Scarlett reached over and slid open the panel.

"Pull over," she said to the driver.

"Oh, come on, Scarlett. Where's your sense of adventure?"

"Adventure is white-water rafting. This..." She held up the can. "...is tuna."

"That was very well phrased. You have a touch of the actress about you, too, you know."

The cab stopped, and Scarlett opened the door and got out.

"You did very well!" Mrs. Amberson called to her as she walked off. "You pass! I think this is going to work out splendidly!"

Scarlett had no idea what that meant, and she didn't care.

DEAL OF A LIFETIME

It took Scarlett the entire walk home to calm down—and it was a long, hot walk. When she arrived at the Hopewell, she pushed right on through the empty lobby, through the dining room, into the kitchen.

The Hopewell kitchen was embarrassingly large for a family that couldn't cook and had no guests to feed. Most of the appliances were from the sixties and seventies, and there were way too many of them. Only about half of the stuff worked. Belinda could make the place behave somehow, but no one else could.

There was something else in the kitchen that refused to behave. Namely, her parents, who quickly moved away from each other and did some quick hair and clothes adjusting. Scarlett knew what that meant. She had walked in on them canoodling. Again. It was kind of nice to have parents who liked each other—she was one of the only people she knew who did. Still, every one of the Martin siblings had caught them making out. There was, after all, a good reason why there were four of them.

"Guys," Scarlett said, wincing, "can't you put up a sign or something?"

Her dad was pretending to be very interested in something behind one of the three refrigerators.

"Is it you or Marlene who freaks out about mice?" he asked casually. "I can never remember. I know one of you is spiders and one of you is mice."

Scarlett responded by backing up against the worktable and pulling herself up to sit on it.

"Oh, right," he said. "It's you. You should ignore what we're doing then."

For once, the sucking face may have been preferable.

"Mrs. Amberson spoke to us this morning," her mom said, opening a box of no-kill traps. "Has she told you her idea?"

"Oh, she told me," Scarlett said, warily watching the floor.

"You don't seem happy about it. I thought you'd be excited about working on a book."

"Wait...what?"

"She wants you to be her assistant!" her mother said happily. "You really seem to have impressed her."

"I thought you said I couldn't get a job," Scarlett said quickly.

Her parents gave each other googely-eyes for a moment.

"Look," her dad said, "we had a long talk in bed this morning about all of you. And we've come to some decisions. We've realized just how much you all try."

"Lola works hard and has voluntarily taken a year off from going to school or moving," her mother said, reaching out for her dad's hand. "Spencer has tried his best at auditioning, and he's really straightened up in the last year—getting up at five every morning to work a breakfast shift. And you...you've never gotten much of a chance at all. And here comes something that is what you love,

104

writing, that would pay a really generous amount."

"It would?" Scarlett said.

"She's offering to pay you five hundred dollars a week," she said. "Cash. We need the help around here, but she is your guest, and that's a lot of money. And a good opportunity."

Five hundred dollars a week was an *actual, literal* fortune. Some of her friends got almost that much for their cab, clothing, and going out allowances.

"So," he said, "are you happy with that?"

This would have been the right time to tell them about the tuna, and the lying to the security guard. But...*five hundred dollars*.

There was something else lingering here, though.

"What did you decide about Spencer?" she asked.

"Spencer told us that this show is connected to NYU and Juilliard, and that doing it might give him a very good chance to go there, maybe even get another scholarship, this time for something he really wants to do," her dad said.

"We called the culinary school," her mother said. "They said they'd have to let his scholarship go today, but there's no reason he can't reapply, and they'll make a note on his file. There is a strong chance that if he reapplies in the next few weeks, they'll be able to give him the same package. It's not guaranteed, but it sounds like he has a good shot."

"We decided to let him do this show," he finished. "If it doesn't work, we may still be able to get him in. And combined with you getting this opportunity..."

"The two things came at the same time," her mother finished. "With this little bit of extra security for you, we felt better about taking a chance with him."

Of course. *Of course*, her taking this job was tied into Spencer's chance.

"So..." her dad said, all smiles, "happy?"

"Thrilled," Scarlett said.

Okay. So her summer was about to be a minefield. But she would be rich by the end of it. She could buy a whole new wardrobe. A new computer. There would be iced coffees at lunch and cabs when she needed them....

"As for the money," her dad said, "it's way too much to play with. So she'll be paying us directly, and we'll put it away for you. But you can have fifty a week. Now, we just need you to take the dirty table linens to Mrs. Foo's and pick up Marlene's prescriptions at Duane Reade. The linens are behind the front desk."

Scarlett slunk out of the dining room.

The dirty tablecloths and napkins had been bundled into a large plastic bag. Obviously, they had been allowed to collect, because the bag was heavy and a bit hard to carry. She hoisted it up and it partially blocked her view. She used it as cushioning as she slammed her way back out the door.

She staggered her way down half the block, the sun beating down on her.

"Whoa!" a familiar voice said. "That looks heavy."

A pair of hands lifted away her burden, revealing Eric. She laughed, a keening, nervous laugh—sort of like the sound made by little purse dogs when people accidentally catch their fur in the zipper. Not an alluring sound. Combine that with the fact that she was sweating and carrying twenty pounds of dirty linen... it was a pretty, pretty picture.

"Where are you going with this?" he asked.

"Down the block," she managed to say.

"You lead the way. Can't have you carrying this."

She was too astonished to do or say anything when he took the bag from her.

"I'm here working with Spencer," he said. "I just came down to get a sandwich from the place on the corner. So this works out. What's going on today? Any more TV appearances?"

"No," she managed, "but my new boss just tried to get me arrested for shoplifting tuna."

He stopped and set the bag down on the sidewalk to redistribute the weight.

"Is that just a joke I don't get, or did that happen?"

"It happened," Scarlett said. "It definitely happened."

"I've only known you for a day or two, and you've managed to do more weird stuff than anyone I can think of."

He picked up the bag again, but frequently peered at her over it.

"Does crime pay well?" he asked.

"Yes," she said. "But I don't get to keep any of it. It's going to a school fund."

"Ah, the joys of college tuition," he said. "Thank God for my commercial. Two days of work paid for a whole year at NYU. I'd better get another one or I don't know how I'm coming back."

It was impossible for Scarlett to ignore that Eric needing to earn money fit nicely into the promise she had made to Spencer about rich guys.

They had reached the laundry. Eric carried the bag in and set it on the counter.

"I look forward to hearing the stories," he said. "Promise me you'll tell me when I see you. And I will see you. I'll make a point of it."

He gave her one final, devastating, and unlikely smile, then went off in search of his sandwich.

It was at that moment that Scarlett fully accepted her new employment.

ACT II

The very last room completed in the Hopewell refurbishment of 1929 was the Empire Suite. J. Allen Raumenberg worked for weeks on its composition. It was perhaps here, in this hotel room, that he developed his concept of "bringing down the moon"—the principle that would guide the hundreds of Broadway and film sets he would design over the next twenty years.

Raumenberg felt that the most magical time of day was twilight, when the moon hung low and the sky split with color. He had his glassworks create a spectacular moonlike mirror, and he carefully manipulated shades of light and dark in all aspects of the design so that the room would "constantly appear to be suspended in that magical hour when the night is about to bloom and the curtains on every stage rise."

Fittingly, the room's first inhabitant was Clara Hooper, a dancer in the Ziegfeld Follies, and the mistress of a wealthy Wall Street banker. She was sitting at the dressing table in the Empire Suite looking into the moon mirror when she got a call saying that the stock market had just crashed. Hours later, her boyfriend vanished, never to return. She realized that the six dollars and forty-seven cents she had in front of her could now be the only money she had in the world. She certainly couldn't pay the twelve dollars a night the room cost. She tossed her things out of the fourth-story window to a friend who waited in the street below, and then slipped out quietly during the night.

So from the start, the Empire Suite had a strong (if somewhat dubious) connection to the theater world....

—J. ALLEN RAUMENBERG: DESIGNER FOR AN AGE

THE INHABITANT

"How do you write a life?" Mrs. Amberson asked from the window of the Empire Suite. "The tangled web. So many stories..."

She blew some smoke up. It floated back down and settled around her head, like a halo of smog.

"I feel like we're missing something," she said.

Words, Scarlett thought. *Words, on a page, written by you. That's what we're missing.*

But she sighed to herself and said nothing. She just absently read her e-mails from her friends. It looked like work—not that there was any work to do.

There were lots of updates, as usual.

Dakota's French was good enough now that she got through an entire day in Paris speaking no English at all. Chloe had accidentally backhanded one of her ten-year-olds in the head with a tennis racket...but otherwise she was good. She had stopped dating the first guy and moved on to another, and already had eyes on a third. Hunter had gone to LA for the day and had gotten to go on the Paramount lot. Josh had about twenty new English friends, and they tended to spend their weekends partying in London or going off to the country to push each other off small boats called "punts" into shallow water.

Two weeks. That's how long it had been. Two weeks, and they all had new lives and impressive achievements. And she'd been here with Mrs. Amberson, waiting for her to get one cohesive thought together for this book.

There had been plenty of writing preparation. They'd gone shopping at the Montblanc store on Madison Avenue, where Mrs. Amberson spent several hundred dollars on two pens—one fountain, one ballpoint—and a pot of ink. They'd gone and spent a few hundred more on notebooks from some imported Parisian papermaker. There was the ergonomic yoga support pillow that was supposed to induce creativity. The multiple trips to various health food and Asian grocery stores for teas, herbs, dried plums, some seaweed in a bag, organic coffee, special water...

In fact, Scarlett had never been so busy doing so much nothing. Between the shopping, the endless walks Mrs. Amberson needed to "feel out the city again," the days spent in bookstores picking up books on how to write, the lunches, locating all of the services Mrs. Amberson required...Scarlett had had almost no time to herself.

"It's hard to know where to begin," Mrs. Amberson mused.

Scarlett could take it no more.

"What did you *do*?" she finally snapped.

"Do? What? For money?"

Scarlett nodded. That was a good start. This direct questioning was effective.

"My very first job was at the Round the Clock Diner," Mrs.

Amberson said. "I got that by lying and saying I had been a waitress for three years in Cleveland. I suppose that you could call that my first role. I played a New York waitress. I definitely didn't know how to do the job when I started. I copied the walk, the way of speaking. After a few weeks, I was the toughest waitress they had. In fact, I was a little *too* good at being a New York waitress. I scared some people. So I refined it a bit and took the act uptown, to the All Hours Diner. And while I was there, I started picking up shifts at the Ticktock."

Scarlett wasn't sure if she was supposed to write down the names of all of these diners, but she had been sitting here for a long time, waiting for something to come out of Mrs. Amberson's mouth. She typed a few of them out.

"Where did you live?" she asked.

"On the floor of an apartment on Thirteenth Street and Sixth Avenue with a ballerina named Suzie. She was a freak. A good dancer, but she lived entirely on milk and hard pretzels. I never saw her eat anything else, even when I brought home food from the diner. She had this loser drug-dealer boyfriend. Drug dealers had some glamour then, but not this guy. Used to come over and sit in the corner, put on a wizard's hat, and meditate loudly. He made a sound like this."

Mrs. Amberson made a loud, grating *mmmmmmmmm* noise. Scarlett considered making a note of this, then opted against it.

"I only stayed there because it was cheap. Then they both went off to form a macrobiotic commune upstate, and I got kicked out. Then I moved to Second Avenue...."

She leaned backward a bit and stared at something below her.

"Your sister is here with her boy," she said. "What's his name?"

"Chip," Scarlett said, without enthusiasm. Why was Lola home? She was supposed to be doing a long shift at the store today.

"Of course. Chip. Nice enough looking, but he's never going to split an atom, is he?"

"I doubt it."

"You look unimpressed. Not your type of boy? I'll bet you like them a little more swift on the uptake, don't you, O'Hara?"

Scarlett decided to let the question drop in the hopes that she would forget it. But that didn't happen.

"What *is* your type?" Mrs. Amberson asked, leaning in from her perch. "You've never told me about your love life, Scarlett. You're a very pretty girl. You must have a boy shacked up somewhere for your personal delights. I'd bet it's a booky one, with overtones of Harry Potter and a lot of black T-shirts. Come on. What's he like?"

"I don't have a boyfriend," Scarlett said. "I've just...some guys at my school, a few times."

"You left out the verb in that," Mrs. Amberson said. "I *love* verbs."

Scarlett glared over the laptop, but Mrs. Amberson did not look even slightly deterred.

"I have great hopes for you this summer, O'Hara," she said. "I don't buy this stern, determined exterior of yours. There's a romantic underneath. I'm sure of it."

Scarlett had no idea she had a stern, determined exterior.

"What are you talking about?" she asked.

"You almost never smile," Mrs. Amberson said. "Not a real smile. I know smiles. I was in several toothpaste commercials. I know all the varieties of smile."

She turned back and tried to squeeze her head between the rails to get a better look at what was going on in the street below.

"Well," she said, "it looks like your sister isn't making out too badly. If they don't bulge in the brain or anywhere else of interest, the wallet is a good alternate location. And I should know."

Something in Mrs. Amberson had detached and floated away. This effort that Scarlett had put her through had exhausted her.

"I think," she said absently, "that I need a little trip down to the Turkish bath this afternoon. I always used to go there to sweat out the small stuff. Maybe just give the room a light freshening and then take a few hours off. You look a little peaky. Do something frivolous."

Lola jumped about four feet when Scarlett opened the door to the Orchid Suite.

"Aren't you supposed to be at work?" Scarlett asked.

"Aren't you? Where's Mrs. Amberson?"

"She's gone to sweat at the Turkish bath. What's your excuse?"

Lola looked a bit furtive and guilty.

"It's Chip's mom's fiftieth birthday," Lola said. "They're having a weekend event in the Hamptons and a dinner in town."

"It's not the weekend," Scarlett said. "And it's not dinnertime."

"There's a lot to do. There's the jitney to charter, the caterers to speak to, the party planners, the flowers, the band..."

"You know, Chip is a big boy with a high school diploma and a phone and everything," Scarlett said. "Why do you have to take off work for that? It's *his* mom."

"He needs help," she said. "He's no good with that stuff."

"Isn't that what the party planners do? Plan parties?"

"You don't understand," Lola said, digging furiously around her bureau. "Have you seen my pink ear...oh, here they are."

She put the pink studs in her ears with a rapid, stabbing motion.

"What was it last week?" Scarlett said. "Or the weekend before?"

Lola ran her hands through her hair in frustration. She was obviously a little nervous about the whole thing.

"I work in a store," she said. "I can switch shifts. And Chip has to go to this wealth management training thing in Boston... he doesn't have time. Just do me a favor, okay? I was never here this afternoon. I'll owe you."

"You already owe me."

"So, you're building credit."

"It's fine," Scarlett said. "I won't tell on you. I'm not...well, Marlene."

Lola's face blossomed into a smile.

"I'll see you later," she said. "I'll try to sneak you out something good from the pastry sampling we're going to. I'll be back early, anyway. Marlene has a bowling party tonight at seven I have to take her to."

Lola was gone in a moment, only the light fragrance of her perfume lingered. Finally, a few hours to write. Scarlett turned on the air conditioner, opened her computer, and...

Again, the only thing in her mind was Eric.

She hadn't seen him since that day on the sidewalk with the laundry, but he had never once left her mind. Every day she wanted to ask Spencer about him when he got home from rehearsal, but every time she opened her mouth to speak, there was an unfamiliar queasiness.

Scarlett had never had an actual, labeled, official boyfriend. But then, almost none of her friends did. It was an intense place, Frances Perkins. No time for attachments—just fleeting making out between labs, museum visits, more labs, and endless extra-curriculars. Dating was for the weak, for people who didn't plan on doing double chem (which Scarlett didn't), double physics (ditto), or getting into the Right School.

This, she had gathered, had not been the case at the High School of Performing Arts. Every time Scarlett saw Spencer's classmates, they were all over each other, getting together and breaking up as loudly and dramatically as possible. Spencer had wooed and been wooed so many times that Scarlett stopped trying to learn their names.

The point was...this should have been an easy topic, but it wasn't. Not that there was any *point* in asking. She was aiming too high.

Still...

Even thinking about him made her itch.

She Googled Eric's name and, within a minute, she found his commercial. She watched it once, then again, and again.

It crossed her mind that she might be going crazy, or that this might be cyberstalking, but these thoughts didn't trouble her too much.

By the time she had finished her thirtieth viewing, Scarlett couldn't sit still any longer. The YouTube Eric was not enough. Nothing prevented her from leaving Spencer a message and meeting up with him when he was done. And where Spencer was, Eric was likely to be close by.

To her surprise, Spencer picked up immediately.

"Are you a mind reader?" he asked.

"Maybe..." she said mysteriously. "Let me guess what you're thinking about now. Does it involve leather pants and bologna sandwiches?"

"You're good," he said. "I have to give you that. Either that, or you've been reading my *That's So Raven* fanfiction again. How are you with using your psychic powers to solve problems?"

"Incredibly expert," she said. "Hit me."

"I'll meet you in the park in an hour," he said. "Bring your spirit guide."

A MINOR PROBLEM

When she arrived, Spencer was sitting on the Alice in Wonderland statue. Two unicycles sat by his feet.

"You're wondering why I'm not at rehearsal," Spencer said.

"Actually, I was wondering about the unicycles," she said. "But why aren't you at rehearsal?"

"The unicycles are for the show. Ask me about the show."

"What about the show?"

"A truckload of officials showed up in the middle of Ophelia's death scene and slapped us with a vacate order," he said.

"What's a vacate order?"

"As in, get out this very second, this building is full of disgusting, infectious, black death mold," Spencer said, coughing a little. "They came in wearing masks and moved us out, then they put yellow tape and a big sign over the door. Like a crime scene, but less fun."

"But where are you going to rehearse?"

"Ah." Spencer held up a finger. "You've hit on a very exciting point. That was the only place the company could afford. They got a special deal from the building's owner—probably because he knew the place was about to be condemned. The company director is making some calls. But unless he finds something cheaper, immediately...and he's not going to find anything cheaper. So I'm going to let you figure out what that means."

"No show," Scarlett said hoarsely.

"No show," Spencer repeated. "No. Show. Me, off to cooking school. End of any plans to act. Unless we come up with a really good idea in the next few hours. In the meantime, I can enjoy my shiny unicycle before it has to go back to the rental place."

Spencer tried to smile, but it looked a little strained.

"They aren't both mine," he said. "One is Eric's. But he took his scooter to rehearsal and couldn't take his home. I'm good, or I will be once I learn how to ride this thing, but not good enough to ride two at once."

He picked up one of the unicycles, balanced it on an angle, and tried to get into the seat a few times, tipping over and falling again and again.

"What do you need?" she asked. "I mean, for the rehearsal?"

"Basically, we just need a large, empty room to work in. Nothing special. Maybe a place to store our stuff, set up some props. Something big enough to hold about fifteen people with room to move around."

"That doesn't sound too hard to find."

"It's not," he said, steadying himself in the seat by spreading his arms wide. "There are a lot of rehearsal places around the city for rent, we just can't afford any of them."

He looked like he had basically gotten himself in position and was able to ride a few feet.

"Let me play around with this thing for a few minutes," he said. "I have to blow off some steam."

Scarlett knew that when Spencer was frustrated, the best thing to do was let him fall down a lot. He rode off unsteadily down the path, narrowly avoiding running over some small dogs and almost falling over into a stroller as he went.

A large empty space with storage. Something that fifteen people could move around in. It was a shame—they had nothing but empty rooms at their place. But they were too small, too full of fragile things. Except...

A little germ of an idea popped into Scarlett's mind. At first, it seemed like a very bad, weak idea. But it didn't bring any little idea friends along with it, so it was the *only* idea.

Spencer came back into view, carrying his unicycle under one arm. He was much dirtier than when he first rode off a few minutes before.

"You know what?" he said. "People give you really suspicious looks when you emerge from a bush, covered in leaves, carrying a unicycle."

"I know a place," Scarlett said. "It's not pretty. It doesn't have any fancy stuff in it. But it isn't going to be condemned."

Spencer cocked an eyebrow at her.

"And how much does this paradise cost?" he asked.

"It's free."

She definitely had his attention now.

"Our basement," she said. "It's big. It's mostly unused. It isn't covered in mold that will kill you."

Spencer tumbled to the grass.

"I don't think Mom and Dad will let us move an entire

121

theater company into the hotel," he said. "I think Dad would call that something like 'guest disruption.' Also, they might change their minds about my show counting when they find out that we don't even have a place to store our unicycles. I don't even think they should know about the unicycles. Otherwise, I like everything about your plan."

"The trick," Scarlett said, "is that they won't know about it. How often do any of us even go into the basement, except to get to the washing machine or the recycling?"

Spencer thought this over.

"I go down there," he said. "Because that's where I keep my bike. That's about it."

"So, if we make sure that we're the only ones taking the recycling down or doing the wash, no one will actually see."

There was silence for a few moments as Spencer did a little feasibility test in his head. Scarlett could see him sitting straighter as it dawned on him that this just might work.

"Everyone can come in through Trash Can Alley," Scarlett thought aloud.

That was the nickname for the service entrance to the basement, which was a set of concrete steps leading down to a dark doorway. They kept the hotel trash cans chained up to the railing that protected it.

"I can stand by the front door and give you the all clear. As long as you all go in and out at the same time, it should work."

Spencer was looking more and more hopeful every second. He spun the wheel with his hand.

"We might not be seen," he said. "But could be heard. We scream and yell."

"Who pays attention to screaming and yelling in New York? It'll be muffled. No one's going to think it's coming from the basement. It'll at least buy you a few days."

A preliminary test brought excellent results. It would be relatively easy to get everyone in and out of the side entrance with the door propped open. Scarlett sat in the lobby while Spencer went down and screamed for a while. She could hear him, but as she suspected, it didn't sound like anything out of the ordinary. They sat in his room to work out the finer details.

Spencer's bedroom was the Maxwell Suite. It was a small, simple room designed for single, professional men—back when people used to live in hotels, as they sometimes did. It was his private hovel, filled with all the things that made Spencer, Spencer. There were pieces of bike, dog-eared scripts, bizarre pieces of old costumes, a massive pile of books on acting, and a few truly mysterious boxes and containers that Scarlett divined, just by instinct, she never wanted to know the contents of.

"If Lola has to take Marlene somewhere by seven," he said, reaching into one of these and pulling out a crumbled contact sheet, "then we should be good from maybe six-thirty on."

Scarlett's brain was already moving on now that Spencer was working on the details. If the show was coming to the hotel, that meant that Eric was coming, too.

"I'll clear all the crap out of the front room," Spencer was saying. "That's big enough for everyone, right?"

Someone like Eric had to have a girlfriend. Some humans are so beautiful, so perfect, that other humans are instantly drawn to them like magnets. And they always stick.

"It definitely is," he answered himself. He was already busy typing something into his phone and consulting the sheet.

It couldn't hurt just to ask, though. Just for information. After all, Eric was someone Spencer worked with closely, and it was just polite to want to know more about him.

"Spence?" she said. "Is Eric..."

He paused his typing.

"Is he what?"

Nope. She couldn't do it.

"A good actor?" she heard herself asking. Her voice had gotten weird and high.

"Is he a good actor?" Spencer repeated.

"Yeah..." she said. "It's interesting. Acting. How do you know if someone is good?"

He just stared at her, which was fair enough.

"I'm just thinking about the basement," she fumbled. "If they...project a lot. The good actors. Maybe we should put some padding around the basement door."

This was an extremely bad cover, but Spencer was both distracted and puzzled and decided to let it drop.

"Padding's a good idea," he said, turning back to his phone. "I'll hang some of the rain mats in the stairway. We can buffer the sound a little. Anything that reduces echo is good. We can do that this afternoon."

"I'll go start," she said. "I have a plan."

***

There is something about staying in a hotel that makes even the most meticulous and orderly person lose all sense of decorum. It is a place of no shame, where you can use ten towels per shower and dangle them off of anything more sturdy than a wet towel. You can litter the floor with bags, papers, discarded clothing, pillows, wrappers...and *much worse* things. In fact, Scarlett wasn't even permitted to turn rooms over by herself until she turned thirteen, and even then she had to have Lola or Spencer with her. They had a special device known as The Claw to pick up anything really scary.

The fine art of hotel laundry is to wash everything using as much bleach as possible without actually dissolving the fabric. When cleaning, you use the most toxic and alarming products on the market—the ones that kill every living thing they touch. The idea is to always destroy what went before.

Before, Scarlett only did the occasional room clean, just as an exercise to learn the family trade. But she was now well-established in the routine of cleaning the Empire Suite every day, usually when Mrs. Amberson went to yoga or dance class or one of her four-hour lunches.

Mrs. Amberson was not like most guests. She actually filled the ancient drawers of the normally unused furniture. Her wardrobe was bursting with clothes. The dressing table was full of little notes, phone numbers, piles of magazines and theatrical publications, and the bedside stand had a neat stack of books on writing, meditation, and natural healing. She had immediately rejected the use of industrial cleaners and sprays and had Scarlett go out and buy a huge bag of organic products and reusable cleaning cloths. It was actually a nice ritual. Scarlett would put in her headphones and tidy up, using the almond wood cleaner, the ylang-ylang bathroom spray, and the vinegar-and-cucumber glass cleaner.

Most important, she washed the towels and sheets in special environmentally friendly liquid. She even did the occasional load of personal laundry. This gave her a new kind of jurisdiction over the washing machine. Mrs. Amberson was the queen of guests, and her needs came first.

As she worked away that afternoon doing the "room freshening," Scarlett made sure to take everything that could possibly be washed—not just the sheets and towels, but her Egyptian cotton bathrobe, her neatly bundled pile of yoga clothes, her silk pajamas (handwashing was an excellent way of killing time in the basement).

Scarlett had a lot of laundry—and a plan. Not *only* would she keep guard over the basement by doing the laundry and going up and down the steps, not *only* would she have an appreciative guest, but...she would *also* be at the rehearsal.

Because, if she was really being honest with herself...which she only sort of was...this saving-the show-by-sticking-it-in-the-basement idea wasn't just about helping Spencer. It was mostly about helping Spencer, of course. That was eighty percent of it. But there was no harm in a plan that helped her brother while allowing her to see the most beautiful guy in all of creation, even if that meant doing all of the laundry in the entire hotel.

Mrs. Amberson arrived home as Scarlett was wheeling out many of her possessions in the laundry cart.

"Well, well," she said. "Such a work ethic! I leave you alone

126

and tell you to take it easy, and you decide to do piles of laundry. I worry for you, O'Hara."

"I'm fine," Scarlett said, tightening her hold on the cart. "I like laundry."

"That's the most disturbing thing I've ever heard. Put those things back. You and I are going out. My friend Billy is working on a massive musical and he wants me to come by."

"No," Scarlett said. "I really can't. I have plans."

"Plans?" Mrs. Amberson leaned against the Empire Suite door. "What kind of plans?"

"With friends."

"I thought all of your friends went away for the summer."

"One of them came home early. She got stung by bees. Lots of bees."

"How tragic. Well, of course! Go and see your friend. And the laundry..."

"I'll keep it," Scarlett said, quickly wheeling it off toward the elevator. "I'll do it before I go. Have a good night at the show!"

She could feel Mrs. Amberson watching her as she waited.

"Give my best to your friend," she said. "I'll be thinking of her."

THE RISKS OF BEING LUCKY

At six-thirty, Spencer and Scarlett went to Central Park, where he had arranged for the cast and crew to meet, well out of sight of the hotel. The idea of meeting a bunch of Shakespearian actors intimidated Scarlett a little at first, but when she arrived, she saw a bunch of people who looked pretty much like the same people Spencer went to high school with. They were a little older—mostly college students—but looked pretty harmless.

Trevor, the director, was tall and kind of heavy, with red hair, a tiny beard, and a massive voice. Hamlet was played by a Juilliard student named Leroy. He was the quietest. Scarlett thought he was keeping in character and brooding, but then she noticed that he was really just trying to balance a spoon off the end of his nose. Horatio, Hamlet's best friend, was a carefully groomed guy named Jeff who thought he was funny, but wasn't. Scarlett watched him look over in annoyance whenever Spencer did or said anything that was actually funny.

There were only a handful of girls. Paulette the stage manager was a tiny and curvy Texan redhead. She had the group well in hand, barking orders and asking about schedules as she ate cold macaroni and cheese out of a Tupperware container. She was roommates at NYU with Ophelia, who was played by a tall, dark-haired girl named Stephanie. She wore tiny glasses and had the firm build of someone who did a lot of gymnastics or modern dance. She also gave Spencer a lot of looks, but of a different kind than Jeff.

Eric was one of the last to arrive, sauntering along with a smile on his face so warming that he might have been singularly responsible for melting an ice shelf.

Getting everyone down the alley was even easier than they had imagined. Spencer and Scarlett had prepared everything as best they could, stuffing old towels under cracks, hanging blankets from the walls, covering the wooden steps and the concrete floor with everything they could find. It wasn't a pretty effect, but the cast didn't appear to think anything of it.

Except for Trevor, they were all good at self-monitoring the noise level. And with Scarlett in command of the washing machine, demand for the basement was nonexistent. They left at eleven, unnoticed by anyone except Weird Carlos, the guy who walked up and down their street with a nonfunctioning radio, telling everyone that he was Bill Clinton. When the last of them had gone, Spencer and Scarlett returned the basement to a more or less normal state.

"I can't believe this," Spencer said, pulling down an old blanket they had taped to the wall. "If I had realized that our basement was this ignored, high school would have been totally different. I feel cheated."

"Cheated how?" Scarlett said, folding one of the dozens of towels she had washed. "What *didn't* you do in high school?"

129

"I never threw a party. Mom and Dad were always home, or one of them was. I was the only one in my class who didn't throw a party."

"Yeah, but you *went* to about a million."

"It's not the same," he said.

"And didn't you say that you made out with your girlfriend from junior year, I can't remember which one, in every single room, even on the front desk? Actually, it sounded like you did more than that..."

"When did I tell you *that?*" he said, snapping in her direction.

"I don't know. Some night at the hospital."

"I shouldn't have told you that story," he said, admonishing his former self. "And it was *under* the front desk. I told you this in the hospital?"

"Yeah. Some night that Marlene was really sick and we got stuck there all night, and you were working on *Romeo and Juliet*. I think you were sleep deprived. You were trying to stay up to learn your lines, and I fell asleep on your shoulder and you couldn't move."

"Oh, right." He nodded and set to work pulling up the mats from the steps. "I remember that. I still shouldn't have told you. Can you forget that? Don't do that."

"Did you go in *my* room?" she asked.

"It was so long ago, Scarlett. It was back before I took my vow of celibacy. I can't remember these things in my pure state."

Scarlett shuddered and turned her attention to folding Mrs. Amberson's yoga pants.

"Stephanie is *really* pretty," Spencer said. "And really, really annoyingly professional."

"Professional how?"

"She's one of these serious types who believes you can't date anyone you work with. It makes sense, but..."

This would have been the perfect time to ask the question about Eric, but just as she was working up the nerve, Spencer moved on.

"Oh, well," he said. "Things can't be perfect. Besides, this will all be over when we get caught tomorrow night."

But they didn't get caught.

Against all odds, this plan worked for two entire nights. Either the gods were smiling on them for once, or their basement was truly the place where no one could hear you scream. There were a few close calls when Scarlett had to throw herself at her dad trying to take down some recycling or when she and Spencer had run evasive maneuvers around Marlene. But for the most part, it went like a dream. They even stopped meeting in the park. Spencer just propped the side door open, and the cast let themselves in.

The whole time in the basement they only went over a handful of scenes, most of which didn't involve Spencer or Eric. But the third night was different—they had just moved on to a major Rosencrantz and Guildenstern scene. Trevor was arranging the three actors. Eric and Spencer were doing something behind Hamlet where they had to keep passing an object back and forth very rapidly. It was obvious that the final effect was going to be entertaining, but Scarlett couldn't see from where she was sitting. She got up and slipped against the wall to watch.

"Leroy, I think it's going to be hard to hear you if you put your head in your hands like that," Trevor was saying. "And, Eric, come around a little, upstage. There. I think that's better. Frame him a little. Now we can hear you. Try it from there."

"I can hear him fine."

That voice came from the direction of the steps. The cast of *Hamlet* froze in their positions. Scarlett's mother stood there, looking at the large group of actors who had assembled in her basement.

"Can I talk to you?" she asked.

This was obviously directed at just two of them. Scarlett and Spencer stepped forward. She at least had the decency to retreat to the steps and speak in a low voice.

"How long did you think this was going to remain a secret?" she asked calmly.

"Um...forever?" Spencer said.

"Isn't it wonderful!" cried a voice from the opposite corner.

Mrs. Amberson, dressed entirely in black yogawear, stepped out of the shadowy anteroom where the hot water heater was. There was a faint, audible gasp from one of the girls over by that wall—which was totally understandable. Otherwise, absolutely everyone stood in shocked silence.

Mrs. Amberson walked into the middle of the group, as natural as day, dusting a bit of smudge from her sleeve. She was holding one of the small French notebooks and had been scrawling away.

"I think you're right, Trevor," she said, consulting the opened page. "That last line is hard to hear from a distance. We'll need to do some vocal work."

Trevor, who had never met Mrs. Amberson, nodded slowly. He did remarkably well by not going insane when the strange woman emerged from the wall to answer his question.

Mrs. Amberson walked up to Scarlett's mother, who was receiving a double surprise. She flashed her biggest smile, which was longer and more insidious than a holiday traffic jam.

"We were just using the downstairs tonight as there was a little problem with our rehearsal space," Mrs. Amberson said. "It's not a problem, is it? I promise I'll have them moved out as soon as possible. I would have asked...but I hated to bother you. Oh, I hope you're not mad. Please, let's have a talk. You come along, Scarlett. Take a break, everyone. We'll be back."

"Um...sure," Spencer said. "We'll break."

His look to Scarlett said: *Please tell me you know what's going on.*

But, of course, she didn't.

A SPY IN THE HOUSE OF DENMARK

Upstairs, in the dining room, Mrs. Amberson gratefully accepted the offer of a cup of hot water while Scarlett was sent upstairs to fetch one of her organic-ginger teabags and her box of pickled Japanese plums. She bypassed the elevator and took the stairs three at a time. When she got back, winded, Mrs. Amberson was in full conversational swing.

"...I'd been hearing a lot about that theater group, First National Bang, from friends of mine in the business. It's a cutting-edge production, and it's going to get a lot of attention in the industry. Color me amazed when I heard Spencer was part of the cast and *that* was the show he mentioned on the night I arrived!"

She gave her hand a little swirl in the air.

"And naturally, when I heard they had run into a small spot of financial trouble...which *every* worthwhile show does, believe me...I absolutely jumped at the chance to become the company's new artistic director and the main financial backer. It was the ultimate piece of good fortune. This is *exactly* the reason this hotel is recommended. Wasn't I thrilled, Scarlett?"

Scarlett got two stares from across the table—one looking for verification, and one waiting for her to verify. There was no time for her to process this utter and insane lie, so she simply said, "Oh...right."

"It's just that we're a bit...concerned about Spencer's career," Scarlett's mother said. "He won a scholarship to the culinary school and there's a window of time that he can still qualify."

Mrs. Amberson was nodding away gravely and gulping back steaming hot tea.

"I absolutely agree," she said, though there didn't seem to be anything to agree with. "The acting life is not an easy choice, and I think you're handling this with exactly the right attitude. Spencer has obviously gotten the excellent training that the High School of Performing Arts is famed for. I know teachers there. They speak fondly of him."

This could have been true, but Scarlett doubted it. She decided that it was too hard to keep up with the lies and keep a straight face, so she pretended to be interested in an imaginary spot on her T-shirt until she got a better idea of what the hell was going on.

"That's good to hear," Scarlett's mom said slowly. "But Spencer is—"

"A rare and gifted physical comedian," Mrs. Amberson cut in. "But that's no surprise to you."

"Well, no. He's definitely that. He's been throwing himself down the stairs since he was seven years old."

"Exactly," Mrs. Amberson said. "There's a huge potential there. In my thir...many years in this line of work, I've only seen a handful of people like him, and they've *all* gone on to have full, flourishing careers."

Lie or not, it sounded so good. Mrs. Amberson had a way of doing that. It stunned Scarlett's mom into silence. The message was clear—the hotel's most important and highest-paying guest in its history was now connected to this show. Scarlett couldn't help but stare as her mother grappled with this new reality.

"Well," she said, "it sounds...like it's quite an opportunity."

Scarlett had to bite her tongue to keep from yelping in joy.

"I assure you, it is," Mrs. Amberson said. "Now, I'm just going to step outside to indulge my vice. And I promise you, they won't be back here. This was a one-time offense."

Outside, Mrs. Amberson broke into her strange, chin-jerking laugh and snapped open her cigarette case.

"It looks like I just got a theater company," she said.

"But how did you...?"

"Scarlett, I smoke on the balcony. For the last three days, I've been watching a trail of actors sneak around the side of the building at six-thirty every night, like clockwork."

"You knew they were actors?"

"They were carrying unicycles and swords. What else could they be? Circus burglars? Of course, I had to find out what they were doing down there. You should never leave doors propped open in this city. I've been letting myself in the back and observing for the last two nights. This is the most fun I've had in *weeks*!"

"So what happens now?" Scarlett said, almost not wanting to know the answer.

"What happens now? Some decent direction. Vocal work, for sure. And if Polonius doesn't stop playing with his fake beard, I will personally break all of his fingers."

"So...this is real? You're really backing the show? You weren't just saying that?"

"I never just *say* things, O'Hara. I *do* things. And I do them well. All in all, it's a good group. And your brother is every bit as good as I said to your mother. And what a physique! I thought he looked like a scarecrow when I first saw him, but once he gets his clothes off you can see he's really just a bodybuilder who's been stretched on a rack. The things that boy can do upside down..."

Something inside Scarlett put out a faint wheeze of alarm, and this luscious description of Spencer made her want to throw up. But overall, things had taken a turn for the miraculous and good.

"What about your book?" Scarlett ased.

"It's a funny thing, O'Hara, I've been feeling stagnant about the book. You've probably noticed. But as soon as I saw your mother standing there, I knew exactly what I had come here to do...New York, this hotel...I came here to reconnect to my theater roots. I saw it all in one shining moment. The book can wait. For now, we'll find them a space, and we'll *really* develop this show. It won't be one of these little productions that falls through the cracks. I am going to make something of this show and everyone in it. I have tricks up my sleeve, O'Hara. Tricks like you wouldn't believe. Here. Have an umbeoshi plum. They taste like salt. Don't eat the stone. Go on."

She thrust the box of grayish things at Scarlett, who reluctantly took one. They did, in fact, taste like sour little fruits covered in salt. She winced and spit out the stone.

"They're extremely good for you," Mrs. Amberson said. "They're a secret to health and vitality, and I want you vital, O'Hara. Now, let's go down and meet our cast."

The cast of *Hamlet* had not moved much. They had that haunted yet hopeful look in their eyes, like the ones you see in old photos of people crammed into steerage compartments, traveling to some new, unknown land.

Trevor, as director, stepped forward to assume some sort of control over the situation, and Mrs. Amberson met him and shook his hand.

"Amy Amberson," she said, introducing herself. "I've been watching you from over there for the last two nights. I was surprised no one noticed me—but then, you were fully engaged in your task."

She pointed to her spot in the dark vestibule.

"Well," Spencer said, "we also kind of assumed that no one was hiding behind the hot water heater."

"Never assume," Mrs. Amberson said. "This city is unique. Every place you go—everything you do—you never know who's watching. There's always an opportunity, if you know how to spot it."

This would have been an extremely annoying little maxim if it wasn't so literally true in this case. She really had proven her point.

"We lost our rehearsal space," Eric said, flashing Mrs.

Amberson a smile. "We got a vacate order. So we came here. It was Scarlett's idea."

He knew it was her idea!

Eric's appeal was not lost on Mrs. Amberson. This was dismaying. But worse, it was Spencer that she turned to when she let loose one of those slow, creeping smiles.

"Don't worry," she said. "No one understands better than I do how hard it is to find a place to rehearse in this city. I was an actress. You want suffering? I'll give you suffering. I landed a part in the hot new Broadway show of 1976, *Rockabye Hamlet*. It was *Hamlet* staged as a big rock concert. Ophelia strangled herself with a microphone cord to commit suicide. The audience *laughed*. We closed after seven performances. Seven. We were all over *The Times* the next day."

This remark met with sympathetic mumbling and exaggerated interest.

"I have a proposal for you," she said. "Of course, you are free to accept or reject it. I'm offering financial backing in exchange for an artistic say. If you agree to bring me on as codirector, I can offer sound advice and excellent connections."

"Codirector?" Trevor said.

"And you all know my assistant, Scarlett. Her resourcefulness will come in handy as well. Talk it over. Do what feels right."

While Trevor looked thunderstruck, everyone else appeared jubilant. This was precisely the kind of deal that Scarlett had been offered, just on a grander scale. It was no surprise that the group immediately agreed, Trevor's shocked reaction nonwithstanding.

Mrs. Amberson plunked herself down in the middle of the

group and started talking about her "deep love of Shakespeare" (even though she asked Scarlett to get her a copy of the play and every book on the subject she could carry the next morning). As the night wore on, various people started to go. By the end, it was down to the residents—Spencer, Mrs. Amberson, and Scarlett—and Eric.

"Do me a favor, O'Hara," she said, not taking her eyes off her two new recruits. "Run down to the corner and get me a box of green tea? I just remembered I was out."

"You have three boxes," Scarlett said.

"Do I? I don't think so. Best get another to be sure."

She did have three boxes of green tea. She also had two boxes of white, ginger, and rosehips, and a box each of plum, ginseng, spearmint, DeTox blend, Restful Blend, Mindful Blend, and Yoga Blend...all of which Scarlett had purchased. But it was clear that she didn't want to be argued with. Mrs. Amberson wiggled herself into a more comfortable seat on the floor by shifting through a lot of complicated dancer positions that clearly said, "I am more flexible than anyone you know." Sadly, Spencer took careful note of this.

"Fine," Scarlett said, pulling herself up off the floor. "I'll get you another one."

As she headed up the creaky basement steps, she heard Eric say, "You know what? I should head home now. Have to get up early."

She immediately stopped and dove down to do some completely unnecessary maintenance on her flip-flop—just enough to give Eric time to catch up to her. This only bought her a few seconds more with him, but seemed worth the effort.

"So soon?" Mrs. Amberson said. "Well, see you tomorrow. We'll be in touch with the new rehearsal location. Scarlett will call. Are you all right there, Scarlett?"

"Fine!" Scarlett said. She'd pulled the thong from the center hole and was now desperately trying to shove it back in again. She had done such a good job of sabotaging her own shoes that it was looking like she might have killed them and would have to go upstairs for a new pair. She hopped up a few steps to get out of Mrs. Amberson's view and managed to get the thing loosely in place enough to walk, as long as she kept her toes wrapped around the thong. It made her hobble, but she was more or less ready when Eric was behind her.

Her mother was at the computer at the front desk, still looking at the basement door with a look of great skepticism.

"I have to go to the deli and pick up tea for Mrs. Amberson."

"*More* tea?"

"Don't worry, Mrs. Martin," Eric chimed in. "My scooter's up the block. I'll walk her down, ma'am."

The idea that Scarlett had to be escorted up and down her street at eleven at night was ridiculous, and the "ma'am" was too strange to comment on. But it was hard to argue with that honeyed voice and the manners from some other century.

"Oh...thanks, Eric. That's nice of you."

Scarlett shot out the door before her mother could read anything from her expression.

"You look like you're in a hurry," he said, as they stepped outside. "And is your foot okay?"

"It's fine," she said quickly. "I'm just trying to get away from seeing my brother making out with my boss. I think it will save me some money in future therapy."

Eric responded with a gratifying laugh.

"She does lay it on a little thick," he said. "I can see what you were saying about your first day. She kind of comes out of nowhere. Literally. Out of nowhere."

"Welcome to my life."

The deli was sadly all too close, and Eric's scooter was chained to a tree next to it. He was the owner of one very old but still extremely stylish black scooter. Its obvious age and many dings made it seem so much better than the shiny new ones.

"Online ad, six-hundred bucks," he explained. "Another gift from the commercial. It conks out a lot, but I've been able to keep it running. Faster than the bus, you know?"

He made no move to unchain it. Instead, he followed her in and walked with her past the Pringles, the empty steam trays, and giant stacks of cat food. This deli knew its people and kept a large selection of organic things in the back. They charged double for the convenience, but Mrs. Amberson never seemed to care.

Scarlett was feverishly working out a good-bye when they stepped outside, but he made no move for his scooter.

"I hope you don't mind about this," he said apologetically. "I just have this thing about girls walking alone in the city at night. I'd feel better if I could walk you back. I did promise your mother I'd make sure you were okay."

He smiled, revealing that even he knew this was absurd.

Still, no movement. He leaned over her, occasionally throwing his glance in the direction of the hotel.

"I guess we'll be working together now," he said.

"I guess so."

"That's great."

Something was going on, but Scarlett had no idea what. Eric blinked a few times, looked around, leaned against the wall. He was close enough that she could smell him—he had the faint odor of the same heavy-duty detergent they used, and a little oil, probably from the scooter.

"I guess..." he said again, "I can see the door from here, so, yeah. Maybe I should get going. I'll see you around?"

What was this? Offering to walk her a few feet—retracting the offer. If it was anyone else, Scarlett would have been annoyed.

"Guess I'll go," Scarlett said.

She walked back as slowly and evenly as she could. She was too terrified to turn around until she got to the door, but sure enough, he was still watching. He hadn't even started unchaining. He gave a little wave.

This was very, very good.

THE GURU

There was a fervent knocking at the Orchid Suite door around five in the morning.

"What?" Lola groaned, putting the pillow over her head. "Make it stop. It has to be Spencer. Kill him."

Scarlett dutifully rolled out of bed, tripping over her blanket, to kill her older brother as requested. She loved Spencer, but she saw Lola's point in this case. But it wasn't Spencer. It was Mrs. Amberson, dressed in a faintly see-through blue robe and not much else.

"You weren't answering your phone," she said.

Scarlett took a second to figure out what she herself was wearing. She looked down to find it was a stretched out T-shirt and a pair of underpants. She pulled the shirt down as much as she could with one hand.

"Do you need something?" she asked.

"I need you in forty-five minutes."

"I..."

"Make it forty minutes. Do you have any matches?"

"No," Scarlett said.

"Dammit."

She shut the door herself. Lola looked over from her bed, her blonde hair tumbled over her face.

"She's not going to do that a lot, is she?" she asked.

Scarlett half-blindly reached for her shower basket and towel and pulled on some shorts. Out in the hall, she bumped into Spencer, who was unused to seeing anyone floating around when he got up. He was leaning out of the bathroom door and brushing his teeth with a puzzled look on his face. He held up one finger to Scarlett, indicating she should wait. He stepped into the bathroom, spitting out the toothpaste foam loudly.

"Was that my new director, your boss, just now?" he asked. "Kind of naked?"

"Yes," she said flatly.

"Does she do that every morning? Because if she does, I'm going to start being late more often."

"Don't do this to me."

"That lady works out. Do you think she does Pilates? I hear that's very effective."

"Spencer," Scarlett said slowly. "Lola told me to kill you earlier. I'm thinking about taking her up on it."

Spencer held up his hands in surrender.

"I'm just saying, if this is too early for you, she can come to my room at the crack of dawn. I am all about service."

He moved swiftly along when Scarlett gave him a stare. Even as a baby, Scarlett Martin had a stare that could remove a strip of wallpaper at ten feet, and it had not weakened with time.

***

145

Scarlett was admitted to the Empire Suite forty minutes later by Mrs. Amberson, who was now dressed only in a matching chocolate-colored bra-and-panty set. An unlit cigarette hung from her lips, and a pile of discarded outfits were thrown all over the bed, all of them stretchy and dancerlike. Scarlet tried to avert her eyes, but it was impossible not to notice how slender and muscular Mrs. Amberson was, especially since Spencer had been kind enough to point it out.

"Where are we going?" Scarlett asked.

"We are going to see Billy Whitehouse."

"Who is Billy Whitehouse?" Scarlett asked.

"A *genius*. A genius of the first order. Everyone in the theater world knows Billy. I knew him when he was just a poor young actor, right out of Yale. He was always unnaturally gifted with voice—had studied every great vocal technique in the western world. I also used to feed him for free at work, let him stay with me when he lost his apartment. He wore sneakers all the time because he couldn't afford any other shoes. I watched him rise to become the great man he is today."

"Why are we going to see him at six-thirty in the morning?" Scarlett asked. "Don't theater people come out at night?"

"Billy is a busy man. Normally, his time is booked months in advance. But I helped him meet his husband. He makes time for me. Have an umeboshi plum. You look a little tired."

She thrust the box of the disgusting little plums at Scarlett and stood there until she took one. Scarlett ate it, cringed, and spit out the stone. Mrs. Amberson tucked the cigarette behind her ear and pulled on her outfit.

Altogether too soon, Scarlett was being ushered out into

the heavy morning, full of humidity and the first signs of New York morning traffic. Not even the dry cleaner was open yet. Scarlett never went out before the dry cleaner was open. Mrs. Amberson saw a still burning cigarette on the ground and pounced on it, using it to light her own. Then she leapt into the street and easily snagged a cab, palming the cigarette as she did so. She mumbled something at the driver and settled back in her seat, slinking down to surreptitiously smoke.

"This has been the problem all along," she said.

"What's been what problem?" Scarlett said, stifling a yawn.

"My voice. It's like I have a...*cork*...a cork bottling up my thoughts...and keeping them from my head. It's here. Here between my heart and my head."

She pointed at her throat with the cigarette.

"My voice. My voice is locked up."

"You sound fine to me," Scarlett said.

"My *inner* voice! Are you always this literal? It makes me wonder what they teach you."

"They're usually wasting our time with Geometry, French, and American Government," Scarlett said, looking out the window and yawning until her eyes watered. "We don't get to our inner voices until next year."

She could feel Mrs. Amberson staring at her neck.

"Don't be snide, child," she said mildly. "It's bad for your chi. In any case, performers often go through this. When they get blocked, their voice literally locks up. They can't sing. I saw it all the time in the theater. The throat is one of the body's great gateways. It carries blood to the head. It carries nerve impulses from the brain to the rest of the body. When you think about it, we are all about our throats."

Scarlett ignored this and went back to sleep with her head against the cab window. She was jolted awake when the cab pulled to a jerky halt. They had stopped in front of one of the Broadway theaters, terrifying a tourist with a large coffee and an even larger camera. Mrs. Amberson tossed a bill through the opening and sprang out. She led Scarlett down to a door marked CAST AND CREW ONLY.

It was amazingly dark inside that doorway. They were in a little hallway with a warren of rooms, stuffed with racks of clothes labeled with masking tape. Mrs. Amberson picked her way through, finally getting to a staircase leading up into a massive, partially lit stage.

"Over here," a very deep, very crisp voice called. "And be careful or you'll kill yourself on those wires."

A man emerged from the darkness on the other side of the stage.

"Billy!" Mrs. Amberson exclaimed.

Billy was exceptionally tall, with immaculately groomed white hair. He wore a white shirt, light khaki pants, and white shoes. He looked like a librarian, or someone who might run an art museum. He greeted Mrs. Amberson by exchanging cheek-to-cheek kisses. Then, much to Scarlett's surprise, he gently sniffed her head, like she was a flower.

"You've been smoking," he said.

She looked down guiltily. This Billy appeared to have genuine power over her, and that meant he was interesting to Scarlett. He turned to her now and smiled kindly.

"Amy's dragged you out at this hour?" he said. "There's coffee over by the piano, if you need it."

"O'Hara," she said, "this is Billy Whitehouse. He can unblock the best, and if anyone needs an unblocking, it's you. No offense."

Scarlett said hello and made her way to the pot. She took a seat off to the side, looking around at the endless depths of the ceiling, the miles of cords and cables, the taped Xs all over the floor, the cherry picker in front of the stage. Broadway kind of looked like a construction site during the day.

She had no idea what unblocking was, but it was pretty enjoyable watching Mrs. Amberson getting ordered around for a change. For the first few minutes, Billy had her run in a circle, barefoot, in the middle of the stage. He started to command her to say single words, like "home," "feel," "kill," "love," all at different volumes. He made her cling to the wall, crawl across the floor, run laps from side to side on the stage. All the while, he stalked around her like a lion tamer.

Scarlett watched this for a while, until the cool darkness of the theater lulled her back to sleep. She woke with a crick in her neck, her head hanging heavily off the back of the seat, to see Mrs. Amberson rolling from side to side on the floor, yelling the word "endless."

"I needed that," she said, getting up and dusting herself off.

"Why do I feel that you didn't just come down here at the crack of dawn to do a tune-up?" he asked.

"You have an uncanny ability to read me, Billy. As it happens, I have acquired a show."

"What do you mean you *acquired* a show?" he asked. "Wait. Never mind. Don't answer that. I genuinely don't want to know."

"These are good actors," she said. "Very good. But they need molding, solid vocal training. And you are the best..."

"Amy..."

"I would never ask this from you on a whim," she said. "Not you."

A grave moment passed between them. Billy walked over to the piano and picked up a datebook and flipped through some pages.

"How many?" he asked.

"Fifteen."

"Doing what?"

"*Hamlet.*"

"And I take it you need me immediately?"

"Today."

More flipping.

"Okay," he finally said. "You've run into a little luck. I wouldn't be doing this for anyone but you, but...I can do two evenings this week. Tonight and Friday. Four hours on Saturday during the day. That's all I've got. Then I have to spend some quality time with my long-neglected family at the beach. I haven't had any time off in months."

"Billy!"

She embraced him aggressively.

"You're out of practice," Billy replied, shaking his head. "The smoking makes it worse."

"I know, I know. No lectures, please."

"It's my job," he said.

"No," she said. "You are just a nosy bitch."

"Also my job. I'll expect to see you and your new company at my studio at seven."

THE OTHER FAMOUS WHITEHOUSE

After the early morning session, Scarlett was released at nine-thirty in the morning with one order—contact every single actor and crew member and make sure they got to Billy's studio on time. That meant waiting for Spencer to get home from work, which really meant going back to sleep for an hour or so.

The lingering smell of overly strong coffee and burned toast wafted through the lobby as Scarlett entered it. Their father was on his knees in the far corner of the lobby, by the elevator, hammer in hand.

"Some of the boards are coming up again," he said. "I can't hammer them down. Oh, well. I'll do what we always do."

He pushed one of the canary-yellow chairs across the room to the spot. It didn't quite fit there, but he seemed content.

"If you have time," he said, "I could use a hand cleaning up and resetting the Sterling Suite. We have someone coming tonight."

"Sure," Scarlett said sleepily. "I'll do it in a few."

"Oh, and Lola's upstairs. I don't think she's feeling well."

Sure enough, Lola was in bed, but she didn't look sick. She was sitting with her knees tucked up, and she looked more pale than usual.

"I have a problem, Scarlett," she said.

Scarlett sat down on the edge of her bed and waited. It took Lola a moment to bring herself to speak.

"They told me not to come in today," she said. "They fired me."

Scarlett wasn't about to say "I told you so." Lola had obviously been chastising herself all morning. She shook her head over and over.

"I'm such an idiot," she said. "I honestly didn't think they would. I have one of the best sales records on the floor. I really thought I was fine. I would never have taken the days off otherwise, I swear."

Scarlett reached over for her hand.

"You don't need to convince me," she said. "I know you wouldn't have."

"Mom and Dad are already so worried. About the bills, Marlene, Spencer's career...I can't *believe* I let this happen. Especially with Spencer doing this stupid show now. This is such a bad time."

It didn't seem necessary to slam Spencer in this, but Scarlett let it go. Lola had truly loved her job. She was good at it.

"You can get another one in a second," Scarlett said, trying to sound cheerful. "You can tell Mom and Dad you got a better offer."

Lola took a long, slow breath and wiped at her face.

"You're right," she said. "I was thinking it might be better if I worked in a spa. This could be a good opportunity."

She changed the head move to a nod, to affirm herself.

"I have another favor to ask," she said. "And I know I already owe you. I've decided to go to Boston with Chip this weekend."

Scarlett contained a groan.

"I know," Lola said. "This is what caused the problem in the first place. But I have no job now. Let me just do this, and then I promise..."

"You can go wherever you want," Scarlett said.

"I know, but...there's a big Powerkids event on Saturday night. A dinner at the Hard Rock Café."

"Let me guess," Scarlett said. "You want me to take her."

"I think that it's good that you and Marlene...bond more. I mean, I won't be living at home forever. Neither will Spen... well, Spencer may."

Scarlett was much more tempted this time to reply to the Spencer-bash, but Lola really did look contrite.

"What are you going to tell Mom and Dad?" she asked.

"That I'm going to Boston to do a weekend intensive on skin care for one of the product lines. You don't have to worry about a cover story. You don't have to lie."

"Fine," Scarlett said. "But just this time."

Scarlett tried to sleep, but Lola was still sitting there, palpably fretting and talking to Chip on the phone. She went down the hall to Spencer's room to sleep on his bed, but he returned soon after.

"You're going to see someone named Billy Whitehouse," she mumbled. "Can you call everyone and tell them?"

"Don't mess with my head," he said, dropping his bag on the floor. "I'm still nervous after last night."

"I'm not messing with you," she said. "You're going to see some guy named Billy Whitehouse."

"*The* Billy Whitehouse?"

"Well, it was *a* Billy Whitehouse," she said. "He was in a theater on Broadway."

Spencer got very agitated and started pacing in the three empty feet of floor space.

"You're not messing with me?" he asked seriously.

"Why would I make this up? Do you know him?"

"Billy Whitehouse, founder of the Whitehouse Method?" he said. "The guy who almost single-handedly changed the way live theater was performed in America? Former director of The Simply Shakespeare Company, pretty much the most famous Shakespeare group of the eighties? Former Juilliard professor? The person the best celebrity actors go to for guidance when they can't nail a part? This guy?"

He whipped a book from one of his lopsided bookshelves called *You Are the Voice* and flipped to the back, revealing a picture of the same man she had met a few hours before. He was looking coolly at an actor writhing on the floor.

"So...that's a yes?" Scarlett said.

Billy's studio was in a large and nondescript building, the kind that grow all over the middle of the city, like dandelions, and can be used for seemingly any purpose. They passed a nonresponsive guard on their way to the elevator, which creaked and groaned its way up to the eleventh floor. The hall they emerged on was fairly bleak, with a series of blue industrial-strength doors. Mrs. Amberson strode along to the very end of the hall with great purpose. Billy opened it in greeting before she could even knock.

"You have a distinctive walk," he said. "Hello, O'Hara! Come inside."

The room was massive, with a hardwood floor and a mirrored wall. There was a piano in the corner, blanketed by a quilted cover. Over by the mirrors were dozens of thick blue tumble mats, along with exercise balls, hoops, straps, beach balls, and jump ropes.

"Let's get rid of this," Billy said, switching off the overhead light. "Nothing kills the soul quite like fluorescent light."

He walked around and switched on a number of standing lamps around the room, giving it a cozy glow.

All the actors looked as dazed as Spencer as they arrived. Billy was known to them all. They obeyed his every word, though he was extremely soft-spoken. He had everyone sit on the floor in a tight circle.

"Tonight," he said, circling the group and distributing long strips of cloth from a box. "We are just going to speak the play to each other. Blindfolded. Please tie the cloths around your eyes, then join hands with the people seated next to you."

Scarlett was mentally preparing herself for a night of intense boredom when Billy gestured in her direction.

"Amy," he said, "please step in and join the group. You, too,

O'Hara. Let's get all of our energy down here, together."

It seemed way too obvious to insert herself next to Eric, so she dropped down one spot over, between Spencer and Stephanie, the girl playing Ophelia. Billy passed her a blindfold, which she dutifully tied around her eyes. Spencer gripped her hand. She expected him to do something to make her laugh, like tickle her palm or try to make those farting noises from the suction, but he was all business. The grip was firm and serious. Ophelia had a cool, tiny hand.

"I will read the stage directions," Billy said. "If you get confused at any point about when to speak, just give yourself a moment and feel it out. Try to work with the energy of the room, your fellow performers, instead of the visual cues you may have been relying on."

The reading of the play took three hours. A three-hour reading of Shakespeare, blindfolded, on the floor, should have been deadly. Instead, it was one of the most electrifying things Scarlett had ever experienced. Sitting together so close, everyone connected...she hated terms like energy...but that's what it was. The longer she sat there in the dark, holding hands with Spencer and Stephanie and by extension, everyone—her world physically seemed to expand.

Billy's normal speaking voice was pleasant and smooth, but his performance voice was massive—not loud, just able to take over all the empty parts of Scarlett's brain that she didn't even know were listening. The events unfolded in her head. She could see the ghost of the dead king approaching the guards on the tower. There was Hamlet, arriving in the cold castle hall to find that his uncle had taken his dead father's place, both as king and husband to his mother. Hamlet was young—not much older than Spencer or Eric—a university student with a lot of problems and a bunch of actor friends. He was in pain, confused, angry...and everyone around him was playing him.

Scarlett could hear Billy walking around the group as the play went on. She felt him brush her shoulder as he adjusted Spencer's posture somehow. His voice came out clearer, more confident. And from across the darkness, she heard Eric reply. He spoke without a Southern accent now, dropping it with ease. Actors had other people living inside of them...lots of other people, other voices. There was something wonderful about this, this unfolding possibility.

When it was over, Scarlett reluctantly peeled off the blindfold. Billy had the lights way down, but still, it was a shock to see again. Everyone stirred like they were waking from a long sleep, one in which they had all dreamed the same dream.

Like several of the other actors, Spencer clustered around Billy when they were done, pelting him with questions. Eric, however, had slipped out with a few of the others, without so much as a good-bye.

"I can't believe that just happened," Spencer said, as they rode the bus home. "I've told you that you're the best sister in the world, right?"

"You can repeat yourself. I will allow it."

"I just spent the night working with Billy Whitehouse. Billy Whitehouse. Do you have any idea what this means?"

Scarlett smiled. It was good to see Spencer feeling like he

was on top of his game again. But why had Eric left so quickly? Obviously, there was nothing going on between them. He barely knew her. Still...

"It means," Spencer went on, "that something is going right. When I get rich and famous, I'm going to get you anything you want. Name it. Helicopter. Airplane. One of those hairless cats."

He had no idea how close he was to what she actually wanted. He could probably even help. All she had to do was open her mouth and ask.

"An indoor pool," she said instead. "With a shark in it."

"You," Spencer replied, throwing an arm over her shoulder, "are clearly my sister. We share the same practical streak."

THE EXCITING LIVES OF NEW YORKERS, REVEALED

For two nights, Scarlett had watched the famous Billy Whitehouse lead the cast through their paces. Sometimes he just ran them ragged, forcing them to run the room while they said their lines, sometimes he put them facedown on the floor, or had them stand on chairs. Random as it all seemed, it was amazing what could come out when Billy was ordering everyone around. Lines that had sounded like gibberish to her before (either because she didn't understand Shakespeare or the actors were saying them wrong) suddenly had meaning. Little gestures could produce laughter or tears. Hamlet became more menacing, the king more duplicitous, Ophelia more tragic. Billy tempered some of what Spencer and Eric had been doing, giving them a winsome edge.

By Saturday, they had come to the last of the sessions. Billy had the cast gather together in a huddle in the middle of the room. It was kind of an intense moment, and sort of not for observers, so Scarlett let herself out quietly to wait in the hall. She walked around, trying to get cell phone reception.

When she looped back, she found Billy and Mrs. Amberson standing by the stairs, at the dark end of the hallway. They couldn't see her.

"You'll never guess who's coming in later," Billy was saying.

"Someone famous? Someone amusing?"

"Donna Spendler," he said.

The name crystallized Mrs. Amberson. The smile fell from her face like it had come unglued.

"I thought you might react that way," he said.

Something in the air changed. Maybe it was the air conditioning cranking to life, or the opening of the door in the background as the cast left, but something wasn't right.

"Why is she coming?" Mrs. Amberson asked quietly.

"To get herself ready for a final audition on Sunday."

"Final audition for what?"

"A new musical. She's up for the lead," Billy said. "I'm just getting her ready. I wouldn't normally, but the producer is a friend. It's purely professional. I plan on not helping her very much."

"You should do what you have to," Mrs. Amberson said.

"I'll do the minimum. Was I right to tell you?"

She did not reply.

The full cast was coming out now, and everyone stopped to thank or hug Billy. Scarlett stayed in her spot, trying to figure out what she had just seen. It was a moment before Mrs. Amberson noticed her standing there.

"Is everything okay?" Scarlett asked.

Mrs. Amberson fumbled around inside of her bag for her cigarette case.

"Change of plan," she said. "I was supposed to see some potential rehearsal sites tonight. I'll call and reschedule. Just tell the others—Trevor and Eric. They're still inside. They were going to come with me."

With that, she left. Scarlett went inside to tell Eric and Trevor the news. They were lingering with Billy a few more moments as he locked up the room. When Scarlett told them the message, Trevor left, but Eric walked with her.

"Nothing to do now," he said. "I canceled my plans for tonight because of this. Are you doing anything?"

Was this really happening? Was Eric actually asking her out? And could she really not go because she was taking Marlene to yet another of her many social commitments, because Lola was in Boston lying her face off about being at a skin care seminar?

Yes, Scarlett, she said to herself. *That really is what's happening.* Which meant that there was only one option.

"Do you want to...come?" she asked. "It's free food. And you can be the first of your friends to have a Hard Rock T-shirt! They're really rare."

To her enduring amazement, he said yes.

There are a few places you don't go to if you live in New York. Everyone who visits you will expect that you have gone to them—that you in fact go to them *all the time*, spend every possible free second at them. They include: the Statue of Liberty, the Empire State Building, F.A.O. Schwartz, the skating rink at Rockefeller Plaza, Times Square (unless you have to change subways there, but then you never go above ground), and any theme restaurant. It was a source of constant bafflement to Scarlett as to why the Powerkids always seemed to end up at these places. It wasn't like cancer turned you into a tourist.

Eric, as an outsider, hadn't gotten any of these memos. He was delighted to be at the Hard Rock. His enthusiasm made Scarlett view it in a more charitable light, as they negotiated their way through the huge gift shop with its 20,000 varieties of T-shirts.

"Do you come here a lot?" he asked.

If any of her friends had asked her that, she could have smacked them with impunity...but there would be no smacking of Eric.

"With Marlene, sometimes," she admitted.

"God, I wish my life in high school was as exciting as yours. I wish I grew up in New York."

Scarlett looked over a vista of Hard Rock shot glasses, unsure how to respond. He was so impressed with her now. What if he found out the truth...that *everyone* else in New York was leading a much more exciting life than she was? He would learn soon enough. Until then, she was ready to embrace the Hard Rock in all its kitschy glory.

The Powerkids were seated together at a massive, long table. The parents and escorts were relegated to whatever seats were left in the general area. Scarlett and Eric were given a small table by the kitchen door. Scarlett got hit in the head with a tray twice, but Marlene couldn't see her, so it was a pretty good trade-off. It was just the two of them, tucked in a corner.

"Can I ask you something that's potentially kind of rude?"

he asked, after they had ordered.

This sounded very promising.

"How is it that you live in a hotel in New York, but you aren't rich? From what Spencer's told me, it's kind of hard for you guys right now."

Okay. Not what she was expecting. Still, a fair question.

"You could say that," she said.

"I don't want to pry, but I'm just curious about your life."

"My dad's family started the hotel. I don't think my dad wanted to run it. But then they had us, and my grandparents wanted to retire, so that's what happened. I think things were okay—not great, but okay—until..."

She looked down at the ketchup, unsure whether or not to continue.

"Until?" Eric prompted.

Scarlett nodded in the direction of the table of Powerkids.

"Until that," she said.

This was the truth never spoken among the Martins. No one talked about the fact that the financial troubles were directly related to Marlene's long illness, the piles of bills that medical insurance didn't cover, the single injections that cost thousands a dose, the hospital costs that ran into the hundreds of thousands. Obviously, there was no price too high for her cure—but it had taken its toll. If Marlene had been well, life would have been very, very different.

"Oh...right," he said, understanding.

"She doesn't know," Scarlett said. "We're never supposed to say it. I mean, she's alive."

"That must have been so scary," he said. "I can't imagine

my brother getting that sick."

"It kind of wasn't," she said. "Actually, that summer was kind of fun. I knew *something* was going on, but they didn't tell me the whole story until she had to be moved into the hospital."

"Kind of a tip-off that there was a problem."

"Yeah. Kind of. I always felt bad, though."

"About what?" he asked.

There was real concern in his voice. Eric was having a *conversation* with her—a real one. She never talked about the Marlene stuff except with Spencer, and occasionally with her friends, but never in much detail. There was one fact she often left out of those talks.

"For not feeling worse," she said.

"You feel bad for not feeling bad?"

"My parents told Spencer first," she explained, "since he's the oldest. He just went into his room for a while. I think he really *got* it, how bad it was. Then they told Lola, and she got really upset. My parents couldn't calm her down. That was bad."

The food arrived, but he waved his hand to show he was still listening.

"Everyone was terrified of telling me," she said, "but I'd figured it out by then, and I guess I was...okay with it or something. I just thought that if you got sick, you went to the hospital and someone made you better. Which is kind of what happened. I'm the mean one, I guess."

"You're not mean," he said. "You're just kind of...fearless."

Was he *high*? Fearless? There were a lot of words that Scarlett

165

could have used to describe herself...well, actually, there weren't, but...if she had had a few, fearless would definitely not have been one of them.

"You just seem like you'll tackle any problem put in front of you," he said, thickly spreading ketchup on his burger.

"They don't go away if you don't," she said. "And my ideas are usually bad."

He shook his head.

"I don't think you get my point," he said. "See, I lived in fear of coming here. I come from this little town where everybody knows each other. I was a big star there. I was, like, *the actor*. Here, there are real famous people. Every other person you meet is an actor. You go to auditions, and there are a hundred people in line ahead of you. Everyone's talented, everyone's good-looking, everyone has a good agent. Everyone has a story. Like you."

Before, liking Eric was like a mirror—it was just a shiny thing, and it only went one way. But he was looking back at her now, and with interest. This was it. This was what people were talking about when they described falling in love. She was almost watching it happen to herself, like she was on the outside of her body.

So it was a bad time for her phone to ring. Mrs. Amberson's name popped up on the screen.

"She never leaves you alone, does she?" Eric said, pointing at the screen with a fry.

Scarlett slipped away from the table to answer, just on the outside chance that Mrs. Amberson could somehow sense the fact that Eric was nearby.

"I need you, O'Hara," she said, urgency rippling through her voice. "Whatever you're doing, I need you to drop it at once."

"Are you okay?" Scarlett asked. "Do you need a doctor or something?"

"I need you! Be here within the hour!"

Scarlett returned to the table, completely frazzled.

"Something's wrong with her," she said. "She was telling me she needs me, now. I've never heard her like this. But I can't..."

"Don't worry," Eric said, all too quickly. "It sounds important. I'll bring your sister home."

Oh, no. This could not turn into playtime with Mrs. Amberson and bonding time with Eric and Marlene. But Eric was being his absurdly courteous self and was already on his feet, offering to get someone to wrap up her food. Before she knew it, he had introduced himself at length to the head Powerkid parent and been taken into the fold. He even walked Scarlett out and hailed the cab for her.

"I'll take good care of her," he promised, as he helped her in. And with that, Scarlett was speeding across Forty-fourth Street, away from Eric.

THE PLAY'S THE THING TO CATCH THE KING

Mrs. Amberson was sitting up in her bed for once—not smoking on the balcony. She was dressed in a long, vaguely oriental set of baby-blue silk pajamas and a never-before-seen pair of glasses were balanced on the edge of her nose. The silver drapes were closed and the wall sconces were lit, giving the room a warm, rosy glow. The expensive Parisian notebooks and papers were all over the bed, and the Montblanc pen (the one without the inkpot) was out of its box.

It appeared that she had actually been *writing* something. Even in Scarlett's flustered, heightened state, this registered as being unusual.

She was also not, as Scarlett had been led to believe, dying.

"I need to talk to you," she said. "Sit down."

Scarlett sat down on the dressing table stool opposite the moon mirror. Mrs. Amberson took a moment before speaking, opening and closing the red cigarette case several times. She held it up.

"Did I ever tell you about this case?" she asked. "It's a very special item...from the thirties, made in Berlin. I saw it in the window of an antique store when I first moved to the city. I promised myself that if I got a big break, I would buy it. I checked on it for months, making sure no one took it. And then one day, I got that big break. I went over to buy it. And it was gone! Gone!"

Scarlett was getting the very annoying feeling that she'd been dragged away from something that might possibly, maybe, have counted as a date with Eric to hear a story about a cigarette case...and this did not make Mrs. Amberson more endearing.

"So how did you get it?" Scarlett asked dutifully.

"Someone bought it for me," she said. "That very day, to congratulate me. I'd never even told him about it. He just happened to pass the store and saw it. I don't know how he afforded it, either..."

"Who?"

Best to keep this story motoring along.

"A friend," Mrs. Amberson said. "Funny thing is...this is the only reason I still smoke. I can't bear to be without it. It was the first truly beautiful, special thing I'd ever owned."

She removed a cigarette from it, then tossed her beautiful, special thing across the bed.

"It's very sturdy," she said. "The Germans build things to last."

She went over to the window, but instead of climbing over the desk onto her perch, she sat on the edge of it, lit the cigarette, and held it at arm's length out the window. She exhaled smoke into the room.

"What I'm about to tell you requires some delicacy, Scarlett," she said. "I need to know I can trust you. Before I say any more, you have to promise me that what we talk about tonight will never leave this room. Your trust will be rewarded, I promise you."

She looked at her just-lit cigarette, tossed it away, and shut the window. She slipped back to the bed. This was mysterious behavior, even for her.

"I promise," Scarlett said.

She snapped the case open once or twice.

"I presume you heard a bit of the conversation I was having with Billy earlier. He mentioned a woman named Donna Spendler."

Even saying the name seemed to cause her discomfort.

"There are some people who will do *anything* to get ahead," she said, "no matter what the cost to other people. You find them in every walk of life. Donna Spendler falls into this category. What I'm about to propose may sound a little... unethical. But it's really just a joke, and it's nothing...*nothing*... compared to what she deserves."

"What is it?" Scarlett asked, nervously.

"The fact that we're doing *Hamlet* made me think of it," she said, getting up and pacing the floor in front of the moon mirror. "Hamlet knows his uncle is guilty of murdering his father, but he can't prove it. So when a group of traveling actors appears, he hires them to perform a play that will trigger his uncle, make him realize he's caught, and force him to confess. Drawing from that idea, I want to stage a little play..."

"A play?"

"Tomorrow," she said, "Donna goes up for the final audition for a very big Broadway role, which she may get. There is only one possible thing that could tempt her away from that room—and that's the possibility of a television show. So tomorrow, at the crack of dawn, her agent will get a call telling her there is a casting emergency. An immediate opening for a female lead role in a new show."

Scarlett remained silent, unsure what to make of what she was hearing.

"I know an out-of-work television writer who sent me some pages of a failed pilot called *The Heart of the Angel*," she said. "It was originally set in LA, but a few tweaks of the lines will relocate it here, and it will be called *The Heart of the Empire*. Good title, huh? The main character is currently a man, but by tomorrow afternoon, it will be a woman. A woman of about Donna's age. She becomes a cop after she turns forty to avenge her daughter's murder. She saves kids. The actress who got the part has been horribly injured in a car accident, and someone else needs to step in, immediately. A big, golden opportunity...one that will take *all* of tomorrow afternoon. If she doesn't take *that* bait, I'll eat my yoga mat. Television trumps Broadway every time."

"Why?" was all that Scarlett could think to say.

"Don't think that I don't know this is a lot to ask. I promise you, Donna Spendler deserves this and more. A lot more."

"She deserves not to get a part?"

"Answer me this, O'Hara. What if someone used Spencer, took away his chance to perform? Actively killed his career?"

"I'd be...really mad?"

"You'd be more than mad," Mrs. Amberson said. "That's what I want you to imagine."

"Who did she do this to?"

"That's not important." She sat on the dressing table, and it shifted, just a touch. "What is important is that this is someone who does not care about the careers of other actors. She will do what she has to to get ahead. And as you know, I take an active interest in *promoting* the careers of young actors, like I have with your brother's theater company. Their continued success is largely in my hands right now."

It wasn't precisely a threat, or a guilt trip, or blackmail. It was a statement of fact wrapped in a thin coating of warning.

"Would this ruin her career?" Scarlett asked. "Like you're saying she did to someone else?"

"I could only wish! No, O'Hara. It's just letting the air out of her tires a little. No one will be hurt. No one will even know. It's just a little prank to get some justice for someone that was hurt a long time ago. Plus, it will be fun. What do you say? Are you in? Don't you want to do something big this summer? Something you'll always be able to talk about?"

There were a few perfectly sensible reasons to walk away from this, which Scarlett felt deserved a few moments of consideration. Overriding those was the fact that Mrs. Amberson really was the person keeping Spencer's career and dream alive at the moment.

"We'll keep the crew small," she added, giving Scarlett a sly glance. "Just you, me, your brother, and Eric. I think they'll be very enthusiastic about this proposition. We'll make an excellent team."

Scarlett waited a moment before answering.

"What do you need me to do?"

"I knew you would do it, O'Hara!" she said, elated. "Now, to pull this off..."

She picked up her notebook from the bed and leafed through several pages of notes.

"...we will need the following. One, a studio. That's done. Billy has graciously loaned me a secondary studio space of his for a few hours, no questions asked. Two, a camera. Easily purchased in the morning, I should think. Three, a small group of actors skilled in improvisation. That's Spencer and Eric. And these..."

She took a handful of pages from the bed, printouts of script pages with notes written over them.

"I need you to type these up. This is our script. I'll need five copies of it ready by noon. Do you think you can manage that? And send Spencer down."

Her voice had lightened to its normal, happy, command-giving tone. But there was still something there—something deeper. Respect. Affection. Or just some bond people develop when plotting fake auditions together.

"Tomorrow," she called out as Scarlett departed. "Great things, O'Hara!"

Scarlett was understandably nerve-rattled when she got upstairs. Spencer's door was open. He had his headphones on and was "cleaning," which meant he was dumping the contents of boxes onto his bed. The one he was currently working on contained tubes and pots of well-used makeup, fake body hair and skin, and lots of crumpled script pages.

"Trying to find a blood pack," he explained, when he noticed Scarlett had appeared in his doorway. "Eric and I have been thinking about doing a thing where one of us stabs the other by accident during one of the scenes. We want to run it by Trevor, but it won't look good unless I bleed. I have about seven of them in here somewhere....Marlene said you brought Eric along to some party she was at tonight."

He tacked that on to the end very casually while plucking three noses out of the mess and piling them on his pillow. Scarlett spoke fluent Spencer, though, and knew that this was not just a random remark.

"Just for backup," she said. "It was free food. At the Hard Rock. I would have taken you, but you had gone to work."

"The Hard Rock?" he repeated. "Why do they always pick janky places?"

The matter had clearly made his radar, but he said no more about it. He continued picking through the debris until he produced a small plastic bag of dark red liquid.

"Here we go," he said. "I'm thinking stomach. It's really easy to puncture the bag there and get the blood all over the place."

He pulled up his T-shirt and started poking around his abdomen for possible locations for his wound.

"Mrs. Amberson needs you," she said.

He straightened up, a little too quickly.

"Service?" he asked. "I love to give service."

She narrowed her eyes.

"What?" he asked, all innocence. He jumped up, fished a deodorant from under a stack of clothes, shoved it under his shirt, and applied it liberally. "I am a Martin. Hotel management is in my blood, and customer satisfaction is my life."

"Every time you flirt with her," Scarlett said, "a puppy dies."

PERFORMANCE

The Heart of the Angel (now *Empire*) was about as generic a cop show as you could possibly want. There was a cop with a dark past, fighting crime in the big city. The scene they had was about a teenager who'd been sexually attacked on a date and was refusing to press charges against her former boyfriend. The Donna character, formerly called "Mike Charlane" (renamed Alice by Mrs. Amberson) was screaming at this poor girl like a maniac, trying to get her to step up and "get some justice," "fight for justice," "speak for justice," and (Scarlett's personal favorite) "be the covergirl of justice."

Though Mrs. Amberson hadn't asked her to, Scarlett took the liberty of improving the scene a little, going beyond the basic guy-to-girl, LA-to-New York changes that Mrs. Amberson had penciled in. Scarlett rewrote the bad speeches, tweaked the dialogue, added a bit to the end of the scene. She was surprised to see the sun coming up outside the Jazz Suite window by the time she finished. As she walked back to her room, she startled Spencer, who was on his way to take a shower.

"Why are you up?" he asked. "Are you sick?"

"I was working," Scarlett mumbled.

"Yeah...what is this thing today? I was in Amy's room *all night* talking about it. I didn't get all the details, because we got off topic. You know how it goes. Massages. Long games of I Never. Doing each other's nails."

She was too tired to respond to his joke. He shook her curls as she stumbled past him.

Scarlett was awakened a few hours later by Mrs. Amberson herself, who had admitted herself to the Orchid Suite.

"Rise and shine, O'Hara," she said, giving Scarlett a good shake. "You picked the wrong morning to sleep in. It's almost ten."

Scarlett groaned and mumbled her way through an explanation, shoving the computer in Mrs. Amberson's direction so that she could read the new material.

"This is *excellent*, O'Hara," she gushed. "You've added so much! I knew you were a talent. Now..."

She pushed a fold of bills and a piece of paper into Scarlett's hand.

"...get dressed. Go and print up a few copies of this. Then take a cab and meet me at this address. Bring the computer with you. I need this all to happen fast. Within the hour. I'll explain the details when you get there."

An hour later, Scarlett's cab stopped in front of a massive building off Astor Place. There was a small lobby with no guard. The walls were covered in handwritten signs saying which auditions were in which rooms. She found Mrs. Amberson by herself in a tiny studio on the sixth floor, sitting at a table covered in black-and-white headshots of actresses, all around Donna's age. Each one had a resume on the back.

"Where did all of these come from?" Scarlett asked.

"Call a few agents, tell them you're casting, they'll messenger over all the headshots you need before you can even put down the phone. Now, our mission today is to keep Donna here until the other audition ends. I have a spy over there who'll tell us when they close up shop."

"Right," Scarlett said, feeling queasy.

"Oh, there's one thing, O'Hara. It's best that Spencer and Eric don't know the exact reason they're doing this. It might confuse their performance. I told Spencer I'm helping a producer work out an idea for a new reality program about a fake TV show."

"So, they don't know this is a setup?"

"They know it's a setup," she clarified, "they just don't know all of the details. Imagine trying to improvise for three hours knowing this was all arranged for this one person. Trust me... this is better. And they'll be paid a hundred dollars each for their time."

Before Scarlett could reply, there was a knock at the door.

"I think our cast is here," Mrs. Amberson said. "Let me do the talking."

The door opened to reveal Eric, dressed in a fine light blue dress shirt and black pants. He was actually, genuinely breathtaking.

"Spencer is right behind me," he said, smiling at Scarlett. "He's locking his bike up."

Spencer was completely out of breath when he appeared a moment later.

"Sorry," he said. "So much traffic. I just got off my shift."

"You're fine. And you smell like breakfast. How nice."

Mrs. Amberson went over the setup one more time, possibly for her benefit. Donna had been told that *The Heart of the Empire* had started production when the lead actress was hospitalized. It needed to be recast immediately, and the chosen actress would start work that week. Eric was playing the casting director. Spencer was the general assistant and would be reading the role of young police detective, Hank Stewart. Mrs. Amberson had acquired a video camera, which would be connected to Scarlett's computer—the story being that everything that was filmed was being shown live to a room full of studio executives in LA. In reality, the camera didn't have a battery and the cord didn't even fit into any of the computer ports.

"The goal," Mrs. Amberson told Spencer and Eric, "is to keep her going as long as possible. We really want to give people an idea of how much actors have to go through to get a part. And you, Scarlett..."

Scarlett looked up from her efforts to disguise the unconnected video cable with a pile of papers.

"...step out into the hall with me for a moment while Spencer and Eric prepare."

Scarlett followed Mrs. Amberson down the hall, where she scuttled out of the low skylight and onto a concrete ledge outside. Scarlett stayed inside, leaning on the sill while Mrs. Amberson pulled out her cigarette case and lit up.

"I have a surprise for you, O'Hara," she said. "Guess what you'll be doing while all of this is going on?"

"Going with you?" Scarlett asked.

"And miss the fun? Oh, no. You're going to be reading the part of our young victim."

Scarlett was too stunned to speak. Her refusal came in the form of wide eyes and a backward stagger.

"Half the actresses on these kinds of shows are so wooden that you could build a table out of them," Mrs. Amberson said. "Donna won't know the difference. Just read the lines and don't fall over. That's all there is to it."

"That's not all there is!" Scarlett said. "They're pretending to be casting people! They're improvising!"

"So?"

"So...I'm not an actress!"

"Who cares? All improvising means is *making things up*, which you can do. I've seen the way you and your brother bounce things off each other. You're a natural. Spencer will help you."

"He can't *teach me how to act* in the next fifteen minutes."

"Leave the work to them. Your part is to sit there and look clueless. Couldn't be simpler."

"I can't," Scarlett said.

Mrs. Amberson leaned back through the skylight to pluck the wayward curl from its traditional spot in Scarlett's eye.

"Stop worrying so much, O'Hara. I wouldn't tell you to do it if I didn't think you had it in you. Now get down there. I have to go before Donna arrives."

Scarlett walked back down the hall slowly, pausing by the elevator bank. All she had to do was hit the button and she could get away from this mess.

Sit there and look clueless, she said to herself.

Maybe she could play a completely clueless person. She had typed and written part of the script, so at least she sort of knew it. If she forced herself back into that room...this was a chance to impress Eric unlike any other.

At the very least, she had to go down and let Spencer and Eric know what was going on. She let herself back into the studio, where they were discussing how to stage the scene.

"Mrs. Amberson is leaving," she said. "She has this stupid idea that I should play the girl, but..."

"Why not?" Eric said. "We need another person."

Spencer looked less sure, and looked like he was about to say something to that effect when there was a buzz at the door.

"Showtime," he said, clapping her on the back. "Guess you're in."

THE HEART OF THE EMPIRE

Donna Spendler didn't look very vicious standing there on the threshold of the studio. She looked a bit older than Mrs. Amberson. Her hair was shoulder-length, perfectly coiffed. It had long gone gray, but she had had it colored so that it was a glistening silver, with many highlights and tones.

Spencer ushered her in, looking every inch the assistant.

"I was surprised to get your call," she said. "Pleasantly so. And you caught me just at the perfect time."

"Glad to hear it," Eric said coolly. He stood and extended his hand. "I'm Paul, the casting director."

That was his agreed-upon name. Spencer (who had gleefully renamed himself Dick) extended his hand. Scarlett quickly chose the name Tara.

"Did you get the sides we messengered over to your agent?" Spencer said.

Sides, Scarlett reminded herself. The script pages were called sides.

"Right here," Donna said. "I read them in the cab on the way over, so I'm still a little green."

"No worries. We can go through it a few times before we roll."

182

"Is it just the three of you?" Donna asked.

"There are a lot more of us," Eric said, pointing to the unconnected, dead video camera. "Video feed to LA. They'll be about ten or fifteen people watching on the west coast."

God, he was good. Scarlett's only hope now was that her computer didn't start belching smoke or just explode for good measure.

"We're just going to read through it first," Spencer said, throwing Scarlett a quick look to see how she was coping.

The reading was easy enough, even though Scarlett didn't sound remotely like an actress. She was, however, a natural at the "sitting and looking clueless" part. There was a bit of a snag when they got to the part where the girl was supposed to start crying hysterically. Scarlett couldn't make herself cry. The only person she knew who could do that was Ashley Wallace at school, and Ashley was a well-known psychopath. At that part in the script, Scarlett just slapped her hand over her eyes to represent crying.

Donna and Spencer actually did read the parts like actors. It was strange for Scarlett to hear her words spoken back to her. She fought the urge to correct them, to tell them how it sounded in her head.

"Good," Spencer said, when they were done. He said it with as much enthusiasm as he could without seeming like her brother trying to be nice about a terrible performance.

Donna was eyeing Scarlett carefully. The one thing that must have been one million percent clear was that Scarlett was not an actress. A small, very dim child could have figured that out.

"Are you..." she began, "are you *in* the show?"

"Tara is the coproducer's daughter," Eric chimed in quickly. "She's doing us a huge favor today. You have *no idea* how tight this situation is. We've never had to cast a lead in one day before."

It was a breathtaking save, and one that brought instant warmth from Donna Spendler. Now that Scarlett was Tara, daughter of a producer, and not just Tara, general idiot...there was a warm, almost maternal vibe.

"You're doing an excellent job," she said sweetly. "I'd never have known you weren't a pro."

"Thanks," Scarlett said dryly.

"Now let's do it for real," Eric said, pretending to switch on the camera.

So they did it again. And again. And again. Eric watched and called "LA" (Mrs. Amberson) a few times to see if more was needed. LA always needed more. Scarlett was so fried she thought she'd cry if she had to read those lines again. Spencer and Donna, being professionals, kept going strong. After the eighteenth take, though, Donna called proceedings to a halt.

"I feel like I've done all I can with that," she said. "Without direction, I mean. At this point, we're just repeating ourselves."

That's the point, Scarlett wanted to say. But secretly she wanted to hug Donna for making it stop.

"Sure," Eric said confidently. "Let me give them a call."

He vanished into the hall with his phone. Donna went to the corner to drink from her bottle of water and do some neck rolls. Spencer gave Scarlett a sly shoulder bump of support as he went over to the table to move the headshots around, as if he was doing something useful with them.

"Okay," Eric said, returning. "They just need to see one more thing. We're going to need to try a little improv scene with you and...Dick. Tara, you can come and sit over here with me."

This was new. Mrs. Amberson clearly needed time. It didn't matter to Scarlett as long as she didn't have to be in it anymore. Now her job was to sit next to Eric. That, she could do.

"This character has a violence problem," Eric explained. "We want to see a scene in the station where Alice really oversteps the bounds. Can you get rough with him?"

As Donna and Spencer squared off, and Eric made up a situation, there was a convulsion in Scarlett's abdomen, a physically painful twinge.

Oh, no. This was bad.

The hysteria finally hit Scarlett. She was going to start laughing, and she was never, ever going to stop. It wasn't a joyful feeling, it was a horribly terrifying one.

"Don't worry," Spencer was saying to Donna. "You can come right at me."

The heave of laughter was building in Scarlett's chest. She put every ounce of energy in her body into pushing it down. She tried not to see, not to hear, not to think...even when Donna was throwing Spencer up against the wall and screaming the words, "Do you want to know what it feels like to be a victim?" into his face.

The laugh was just at the bottom of her throat, and when it came, it would be loud, and it would never, ever stop. It would be laughter vomit.

Just as it was all going to come out, Eric reached over and took her hand under the table.

"Squeeze," he whispered surreptitiously. "Hard."

Scarlett squeezed. She squeezed so hard that she worried that she might break his fingers. He didn't wince. Didn't blink. Just kept his eyes straight forward on the scene like it wasn't even happening.

She felt herself relaxing. The laugh eased itself back down. Scarlett released some of the pressure, but kept her hand in Eric's for safety as Donna raged on, cycling through every emotion, showing them everything she could. She fought, she cried, she swung. Spencer weaved and dodged and held her back. And all the while, Eric squeezed Scarlett's hand gently. Something real passed through that squeeze. He wasn't doing it for the scene anymore—he was holding her hand because he wanted to, and he extracted it reluctantly when things drew to a close.

"That was great," he said, when Donna had finished. "I'll just check with them...."

"LA" was apparently satisfied, and Donna was thanked and dismissed, with promises that someone would be in touch soon. When she was gone, the three of them were quiet for a moment. They heard her footsteps going off in the distance, the ding of the elevator, the close of the door.

Eric put his head down on the table. Spencer sprang up, grabbed Scarlett, and threw her over his shoulder.

"You were amazing!" he said.

"I sucked," she replied, upside down. "I almost laughed."

"No," Eric said, rubbing his crushed hand with a knowing

smile. "You covered yourself really well."

"Seriously," Spencer said, shifting her into piggyback position. "I have to admit I was worried when you got thrown into it, but you totally pulled it off like a champ. I could tell you were scared, but you did it, anyway."

This praise felt good...maybe better than anything in recent memory. She had made her brother proud and impressed the guy she liked. The mood only improved when Mrs. Amberson returned to see how it all went. She was effusive in her praise.

"Now," she said, passing some money to Spencer and Eric, "my friends didn't want to bother with a confidentiality agreement, but it's important that you don't tell anyone about this. Word gets out way too easily. So, lips sealed! You two can head off. Scarlett and I will finish up here."

Eric looked like he wanted to linger a bit, but with Mrs. Amberson shooing him out and Spencer going as well, he couldn't really stay.

"I knew you had it in you," Mrs. Amberson said when they were gone.

"I guess," Scarlett replied.

"You guess? Learn to take a compliment, O'Hara. I asked for your help, and you came through. I won't forget this, mark my words."

It was only now that Scarlett remembered what this was all about. For better or for worse, she had just helped to destroy Donna's chance at a Broadway role. And though she knew that Mrs. Amberson's words were meant in a friendly way, she couldn't help but feel a faint sense of alarm, as if the sirens in the street below were headed in her direction.

THE NEW SPACE

"Billy called me," Mrs. Amberson said, when Scarlett walked in the next morning. "It seems that Donna has walked away from her new musical because of a major television opportunity that's come up."

She was sitting on her bed, in a meditative position, grinning like a serial killer who'd just been given all the keys to a dorm building. She got up and climbed onto her perch so Scarlett could change the sheets on her bed.

"We have to get going in a minute," she said. "I have a lead on a place for rehearsal. It sounds absolutely ideal."

The ideal place was a former church in the East Village. It looked like it had been repurposed long ago—there was nothing left on the inside to hint at its previous function except the stained glass windows. The main room had been gutted and a low stage installed at one end. The stage felt hollow when Scarlett walked on it, and there were small holes dotting its surface. The rest of the room was hard to walk through, as it contained a hundred or so folding chairs, countless boxes, folding tables, fake trees, broken clothes racks, and for some reason, a lawn mower. In the back, there was a large closet with exposed insulation that they called the "workroom." There were two tiny bathrooms and a dirty window facing an unused playground.

Mrs. Amberson wrote out a check for two thousand dollars for two weeks without blinking an eye.

"It's gorgeous," she said, carefully negotiating around the holes on the stage. "It's a miracle we got it on such short notice and for such a short time. I wish we could just do the show here, but someone has it booked starting next week. Still. It gives us a good place to work out the new concepts. I have fabulous ideas."

"Ideas?" Scarlett asked. "What are you..."

Mrs. Amberson held up a silencing finger.

"Scarlett, let me tell you the one thing I've learned in life. You have to tell people what they want. Most people don't know. They mill around through life, bumping into things, waiting for someone to give them some *direction*. Trevor's a sweetheart, but without guidance, this show will go nowhere. That's the trouble with so many of these groups—they have no one to tell them the big things they have to do. And this works so well for us!"

"It does?"

"This is the second part of the story that will frame my narrative. I meet the theater group, pull a stunt out of *Hamlet* to right old wrongs, then save the show. This is part of my story! And you're my Boswell."

"Your what?"

"My Boswell. My right hand. The recorder of my adventures. Now, let's wrap up some business. We need to call Donna and tell her there's a delay for a few days while the script is being rewritten. Tell her that the studio will be sending someone over to cut her hair short. It's a nice touch. She's always been a hair diva. It will be a very, very nice buzz cut."

For some reason, this caused Scarlett to hesitate.

"It's *hair*, Scarlett," she said. "I'm not cutting off a finger. Now, I have a contact at the Roundabout who has access to the most amazing costumes. I'm going over to meet her. Move all of these things off the stage and the floor. I want this space completely clear and open. I'll be back in a few hours."

Scarlett looked around at the chairs, furniture, boxes, and heavy pads.

"You want me to move all of this?"

"Oh, don't worry," Mrs. Amberson said. "I'm sure you'll be fine."

She grabbed her purse and waved, leaving Scarlett alone in the sweltering room. This didn't precisely seem like the copious thanks she'd been promised. Scarlett folded a few rows of chairs in a disgruntled manner, then planted herself on a pile of them to send some messages to her far-flung friends. She was so engrossed in this that she didn't notice when, a half hour later, the door opened and someone walked through the mess in her direction.

"Hey," Eric said.

Scarlett literally fell off the chairs in alarm. Profuse apologies from Eric followed. They weren't needed. What she needed was some dignity and poise, but you can't just get them at the corner deli.

"So we have to get this cleared out?" he asked, once he was sure that he hadn't caused Scarlett any permanent damage. "I just got the call. I hope you didn't do too much on your own. I have to change my shirt. I'll be right back."

He took a shirt (perfectly folded) from his bag, and went into the corner behind a box.

"I realize this is ridiculous," he called from his impromptu dressing room. "Guys take their shirts off all the time in public, but I have the Southern thing going on, remember?"

He emerged, wearing a T-shirt so snug and perfect that Scarlett first thought that someone was playing a joke on her.

"It's how we show respect," he said. "We don't flaunt our nakedness in front of ladyfolk."

This was both a staggering disappointment and a touching show of thoughtfulness.

"I guess we should start moving this stuff," he said, looking at the disaster around them. "And I guess there's no chance there's an air conditioner in here, is there?"

He poked around for a moment and eventually produced a small dolly with an unstable wheel.

"This should be fun," he said, giving the dud wheel a spin. "Why don't we move most of it toward the back? We'll just pile it high. If you can move chairs, I'll get the big stuff back there."

It was clear from the first moment that Eric was going to try to keep Scarlett from doing the heavy work. She was torn between wanting to throw herself in and show that she was just as capable and, frankly, not wanting to get absolutely disgusting in the painful heat of the church. She decided the best idea was to fold as quickly as possible and help move the chairs. This also gave her the opportunity to watch Eric work, which was admittedly pretty engrossing.

"Do you know anything about what that thing yesterday was for?" he asked, shoving a refrigerator-sized box onto the dolly with only a little difficulty. "All Amy told us was that she was helping out someone who's developing a reality show."

Scarlett bit down hard on the tip of her tongue before answering.

"I think it's just a test," she said. "They're just trying out some ideas."

"Spencer and I were just talking about why it was done. We were thinking that maybe it was some kind of audition that Amy set up...."

The hope in his voice was depressing.

"I don't think so," she said. "I'm pretty sure it was just... something to work out some ideas."

"Oh." He didn't show any disappointment, but Scarlett still felt swamped with guilt. He worked quietly for a while on the other side of the room, and she finished up with the chairs. It seemed that he had nothing else to say to her, but then he abruptly stopped stacking boxes and came over to where she was.

"You two are a lot alike, you know that?" he asked, helping her with her halfhearted effort. "You and Spencer. You don't look alike, but you act alike."

"We're close," she said. "But we don't seem alike. He can act. He likes to throw himself over walls. I can't do anything that Spencer does."

"He's good at that," Eric said, his voice getting twangy and soft and Southern again. "I think he's the best I've ever seen. But you are alike. You're both...personalities. Half the girls in the cast are after your brother right now. I'm not sure if you want to know that or not."

"He was like that in high school. But you should tell him that. He thinks he's losing his touch."

"Stephanie—Ophelia. She has it really bad. We walked home the other night, and I promise you, she didn't shut up about him for an hour. 'Spencer's so funny.' 'Spencer's so good-looking.' 'Spencer sang today and he has a great singing voice.' 'Spencer can fall over a half a dozen trash cans.' I started to get a complex."

"Why would *you* get a complex?" Scarlett said, without thinking.

Eric stopped in midreach for a pile of chairs. His shirt was soaked through in spots.

"I'm not smooth," he said plainly. "I don't have that natural... whatever it is that your brother has. I'm a hick, Scarlett. A hick in the big city who doesn't know what he's doing half the time."

Was this how he saw himself? This gorgeous person with so much talent?

"But you're...amazing," Scarlett said. "You're the most amazing person I've ever met."

He looked up at her and visibly worked through some kind of mental calculation. Then he stepped over to her, coming so close so quick that for some reason Scarlett assumed it was because something was wrong with her—like a spider on her arm.

"I really hope I don't mess this up," he said.

"Mess what..."

He kissed her. First on the nose, as if testing for approval, working down to her lips. He kept his mouth firmly closed, but that didn't take away from the intensity of the moment at all.

He broke contact when her phone began to ring.

"I'm getting really sick of your phone," he mumbled good-naturedly, gesturing for her to answer it. "I'll bet I can guess who it is."

Mrs. Amberson was maddeningly chipper on the other end.

"How're things?" she asked.

"Fine..." Scarlett said, her teeth sightly clenched.

"I'm on my way back in a cab, with yet another cab behind me full of outfits. You should see this haul! Well, you will, in about fifteen minutes. Just giving you a little heads up to...set up a clothes rack or two."

This remark was punctuated by a tiny snicker. Scarlett could hear her sucking on a cigarette in satisfaction.

"You know what I think, O'Hara?" she said. "I think I do know your type after all."

She hung up.

"I've wanted to do that pretty much since I first saw you in the park," he said. He almost sounded nervous. "I hope that was okay."

Scarlett clutched the pile of chairs behind her in what she hoped looked like post-kiss casualness as opposed to just, well, collapsing in shock.

"I'm okay," she said.

"I don't want to be weird, but...we should maybe not tell your brother about this. Just because we work together, you know? Is that all right?"

"Sure," she said, not even processing the question. Her brain had gone all soft and floppy. Something about not telling Spencer. Whatever. It was probably a good idea.

"So," he said, "is she on her way?"

Scarlett nodded.

"Well, we probably have time...."

And then he did it again.

CRACKS

The train home that night was packed.

A crowded New York subway car in the summer is a wonderful place to meet new people. There is no decorum, no breathing room, and often, no deodorant. You survive by keeping yourself small and taking short maintenance breaths and making them last, like divers do.

Scarlett was well versed in the art of subway riding and could handle even the worst of conditions—but today, she was simply overloaded. Her brain was scrambled as they sped along, the train shaking back and forth. All she could see, all she could think about was the kissing. It had become overwhelming—it was taking over everything. It had passed over feeling good to that superintense feeling that is just too much for the brain or body to hold. She pushed her face, lips and all, against the subway pole to keep herself upright, even if that was almost a guarantee of catching something truly horrible.

"Are you going to puke?" Spencer asked. He was standing next to her, holding his bike upright with one hand and carefully balancing himself by holding onto the pole high over her head.

"Huh?"

"You look like you're going to hurl," he said in a low voice. "Should we get off?"

The man Scarlett was pressed up against on the other side looked down warily.

"I'm fine," she said. "It was just warm in there today. Must be dehydrated…"

…from all the kissing I was doing. Shut up, brain!

"What's wrong with you today?" he asked, unsatisfied. "It wasn't just the heat. You seemed…I don't know. Like something was up."

When she was little, Spencer told her that he could see pictures of her thoughts in her eyes. Obviously, she had figured out this wasn't possible, but there was still something in her that believed that he could get at her thoughts if he wanted to.

He was doing it now. He was looking her in the eye and seeing the truth there.

"Is there something going on?" he asked.

"Going on?" she repeated. "Going on with what?"

This was idiotic. She knew what Spencer meant, and he knew that she knew. This was her moment to come clean. So what if Eric had asked her to keep quiet? There was no need to keep things from Spencer.

Scarlett opened her mouth to tell him, but something strange flashed across his expression—something so fast and so subtle that anyone else would have missed it. But Scarlett saw it. He wasn't going to like her answer.

"I got my period," she blurted out, much to the continuing delight of the man pushed up next to her. "It's catastrophic."

"Oh," Spencer said. "Why didn't you say so? That's it?"

"That's it."

He didn't look convinced.

"You would tell me if there was something else, right?"

"Of course!" she said.

This was the first time she had ever really lied to Spencer. It was upsettingly easy. He turned back to the Manhattan Storage ad that he'd been staring at before this doomed conversation started. He had asked, and he had taken her at the word. Which made her the worst sister, ever.

Then again, she thought, she hadn't really lied—she'd just *switched topics*. It wasn't like Spencer told her every *little tiny detail*. She didn't want to know every tiny detail. She had once seen an open box of condoms poking out from under a pile of his clothes, for example. She never whipped them out and said, "What, or who, have you been doing with these?" He told her the stuff that mattered to him. She had known about his major crushes, his biggest frustrations. The gory details weren't important. He had to have left out some pretty big things along the way.

But he had never *lied*. If she had asked him something, he would have told her, no matter what it was. She knew that for a fact. If she had wanted, for some insane reason, to hear the gory details...he probably would have given them to her. Or, at least, he would have told her as much as he thought a younger sister could hear without her head exploding. He would not have looked her in the face and denied something.

And she didn't have her period. That *was* actually a lie.

The train stopped, and he began to wheel off his bike. She followed him as he lifted it up the stairs into the heavy, humid night. He was already talking about something else—something that had happened to him at work that morning. But she wasn't listening. There was a low pounding in her head, like a pump gone haywire.

She had to tell him. No matter what Eric said. It would be fine. He wouldn't care. It would change nothing.

Her phone beeped, registering a message that had come in when they were underground. Her hand shook a little as she flipped it open. It was from Eric.

You've made a country boy very happy, city girl, it read.

"Who was that?" he asked. "Mrs. Amberson?"

She flipped the phone shut and shoved it into her pocket.

"Yeah," she said, amazed at how quickly another lie flew from her mouth. "You know what she's like."

She would have cracked—started laughing uncontrollably, started screaming. It was unclear. But fate dealt her one other kind hand. As they approached the hotel, they noticed the black Mercedes lolling in front of it with the hazards on. The driver was out of the car and up the street a bit, talking on his phone.

"What's going on here?" Spencer said, jumping on his bike. "I think we need to go and have a look."

He rode off ahead. Scarlett walked slowly, trying to catch her breath. She'd made him happy. That was the kind of message you sent if there was a *thing*—a real thing. She was barely paying attention as Spencer circled the car like a shark, tapping on all the windows to torment the occupants. They didn't respond to his efforts. The doors and windows remained closed when Scarlett approached.

"What do you think they're doing in there?" Spencer asked, jumping off his bike and wheeling it to the curb. "If you were going to pick a place to have sex in a car, would it be in front of your own house, blocking traffic?"

"Probably not," Scarlett said.

She suddenly felt a weird affection for Lola and Chip and their cozy little life.

The door flew open, and Lola got out. She was wearing the Dior dress. Chip looked like he was about to get out after her, but then he caught sight of Scarlett and Spencer standing there. His face was a mess—red, wet. Lola looked comparatively composed, though her eyes were clearly a bit on the runny side and her mascara was smudged a little under the eyes.

"Are you okay?" Spencer asked, as she approached them.

"I'm fine," she said, brushing back some hair that had stuck to her damp cheeks. "Can you just ask him to go? And be nice to him, Spence. Okay?"

She said it so quietly and with such obvious discomfort that there was no way that Spencer was going to say a word in reply.

Lola went inside. Spencer passed his bike over to Scarlett and went over to the car and leaned over the door. Scarlett couldn't hear what he was saying, but clearly he wasn't mocking Chip. Chip put up no resistance. The driver got back into the car, and the Mercedes pulled off.

"I don't believe it," Spencer said. "She finally did it. She actually dumped him. I think...I think I feel *bad* for him. That's annoying. But also, how great is this?"

As he went toward Trash Can Alley to lock up his bike, a glowing cigarette butt came sailing down next to Scarlett, striking itself out on the pavement on impact. She looked up, and was not surprised to see a thin trail of smoke and a shadow above.

"Interesting night, O'Hara?" a voice asked. "I have a feeling they're only about to get more so. See you in the morning."

LOLA SEES A DINOSAUR

Lola was in the Orchid Suite, stripping off her dress when Scarlett opened the door.

"Here," she said, as Scarlett came in. "This is for you. I think it looks nicer on you, anyway. I'm not sure I can really wear black. Not everyone can. It's a myth. I'm too pale."

Scarlett accepted the dress and watched as Lola pulled on a pair of pink shortie pajamas and then set to work dumping out the contents of her underwear drawer onto her bed. She began refolding her panties into perfect little squares, which was something she usually did to relax herself in times of stress.

"Do you want anything?" Scarlett offered quietly. "Tea, or water, or something?"

"I'm fine. Thank you."

Scarlett put the dress on her bureau and sat down on her bed opposite. She waited until Lola had folded everything to her satisfaction and sat down, squishing the pile of panties between her hands, like a delicate pastel accordion.

"We were at a benefit at the Natural History Museum tonight," she said. "Some friend of theirs rented out the lobby for something—I don't even know what—and everybody paid about a thousand bucks to be there. There was a girl named Boonz there. I've seen her at a few things. She dates this other guy from Durban. She walked right up to me, like she wanted to make small talk, because there's nothing else to do at these things. And do you know what she said to me?"

Scarlett could have come out with a few amusing possible answers that Spencer would have loved, but this was definitely not the time.

"She said, 'Don't you have a second dress?' I kept waiting for her to laugh, to show that it was some kind of weird joke. But she didn't. She said, 'You've worn that every time I've ever seen you.' And she smirked and walked away."

Scarlett felt a flush coming to her cheeks. There was no reason for someone to cut Lola down. Lola, who could be one of those snotty and horrible people, but who never, ever was.

A few tears dribbled down Lola's cheeks.

"I barely know her. There was no reason for her to do that. She just had to make a point of the fact that I wear this one dress a lot, because *they* get rid of them after they've worn them one or two times. I was trying not to cry, and I looked up at the dinosaur skeleton, and all of a sudden, I just had this horrifying image of...forever. Being around these people for the rest of my life. I put down my drink and walked out."

"Good," Scarlett said. "You should have. Did Chip leave, too?"

"He followed me out," she said. "He tried to make me feel better. He said that he would get me a new dress. And that's the problem. The solution is always going to be 'buy another one.' The people are always going to be the same. They're so smug, and most of them are so *stupid*, and they think they deserve everything they have. They'll never have to work, never have to do anything they don't want to do. They can't understand not having money. They see it as a flaw. Chip doesn't...but I just realized he'll never, ever *get* it. He would never get that, to most people, getting a dress like this is a huge deal."

She looked at the once-beloved dress, now lying limply on the bureau.

"He wanted to take me out somewhere else. Go downtown to a club, or over to the boat, and I just wanted to come home. We pulled up, and I broke up with him. Just like that. I always thought that was what I wanted. I always thought that's where I wanted to be—with the people who really lived that life. And then I didn't anymore."

There was a knock at the door, and Spencer let himself in, slightly more subtly than normal. He dropped down next to Lola and leaned low over his knees to look up at her downturned face.

"You must be thrilled," she said. "You don't have to lie."

"I wouldn't. But I'm not saying a word. I was nice to him. And I will be even nicer to you, and your weird underwear sandwich."

"Thank you." Lola set the pile of perfectly folded panties on her bedside stand, then reached over and gave his hand a little squeeze. "I appreciate it."

Both of them sat there watching Lola, waiting for something dramatic to happen, but nothing did. She sniffed a little, straightened the underwear pile, then stood.

"I should go tell Marlene," she said. "And then I'll tell Mom and Dad. About this, about the job. Might as well. I just broke up. They aren't going to kick me when I'm down. I'll be back in a minute."

She floated off, closing the door quietly behind her.

"Did you see that?" Spencer said in a low voice. "That's not what you look like when you break up with someone you really like. Remember when Gillian broke up with me last year, during our final production?"

"Which one was Gillian?"

"The one with the really long red hair. She broke up with me right in the middle of *The Music Man*."

"I remember," Scarlett said. "You sat in your room for three days over the long weekend and got drunk on that Johnnie Walker you stole from her apartment and told Mom you had the flu, except you smelled like booze. And you threw up a lot. And you never changed your clothes."

Spencer nodded, not even a little taken aback by the description.

"Exactly. That's what it feels like. I know."

"Didn't you go out with her best friend a week later?" Scarlett asked.

"That's not the point..."

"And *she* broke up with *you*, so it's not really the same."

"All right. That was a bad example. Do you remember Emily, from junior year?"

"From *The Glass Menagerie*?"

"That's the one. *I* broke up with *her*, and I felt horrible. I was a big, hot mess."

"Yeah, but didn't you break up with her because she was

gay and about to break up with you anyway to date that other girl in your class?"

"Scarlett," Spencer said, drawing himself up, "I am trying to teach you a lesson."

"Sorry."

"Lola's way too calm."

"Lola's always calm," Scarlett replied.

"Lola isn't *always* calm."

He said it like he knew what he was talking about, but Scarlett couldn't figure out what he was referring to.

"You only look that calm when you feel relief," he went on. "When you didn't care in the first place."

This was punctuated by a slamming door and heavy footfalls down the hallway. Marlene came tearing into the Orchid Suite and made right for Lola's bed, clawing at the sheets and pulling them off the bed, then knocking things off the dresser. It was a very uncoordinated effort, one that screamed of a general frustration. Spencer caught her around the waist and hoisted her up. She flailed at him, but the blows were ineffective.

"Marlene," he said, "you must chill a little, okay?"

He kept her dangling there until she gave up and went limp. Lola rejoined them and looked at Marlene sadly.

"I'm sorry," she said. "Marlene, I really am."

Marlene wasn't interested. She wiggled her way out of Spencer's grasp and stalked out of the room.

"Why is she more upset than you?" Scarlett asked.

"I think she sees Chip as an older brother."

"She has an older brother," Spencer said. "*I'm* her older brother."

"Her older brother with a boat and a driver," Lola clarified. "She got attached to him. She'll be all right. I'll talk to her when she calms down. Don't let her break anything, okay?"

Lola went off again, and Spencer just shook his head in amazement.

"That's enough drama for tonight," he said, peeling off his shirt. Even he was struck by the powerful odor that had been caused by the long day in the church. He held it at arm's length. "I'm done. I'm going to go to bed and read important books about theater."

"It would be easier if you just said porn," Scarlett said.

"No idea what you're talking about. But knock first if you need me."

When he had gone off, and the room was quiet at last, Scarlett went over and picked up the black dress and held it up to herself. It was hers now. And she had Eric. And Lola was single.

She went to the window and pulled it open. The windows of the Hopewell were old, made of thin glass, and largely uncared for wood frames that coughed up paint and pigeon feathers when you touched them. But the night air was warm and sweet, and didn't smell too heavily of garbage from the alley below. There was a white full moon hanging over Naked Lady's building.

She read the message on her phone again.

You've made a country boy very happy, city girl.

She was the city girl. This was her city. And for the first time that summer, maybe ever, Scarlett felt so full of contentment that she would even have been happy to see Naked Lady and wish her well.

CELEBRATION

The cast was fading in the heat the next day. They lounged on one another across the big, empty floor, treating each other like pieces of furniture. Scarlett had always noticed, when dealing with her brother's friends, that actors were touchy. She now appreciated this fact completely. She smiled benevolently as she watched Ophelia share her bottle of water with Spencer.

She didn't sit next to Eric. It was too soon for that. She took her place over by the wall, next to where Mrs. Amberson had planted herself during the actors' warm-ups. She had now taken the low stage.

"Trevor and I have been talking," she announced to the group. "And *we* think..."

Unless she was seriously imagining things, and she might have been, Scarlett detected a very slight, very fake British accent creeping into Mrs. Amberson's voice. It wasn't constant—it would just twang Scarlett's ear from time to time, sharp as a flick of the finger. No one else seemed to register it. Or, if they did, they weren't letting on. They were a bunch of actors, so they could have been *acting* like they didn't hear it.

"...that we need to push the dramatic stakes a bit. We need to give this performance a real sense of style, so we're going to take what you've been doing and extend it a bit. Think classic film. Think silent movie. Hamlet and Ophelia, you're going to be like classic screen legends. Think Bogart and Bacall. Valentino and Garbo. Spencer and Eric, you'll be our Keystone Cops, our Marx Brothers."

There was a warm reception to this idea.

"I have one other piece of news," she said. "Tonight, to celebrate all the work we've done, I want to have a little party."

This was a surprise to Scarlett. She glanced over to Eric, who beamed widely at her.

"I'll supply all the food and drink," she went on. "So, we break at five and reconvene at eight."

The idea of the party roused the group, and they threw themselves into the work. At five, Mrs. Amberson forced everyone out except Scarlett.

"You didn't tell me you were doing this," Scarlett said, as they stood outside and Mrs. Amberson waved toward a van that was pulling up at the curb.

"I like surprises," she said. "And I certainly owe you and your brother and Eric some thanks. Now, let's get these things inside."

Mrs. Amberson had ordered a substantial amount of food, along with several cases of beer and two cases of wine.

"For the over twenty-ones, of course," she said with a smile. "As for you, there is underage, and then, there is *underage*. I believe a taste of wine is perfectly acceptable, but please stick to one glass tonight. Now, let's work on ambience."

It was a strangely pleasant interlude. If there was one thing Mrs. Amberson was good at, it was creating a good atmosphere. From one of the many boxes in the back, she produced a hundred or more tealight candles and strings of lights. Together, they created a bar out of crates and chairs, which Mrs. Amberson draped in fabric. They dangled the lights around the room, lined the stage with candles, created a center stage area and a few little clusters of chairs along the sides of the room. Slowly, the big dusty room was transformed into a softly lit hall.

Even her stories got more entertaining. Broadway flops, discos, schemes she'd used to get auditions....Mrs. Amberson was actually an interesting person when she wasn't barking out orders or using Scarlett for one of her schemes. She was deeply engrossed in a story when the actors came drifting back, correctly guessing that all of the supplies had already arrived, and the sooner they got there, the quicker they could get at them.

Scarlett hadn't really talked with the other cast members much before, but they all proved to be nice, and surprisingly interested in her. Over the course of the night, there was some impromptu singing. Hamlet got up and did a hilariously overdone version of the "To be or not to be" soliloquy. Eric and Spencer were called upon to do some of their usual routine, which they did with more manic energy than normal, throwing each other all around the room. Annoying Jeff tried to join in, but was rapidly frightened off by the speed and genuine skill it took not to get hurt. Scarlett kept an eye on Stephanie while this was going on, and sure enough, she was watching

Spencer with a rapt expression. Scarlett felt a flush of pride—she really did have the best brother in the world.

Then the room broke into smaller groups. Mrs. Amberson sat with Trevor and some actors and told stories of her Broadway days. Out of the corner of her eye, Scarlett saw Spencer leaning in to talk to Ophelia. From the way he was smiling and joking with her, Scarlett could tell that he was in heavy flirting mode. While she was glad for that, it really wasn't something she wanted to watch. She drifted around, standing with various groups and listening to them talk. They all accepted her, but she couldn't really join in with any conversation. It was all very theatery. She was starting to feel out of place, when Eric popped up from behind one of the poles that lined the edge of the room.

"I need to talk to you," he said. His voice was slurring just slightly, but not enough that the words slid out of place. "Meet me out front in five minutes?"

He vanished before she could answer. Scarlett had to take a heaving breath. Five minutes. She looked around to see if anyone had just noticed what transpired, but everyone was busy talking. She quietly got her bag from the corner of the room. When she went outside, Eric was there, staring into the driver's window of someone's car.

"Come on," he said, taking her by the hand and hurrying her down the block. "I should have showed you this before."

They went four blocks to see whatever it was that Eric wanted to show her, finally stopping in front of a fairly run-down apartment building, one of hundreds that dotted the East Village.

"Wait," he said, throwing himself up against the door. "Wait a second. Before you go in. I just want to say, you don't have to worry."

"I'm not worried," she said. This wasn't true. She was experiencing a kind of terror, but a pleasant terror.

"No," he slurred. "Remember. I am Southern. I am a gentleman. I just need you to know that. If you feel uncomfortable, you just tell me, and we go back in a second, okay? I've got iced tea and a television, and we can just drink iced tea and watch TV if you want. That's all I'm saying. Or we could not go up. I wouldn't be offended."

He was drunk, possibly even playing it up to make his point, but it was all very sincere. He looked both hopeful and worried.

"It's okay," she said.

He smiled so deeply she felt her eyes water.

The lobby had a cracked mosaic floor and smelled like old pizza boxes. There were stickers for a political rally pasted all over the circuit breaker box. He didn't let go of Scarlett's hand or slow down the entire way to his apartment. He took the steps two at a time and had the door hanging open when she got there. It was dark inside the apartment. He went in first and turned on all the lights.

"Welcome to the palace," he said, backing up against the refrigerator to let her past.

Eric's apartment was a tiny studio, the kind that reminded Scarlett that most people in the city didn't live in five-story hotels, no matter how decrepit they were. The room had an uneven floor and was just wide enough for a bed and a canvas chair. Those were the only real pieces of furniture. The kitchen—it if could be called that—was about the size of the back seat of a car and was full of miniaturized appliances. There was only one small set of shelves, and they were packed to the point of groaning, so most of his things were piled neatly and pushed against the walls—books, scripts, DVDs, piles of clothes. Everything was careful and neat.

"This is where I live," he said, offering her the room's only chair. "It's not as nice as where you live."

"I like it," Scarlett said. And it was true. Eric could have lived in a box behind a pizza place, and she would have said she liked it and meant it.

"You know what? If I went to school in North Carolina, I could rent an apartment about twelve times this size for about half as much. Anyway, I have something to show you. Just sit there. Don't look. Close your eyes."

Scarlett slowly closed her eyes. She heard things being shifted around.

"Okay, open!"

He was holding up a boxed set of *Gone With the Wind* DVDs.

"This isn't the normal version," he said gravely. "Oh, no. This one has everything, all the extra footage. It has like... nine hundred hours of footage. If you're in my family, this is what you watch on Christmas. My grandma gave this to me when I moved here so I wouldn't forget the glorious cause."

He set it on the floor by her feet and then went and sat on his bed, which was the only other piece of furniture on offer. Then he seemed to think better of it and sat in the middle of the floor.

"When I first met you," he said, "I was so amazed to meet someone named Scarlett. I thought it was a sign or something. I had come to New York, and there was Scarlett, and she lived in a hotel. And she had beautiful blonde curls…"

He put the tips of his fingers together and touched them a few times. For several minutes, he said nothing at all. Then he dragged himself over to the foot of the chair and moved the wayward curl out of her eye.

"That's always there," he said. "I always want to move it. Hope that's okay."

"It's okay," she replied, her voice dry.

"The thing…from the other day…"

He waited, as if thinking that Scarlett would need some time to recall the kissing.

"In the theater?" she asked.

"Yeah. That. Did you…like that?"

"It was the best thing that ever happened to me," she replied, with a sudden and surprising candor.

"So, if it happened again…you wouldn't be upset?"

Only a shake of the head this time. Saying "no" was way too complicated. He reached up his hand, offering her help down from the chair. When he kissed her this time, he leaned her back against the floor, guarding her head with his hand. Scarlett lost all sense of where she was, or anything else that could possibly have been happening when the whole thing was broken by the most horrible buzzing noise that she had ever heard.

"It's okay," he said. "It's just my door. Hold on."

Spencer's voice entered the room, very loudly.

"Hey," he said. "I can't find Scarlett. Is she up there with you?"

"Uh..." Eric looked down at Scarlett. "Yeah. She is. We're coming down now. Meet you in a second."

Scarlett looked at the clock. It was one-thirty in the morning. That had to be wrong. She looked to her watch for confirmation, and the DVD display, and the readout on the little orange microwave. They all said a variation of the same thing...1:32, 1:33, 1:34. How had it gotten so late? They must have been there for over two hours.

Eric leaned against his door and banged his head lightly against it in concern.

"That was your brother," he said. "He didn't sound very happy."

"It'll be fine," Scarlett said. A quick glance in the mirror as she stood revealed a head of curls standing on end and a lot of makeup smudges around her eyes. She flattened the curls as best she could and rubbed away the blotches.

"Do you want me to go down with you, or...?"

"I should probably go by myself," she said.

"But you're okay?"

"Don't worry," she said taking a deep breath. "It's just Spencer. It'll be fine."

He reached for her hand and rubbed a little circle on her palm with his fingers.

"I..." He shook his head. "I guess you have to go. I'll see you tomorrow."

THE IMPOSSIBLE BREAK

Spencer was outside on the sidewalk, sitting on the stoop and drumming his fingers on the lid of one of the trash cans chained to the front of the building. His unicycle was balanced against his knee. There was a look in his eyes that Scarlett had never seen before—a distant, dim stare. She saw him notice her tousled hair and slightly rumpled clothes.

"You didn't answer your phone," he said. "I called you about a dozen times."

Scarlett looked at her phone in confusion. The answer was depressingly dumb—it had run out of charge.

"Oh, it..."

She held it up to explain. This didn't impress him much.

"Come on," he said.

He said nothing as they waited five minutes for a free cab to come by. Spencer tossed the unicycle into the trunk. She got in and he slid beside her, keeping close to his side of the seat.

"I called home and covered for you," he finally said in a low voice when they were halfway uptown. "That wasn't easy. You were supposed to be home two hours ago. I told them we were working late and that I was with you. It's a good thing I didn't have a lot of time to think about it, because I might not have."

"You're angry," she said.

"Yeah," he snapped. "I am *seriously* pissed."

The cab made a frighteningly fast turn. She slid into him and then edged her way back.

"Why didn't you tell me?" he said.

There was no point in denial.

"I...couldn't."

"What do you mean you *couldn't*?"

She was about to say, "Because Eric said not to." But no matter how she put that, it was not going to come out well. She left the question unanswered as they rode up Third Avenue.

"Then you took off from the party without telling anyone where you were going. So, suddenly, you just aren't there, you're not answering your phone, you're just gone. No one knew where you were, not even Mrs. Amberson. To be honest, Scarlett, it scared the crap out of me. I only went to Eric's because I had no idea where else to look."

The cab jerked to a halt in front of the Hopewell. Spencer reached into his pocket, pulled out some crumpled bills, and shoved them through the window to the driver. He kept three steps ahead of her while he unlocked the front door and didn't say a word in the elevator. When they hit the fifth floor, he dropped the unicycle and stalked down to their parents' room, the Diamond Suite, knocked on the door, and mumbled a few words of explanation.

His entire body stiffened as he walked past her to his room. She followed him inside. He started undressing, as if the conversation was over and she wasn't even there.

"I'm sorry," she said quietly. "I am. I swear."

"I'm tired," he said, tossing his shirt into the corner. "I get up early, remember?"

He climbed into bed, still in his shorts and shoes, but she didn't leave. He folded his arms over his chest and stared at her. Spencer mad was actually a scary, but infrequently seen thing, like the Loch Ness Monster. He could hold a lot of emotion in the narrows of his face.

"Do you want to know what really bothers me?" he said. "What makes me mad is that you couldn't just tell me. You looked right at me and lied to my face."

"I..."

She was going to say *had to*. But she didn't have to lie to Spencer. She just did. He had her dead to rights.

"Can I just ask," he said, his voice reaching a sharp edge, "what you think is going to happen? He's about to start college, Scarlett. You're going to be a sophomore in high school. How's that going to go? Do you think he'll have time for you once he starts school?"

There was a meanness to this that was completely unfamiliar. It made her nauseous.

"So, you think he can't like me?"

"Of course he *likes* you," he said. "He's a guy."

"What does that mean?" she spat. "Are you just mad because *you're* not dating anyone?"

Where had *that* come from? She didn't mean that. It just came out.

217

"It means just what I said," he replied. "This is a bad idea, all around. And this is my show you're messing with."

"Messing with?" she said. "This isn't about you. He likes me. So what if he's in your cast? And the only reason there's even a show to go to is because of me."

He rubbed his face hard with his hands, as if trying to make the view of her go away.

"Forget it," he said. "I covered your story. I'm going to sleep."

He flopped on his side, turning from her. She backed out of the room, waiting for any sign that he was going to keep talking. It didn't come. When she was out in the hall, he got up and closed the door. And for the first time, she heard the sound of his bolt sliding shut.

ACT III

Almost every hotel in New York has experienced a death; therefore, it is no surprise that most hotels in New York have had reports of spectral activity.

In 1934, the Hopewell Hotel on the Upper East Side was well-known among the Broadway set. Its small size and au courant design made it an elegant enclave—and it was considerably more affordable than The Waldorf-Astoria or The St. Regis (where the Bloody Mary was invented in the King Cole Bar that very same year). Performers desiring decent accommodation and a friendly atmosphere kept the hotel going during the Depression. (It was also helpful that the hotel's owner tended to turn a blind eye to room sharing. A room filled with too many guests was better than one with no guests at all.)

In June of that year, a would-be actress named Antoinette Hemmings moved into a room in the Hopewell called the Orchid Suite, which she shared with a theatrical secretary named Betty Spooner.

Though Antoinette had done many chorus roles, she had greater aspirations. It looked like she was on the verge of her first big break when she auditioned for the role of Hope Harcourt in the new Cole Porter musical, Anything Goes. A summer cold and a sudden attack of laryngitis derailed Antoinette's dreams on the day of her final, critical audition.

Antoinette was crushed to miss such a massive opportunity. She was determined to get noticed some other way. She returned to the Hopewell and wrote a long note of instruction to Betty, including the name of the closest hospital and the phone number of a friendly newspaper reporter who covered the theater beat. After dressing herself in her diaphanous, pink, feather-edged dressing gown, she took a handful of sleeping pills, and washed them down with champagne...timing the entire event carefully to coincide with Betty's return from work.

Unfortunately for Antoinette, the normally timely Betty was delayed. Instead of finding the elegant but still very much alive Antoinette draped elegantly over the bed, ready to be carried off to the hospital in her pink gown...she found the very dead body of Antoinette by the door. She had apparently realized in her last moments of consciousness that Betty was not going to be able to save her and made an attempt to get help.

In 1974, a guest in the Orchid Suite reported that a young woman in a pink gown knocked on his door. She asked if Mr. Cole Porter had called for her. The man was about to ask her who she was or why the long-

dead Cole Porter would have called her when he said
she "vanished before my very eyes, like a lifting fog."

—FROM *81 BIG APPLE GHOST TALES*, CHAPTER 8,
"HOTEL GHOSTS: THE GUESTS WHO NEVER CHECK
OUT"

PUNCH IN A VELVET GLOVE

It should have been one of the best weeks of Scarlett's life.

Mrs. Amberson was more or less out of Scarlett's hair entirely. She had forgotten all about the book, and was spending the majority of her time running around the city doing what she called "social PR" for the show. She sent Scarlett in her place to watch and help with costumes. This meant that Scarlett had a full six hours a day to hang out with Spencer and watch Eric.

Theoretically, all perfect.

Like the good actors they were, Spencer and Eric kept right on going as everyone's favorite lovable idiots, playing to the crowd. If there was any weird feeling from the night at the party, they weren't talking about it, weren't showing it. As for how they treated *her*, however, each had his own unique method of torture.

Spencer had barely spoken a word to her in a week. He didn't come down to her room. He closed his door when he was at home. When they went home at night, he put on his headphones, if he waited for her at all.

Eric spiced things up by adding the element of uncertainty.

It seemed clear that the discovery had rattled him a little, and his response was to lay very low. He kept his communication to subtle glances, brushes in the hallway, an incredibly covert hand squeeze during a run-through of Polonius's death scene. The major event of the week took place in the costume closet—the tight little space behind the stage with the exposed insulation. Scarlett had gone back to get Ophelia's crazy drowning outfit to rough it up (the term was distress) a little. Eric had swung in behind her, pulled her behind the rack, given her a long, closed-mouth kiss, then grabbed a hat and run right out.

Which was great...but what did you do with that? That wasn't a date—it was an ambush.

By Friday morning, after a sleepless night, Scarlett decided she could take it no more. She planted herself on the floor outside of the bathroom door while Spencer was getting ready for work. If he wanted to ignore her, he would have to step over her.

Spencer finally emerged in his work clothes. He didn't see her at first because he was toweling off his head.

"Remember me?" she asked. She stretched herself wide, blocking his way as best she could. "I'm your sister. The one you used to like."

"Come on, Scarlett," he grumbled. "I don't have time."

"This has to stop. Please."

He leaned against the door frame and sighed, picking at the crack that ran through the wood.

"After rehearsal tonight, want to get something to eat?" she asked. "My treat."

Normally, the offer of free food would have Spencer come running across the hills. Today, not so much. He continued to work at the cracked wood with his nail.

"Come on," she said. "Are you going to let your anger get in the way of a free meal? With *dessert*?"

He looked like he wanted to say something—something other than, "I have to go." But that's what came out. He stepped over her carefully and went off down the hall. Scarlett stayed right where she was, in case he came back, and ended up falling asleep there. Lola woke her up soon afterward.

"I have no idea what you're doing out here," she said, "but since you're out of bed, want to help me with breakfast?"

Lola, in the wake of her breakup with Chip, had decided to take the opportunity to go a little insane. Not fun insane, where you talk to your imaginary friends and put food on your head. Annoying insane. The single, unemployed Lola was evangelical about work, to a painful degree.

"Why not?" Scarlett asked, dragging herself off the floor. "I have a few hours."

Lola seemed thrilled to be able to share some of her new rituals with her little sister. She and Scarlett frosted juice glasses, ground fresh coffee, made napkin sculptures, and ironed linens. All in all, a lot of work to do for two guests who just grabbed pastries and left. Then, they moved on to cleaning.

"The trick," Lola was saying, as she huddled over the toilet-paper roll in the Metro Suite, coaxing the last square into a point, "is to get it even, because if it's not even, what's the point? Then you just look like you're trying and failing. It's almost better to leave it alone. There..."

She completed the fold to her satisfaction.

"Press it flat, so it sort of looks like a little round envelope. And then, the secret touch..."

She pulled something from her apron and squirted it on the roll carefully.

"Lavender water," she said. "It's important to buy a very pure extract. That's the difference between conjuring up thoughts of Provence, or smelling like an old lady's house."

Scarlett watched this from the empty clawfoot tub, where she was lounging, her feet carefully dangling outside so as not to get it dirty.

"Have you considered medication?" she asked politely.

"You laugh," Lola said, "but you want to know something? It's not the big things that people remember about service... it's the little ones. People don't remember what street the hotel was on—but put a Maison du Chocolat truffle and a tiny bottle of Evian next to their bed when you turn it down, and they'll remember that they liked it."

It was hard to tell if Lola was suffering or if she was just *really like this* and had simply been too busy with Chip in the last year to let her freak flag fly.

"What's going on with you and Spencer?" Lola said, polishing the tap with some vinegar on a Q-tip. "You two usually share a brain. Or, at least, he normally borrows part of yours. Something seems weird."

"He's just busy with the play," Scarlett replied. Which was true, if irrelevant to the question.

"Don't you work on that play?"

"Yeah...well...he has to concentrate. Be all actory."

"Scarlett," Lola said, turning around, "Spencer has been in plays since he was twelve. His brand of actory intensity isn't exactly quiet and brooding, and he can't go fifteen seconds without talking to you. So what's up?"

"I don't know," she lied.

"I doubt that. Whatever it is, you two have to work it out. The silence between you is creepy. Dad was asking me about it yesterday, and I had no idea what to say. And Spencer looks miserable. Talk to him. Now, do you want to see my new technique for vacuuming the curtains? It's amazing. You should see what I get off them."

"Have to go," Scarlett said, propelling herself out of the tub.

That afternoon, while Scarlet was on sewing duty, it was pretty much the Spencer and Eric show. Their many hours of unicycle practice, handstands, self-punching, and falling had finally paid off. Their routine was now to be woven throughout the entire play. They had even worked out an elaborate comic fight between Rosencrantz and Guildenstern.

It was a good one, too—a carefully crafted version of what they did in the park, played for maximum comic effect. Spencer tripped Eric, causing him to fly offstage. Eric stormed back and punched Spencer, knocking him down. Then he flipped Spencer and grabbed him by the ankles, forcing him to walk in a handstand.

There was a loud smack from the stage that cut through the empty room like a gunshot. Of course, this was just

Spencer doing the face-first falling trick, but it startled Scarlett so much that she jammed the needle she was sewing with into her thumb. Blood dripped out of it and onto Hamlet's coat.

"Idiot," she mumbled to herself.

"Okay!" Trevor shouted. "Let's take a little break! That was great, guys...."

Scarlett pulled out the needle and stuck her thumb in her mouth. She was digging around in her bag for something to wrap it in when she felt something bounce off her back and land on the floor behind her. It was a towel, marked with the Hopewell monogram. And it was followed by Spencer.

He sank down to the floor, picked up the towel, and began rubbing his face and neck dry. He was drenched in sweat from the fight.

"What did you do to yourself?" he asked. "Lemme see."

The normal ease still wasn't there, but he was talking. He leaned over and examined the injured thumb. That was at least brotherly.

"It's fine," he said. He dug around in his bag and produced a packaged hand wipe, the kind that comes with take-out food. "This will clean it up a little."

He cracked open his water and settled back for a long drink.

"I haven't seen you do that handstand-flip thing in a long time," she said, ripping the wipe open and giving her wound a lemon-scented cleaning.

"I had a bad experience when Dad waxed the lobby floor," he said. "Hand grip is pretty key. But it did teach me that falling on your face is a funny way to end that. When you're faking, at least."

He drained the rest of the water in one long gulp. The bottle crackled under the suction.

"Okay," he said, getting up. "Tonight. I'll go with you. I think Paulette has Band-Aids. She has everything."

He was clearly trying not to make a big deal about it. He just sauntered off to talk to Trevor as if nothing unusual had happened. Scarlett suddenly felt something in her chest—a real, physical sensation like something horrible she couldn't see had just been lifted off of her, enabling her to breathe.

She enjoyed the rest of the afternoon, watching how they worked the scenes together, piece by piece. Hamlet stabs Polonius, the king and queen's spy, through a curtain. Gertrude, the queen, watches this, and thinks he has gone insane. Hamlet drags the body off and hides it. And Rosencrantz and Guildenstern—Eric and Spencer—are given the unwelcome task of making a crazed killer give the body up, which he refuses to do. The fight they made up was over who had to talk to Hamlet, with each move carefully tied to a line of the script.

They slid through the sequence again and again, twisting and tuning each bit, rearranging it endlessly. Scarlett didn't really *need* reminding that her brother was good at this, that he was highly trained and professional, but watching him work filled her with pride. Especially now that he was talking to her again.

"I just have to wash up and change my shirt," he said, when they had finished for the day. "There is no way I can wear this one out to eat, even to wherever we're going. Be back in a minute."

He walked back toward the scary bathrooms in the vestibule.

"I've been waiting for Spencer to walk away," Eric said, out of the side of his mouth. "Are you doing anything now?"

He was giving her that look. The smoky one. Sort of the one he used at the end of the commercial, when he was on... well...fire.

"I..."

Spencer was going to be coming out in a minute, expecting to go to dinner with her. Her brother. The one she loved, and the one she had to make up with. He would always forgive her in time. But *this* chance with Eric...this might not come again.

"No," she heard herself say.

"Want to meet me in front of my apartment? I'm heading there now. There's something I really want to show you, but I can't explain here."

It took about ten minutes of agonizing wait before Spencer reappeared, wiping himself down with the towel.

"Where is this food I've been promised?" he said, throwing himself down next to her in his normal manner. "I'm starving."

"Um, about that. Can we do it...tomorrow?"

"Tomorrow?"

"I can't today," she said, unable to even look at him.

It didn't take him long to get the idea.

"Another commitment?" he asked coolly.

"Kind of."

He sat there for a moment, beating out a little rhythm on his thighs with his hands, deciding what he thought of this.

THAT IS THE QUESTION

Eric was waiting on his building steps when she arrived. He had changed his clothes with astonishing speed, and was now dressed in a light blue dress shirt. He was still wearing shorts, and he wore sunglasses to keep out the late summer evening glare. The effect was ridiculously actor-modely, enough to make Scarlett's heart make an alarming *glurg* in her chest.

He had never looked so good. *No one* had ever looked that good. There was no way that he was actually waiting for her, Scarlett Martin. He was clearly waiting for a trio of models to spirit him off into a montage for a vodka commercial.

"Hey," he said warmly. "You came! This is probably going to sound ridiculous to you, but I want to go up to the top of the Empire State Building. I don't want to go by myself."

Scarlett had been up the Empire State Building before with her third-grade class, but again, this was one of those places you just didn't go if you were native.

"I didn't want to embarrass you by asking you in public," he said, as if reading her mind.

There are probably places in the world where being asked to go on a walk implies that you are going off to do something private and intimate. Maybe it means that in most places. But not in New York. The advantage of walking in New York is that there's lots to see and do—but even on the most private ramble you're bound to trip over at least three Chihuahuas, walk behind people who spit a lot, and maybe set off a car alarm.

Still, Eric had a way of making Scarlett feel like she was the only person on the sidewalk he noticed. He had at least a half-dozen stories about shows he had done in high school— tragically missed cues, actors disappearing before they were supposed to be on stage, malfunctioning lights, collapsing set pieces. It was all very entertaining, but it was difficult for Scarlett to get any meaning from it all.

One thing Scarlett had either not noticed or forgotten—once you actually make it through the lobby of the Empire State Building, you end up in a vicious trap of endlessly weaving lines, multiple escalators that don't seem to go anywhere but across, and hordes of people. Finally, though, they were loaded into the elevator that shoots right to the top, and Eric reached over and took her hand. He kept hold of it as they escaped from the people trying to sell them photos and the crush in the gift shop that led to the observation platform. It really was adorable how excited he was.

It was just getting dark, and the sky over the city was apricot-colored. They worked their way forward to a spot near the edge. (Not that you could ever get near the edge, really.) Eric wanted to see the view in each direction, including the one that faced the Hopewell. It wasn't even remotely visible, but they could see the park and the avenues. They were looking at it, whether they could see it or not.

"This building is based on a building in Winston-Salem," he said. "True story. The Reynolds Building. The people who built that were hired to make this, and they were in a hurry and pulled out a set of the early plans. So, this is the early, rejected version of something near my hometown."

The embarrassment on his face was real. He laughed at himself and wrapped his hands around the protective bars that keep people from jumping or falling to their deaths.

"I only know that because my seventh-grade history teacher told us the story ten times," he said. "Swear to God. I think she was trying to convince us that Winston-Salem was as important as New York."

"Sure," Scarlett said. "That's what they all say."

He turned her around to face him.

"There was another really stupid thing I wanted," he said. "Are you going to laugh if I ask? Because if you are, I am marching right back down those ten million stairs and going home."

"I won't," Scarlett said, keeping a very straight face.

"You get the scariest look when you lie like that," he said.

"I'm not lying. What do you want? Did you want to do a pencil rubbing of the plaque in the lobby? Get a snow globe?"

"It's both scary and sexy," he said.

Now he'd done it. He'd called her sexy, and not in the joking way that she and Dakota and Tabitha called each other sexy twenty times a day, or in the way that Spencer told her she looked very sexy when she got a comb ensnarled in her curls and she had to keep it there all day until Lola got home and could weave it out. He just dropped it right in there, like a quietly ticking bomb mixed into a clock display.

"What I wanted," he said, pulling away the curl that had fully impaled itself in her eye, "was to kiss someone once I got to the top."

He didn't wait for her inevitably stupid reply. He took her chin in his hands and kissed her—fully, unabashedly, right in the middle of the tourists and for all of New York to see, if they could see on top of huge buildings. And not a quick kiss, either—it went on and on, with at least five pauses for breath, and then, when it looked like it might be over, just started up all over again. He kissed her so long that she had to hold him for support.

The tourists didn't care. They just milled around like this was just something else they expected to see. Scarlett even got a flash in the corner of her eye as someone took their picture. As it was finally winding down, they switched the lights on overhead, and the spire that towered above them turned a luminescent purple.

"That," Eric said, looking up at the light, "was pretty much how I imagined it would be."

Scarlett found it a little hard to stand as they went back through the gift shop, to the series of elevators and escalators to take them back down. The whole "weak in the knees" thing, which she always thought was just some idiotic expression back from the golden age of idiotic expressions, was real. Her knees really were weak. Why, she had no idea. Kissing shouldn't produce any particular leg strain, at least once it's over, but there it was. They were all spaghettilike.

Eric had his arm wrapped around her as they rode the elevator back down, as if proudly announcing their coupledom to the world. It was this, combined with the general body weakness, and the g-force of being dropped so many hundreds of feet in a matter of seconds that caused Scarlett to do what she did next. As they emerged on the mezzanine, Eric stepping back to allow her to go first down the escalator, she said, "Are we...you know...dating?"

"We haven't had a proper date yet," he said, good-naturedly. "Where I come from, nothing is official until you've had dinner together in the mall and made out for at least two hours in a car. What do you do without malls and cars?"

Scarlett gave this the expected smile, but wasn't feeling very amused. This conversation was ridiculous. She had never actually imagined how you did this—she thought it just happened. A mutual wave of understanding passed over both your heads, covering you both completely in the warm waters of relationship status.

But no. Like most things in life, it required an unexpectedly awkward moment of bureaucracy.

"I just mean..."

She tried to lift her voice and say that last bit in a joking way—but not *too* joking, as if her entire being didn't *exactly* depend on the answer.

"I know what you mean," he said. "I didn't think people in New York had these conversations."

He was still smiling, but he had taken out his keys and was bouncing them nervously in his palm.

"We don't," she lied, poorly. "I was just kidding."

"Oh, right," he drawled.

Scarlett had no idea what that meant. He was playing with

his sunglasses now, polishing them on his shirt. The ease had disappeared.

She had messed this up very, very badly. If her friends had been here, Scarlett thought ruefully, this would never have happened. Dakota would have come to the stupid Empire State Building, leapt out of the shadows, and tackled Scarlett before she would have let her ask that question. This is why her friends shouldn't have been allowed to go *anywhere*. She got *stupid* when they were gone.

There was only one thing to do—get out of the burning plane. Put on the parachute. Jump. Salvage what she could. Make it seem like she didn't care too much.

"Oh my God," she said. "I completely forgot. I have to go home and…fix up a room. There's a guest coming. I'd better get back."

Again, this wasn't smooth, but he accepted it graciously and gave her a little kiss before she escaped. It was a good kiss, but it didn't have that same incapacitating energy as the one before.

In the Empire Suite the next morning, the silver walls were covered in taped up notes and Mrs. Amberson was in downward dog.

"Media!" she exclaimed. She pushed herself up to stand and folded her hands prayerfully in front of her chest. "We're less than a week away from opening. Can you believe that this company had no publicity plan? Don't answer that. Anyway, we're about to change that. Do you see this?"

She waved her hand at the notes.

"I've spent the last few days reestablishing every contact I have. These are the names of agents, casting directors, reviewers, producers...and do you know what we're going to do?"

Scarlett shook her head and went over and got out the organic cleaning products. She wasn't in the mood for any more fill-in-the-blanks conversations.

"We are going to have a special preview. Very special. Catered."

Scarlett nodded and sprayed the dressing table with ylang-ylang.

"What?" she said. "What is that *face*, O'Hara?"

"I don't have a face."

"You most certainly do. Look at this wonderful work! Do you realize what this means for the show?"

"It's great," Scarlett said.

Unable to rouse any enthusiasm, Mrs. Amberson went back into her position.

"I won't be coming to the theater today," she said. "This is much more important. But I need you to be there. It's the first dress run. Be my eyes. And for God's sake, *smile*. You're representing me! You have to emit positive energy!"

To her credit, Mrs. Amberson had provided fantastic costumes—and there was something fascinating about what happened to the actors once they put them on and did their makeup. Everyone really seemed to change.

Mrs. Amberson's concept was a twenties silent movie, so they all had at least a dusting of white with dark lining around the eyes and coloring on the lips. The female cast members were in sequined dresses, and the guys were outfitted with elegant suits. The silver trim she had sewed onto Hamlet's looked strangely appropriate against all of the other outfits. Spencer and Eric had been directed to apply heavier coats of white makeup, with more lining around their features. They also wore suits, but ill-fitting ones, several sizes too large with the hems on the pants raised up high. This was partly for comic effect, and party for safety when they rode.

Scarlett stood out in her simple summer skirt and T-shirt. Her face felt bare. (Thankfully, in the heat. Also, actors seemed to sweat more than other people—what was that about?) She plastered on the requested smile as well, until Ophelia asked her if she'd hurt her jaw.

There were a lot of hiccups in the run. People forgot lines all over the place (including Eric, three times). The ramp going up to the stage shifted when Spencer was riding up it, and he just barely caught himself when the wheel jammed and he was sent pitching forward. Gertrude went into a panicked meltdown for ten minutes when she couldn't get one of her scenes right. Hamlet bent the tip of his sword when it struck the wall.

It was Paulette's job to deal with most of these things, but Scarlett dutifully wrote them down for Mrs. Amberson, only leaving out the problems with the ramp (it wasn't Spencer's fault, and Paulette was all over fixing it) and Eric's flubbed lines. The group seemed exhausted by the end of the day, gratefully accepting Scarlett's help with their clothes and props. Many of the outfits were pretty foul by the day's end, and Scarlett started to fear for what things would be like when they'd been wearing them for a few days.

Scarlett had been avoiding approaching Spencer directly, but as he sat by himself, removing his makeup with some tissues, she saw a good chance to get a natural conversation going.

"Are you okay?" she asked. "The thing with the ramp..."

"I'm fine. I didn't even fall."

"I know, but..."

But nothing. He hadn't actually fallen.

"The offer for dinner still stands," she said.

"What?" he asked, rubbing hard at the white coating on his forehead. "No plans?"

"No," she said. "Come on."

"Can't. We're all going to Leroy's apartment tonight. It's a cast-bonding thing. Can you tell Mom and Dad I'll be home late?"

As soon as he said this, Scarlett became aware of the fact that everyone was zipping up their bags and congregating as if about to depart collectively. How she had missed this all day—not been aware of the event—was a little disturbing. Sure, she wasn't *exactly* part of the cast, but she *practically* was. She had helped dress them. She had taken their skanky clothes when they were done.

"Sure," she said. There was an audible droop in her voice that he had to have noticed. Either he was still angry, or he was feeling guilty, but he packed up and left even though he hadn't completely removed his makeup.

This wasn't okay. It really couldn't go on. Scarlett followed right on his heels, all the way outside, where he had stopped to talk to Claudius.

"We need to talk," she said, catching him by the arm. He put up no resistance and let her drag him a few doorways over, to a quiet spot in front of a nail salon.

"What am I supposed to do?" she asked. "When do we get normal again?"

He didn't answer for a moment.

"I don't know," he said.

"I don't get it. You like Eric. He's your friend."

"I work with him," Spencer clarified.

"He's not your friend?"

"I'm just clarifying. I have to get along with Eric no matter what in order to do my job."

"That's why he just thought it would be better if we didn't..."

"He thought?" Spencer said. "*He* said not to tell me?"

"You can't blame him. I'm the one who didn't tell you. I'm sorry. I've been sorry every single second since I did it."

Spencer was shaking his head and almost laughing, a grim laugh.

"What?" she said.

"Nothing," he said, still smiling the rueful smile. He rubbed the remnants of white makeup off his eyelids with his hand. "There's nothing I can say."

This was infuriating. For one second, she understood some of the frustration that Lola felt when dealing with Spencer. It had never made sense to her before.

"He *likes* me," she said. "Can you just get over the fact that it's someone you know? I won't hurt your show. Just let me be happy, please?"

This got rid of the smirk.

239

"You don't really look happy," he said.

Which was true—she wasn't at the moment. Not with Eric, and not with life in general. And really not with Spencer. She would have started screaming at him except the other cast members were coming out, so she just turned and walked away from him, back to the theater.

Most of the cast had gone out by now, saying their good-byes to Scarlett as they went. None of them asked her along, but they didn't look like they were hiding anything, either. Maybe they all just assumed that Spencer would bring her along.

Eric was still there, packing away his spare clothes and makeup into his bag. He had done a slightly better job getting all the white stuff off of his face. He gave Scarlett a friendly wave and nod as she approached.

"I heard there's a thing tonight," Scarlett said. Her voice still had a touch of a quiver from the argument with Spencer. She tried to play it off like she had to cough, but it just came out a bit odd.

"Oh," he said. It was an apologetic, long ohhhh. "Yeah. It's a cast thing."

There was a long pause in which an invitation, if it was going to be offered, would have gone.

"I'll give you a call later, okay?" he said.

"Yeah. Sure. No problem."

Those four words strung together were the most insincere in the English language.

As they stepped outside, Scarlett turned one way, and Eric and the remaining actors turned another.

And then she went home.

THE LONELIEST GIRL IN NEW YORK

Lola, still on her campaign to be the most efficient person ever, was both manning the front desk and studying up on career choices. There was a clear plastic file full of brochures and letters about different schools and companies, and she was researching online at the lobby computer.

"You staying here tonight?" Scarlett asked, mooning around the front desk.

"Actually," she said, "I'm going out later with some friends who are home from Smith. You remember Ash and Meg, right?"

"Oh. Yeah..."

"If you're not doing anything, we need all these mailers addressed and stamped. It would be a huge favor."

She pointed to a huge box next to her full of newly minted Hopewell Hotel brochures.

"We're doing a massive mailing to travel agents booking for fall tours," she said. "I tucked the list and stamps into the box."

The box was absurdly heavy. There had to be hundreds of brochures packed in there. Scarlett lugged it on to the elevator and dragged it along to her room. It was much, much too hot in the Orchid Suite. Much too hot, and much too dark. Scarlett peeled back the purple sheers and turned on all the lights, but it still seemed dim and unpromising. She looked out over the view. Saturday night in New York. And here she was.

Her neighbor who could never decide what to wear was fully dressed and obviously preparing to go somewhere. Anything for Breakfast Guy was unloading several six-packs of beer on his kitchen counter. Even Naked (now clothed) Lady made an appearance, dressed in some kind of coordinated blouse and pants thing with beading on it. She was going somewhere, too.

Only Scarlett was staying in to stamp and address.

She fell back on her bed, feeling the heat crushing on her lungs. Why couldn't they live in a suburb where you just got in your car and went to the mall when nothing else was going on...like normal human beings? Not that Scarlett felt like she could have lasted very long in the suburbs. She'd spent two weeks with her grandparents in Florida once, and once the initial shock of all the sun and the proximity to Disney World and manatees wore off, the fact that there was nowhere to walk to except some fast-food seafood place and a pet supply store about a quarter of mile away got a little old.

Really, nowhere was good. Except with Eric. He had both perfumed and poisoned her entire world.

She picked up the box and lugged it down a few more doors to the Jazz Suite, the one room on the fifth floor that was decently air conditioned. She switched on the TV and tried to get lost in a *Crime and Punishment* marathon.

Crime and Punishment was very soothing—the most wonderfully predictable show on television. Murder in the first ten minutes. Police investigation in the next ten. Wrong suspect cleared by half past. By quarter of, the correct suspect was on trial, and after a surprise twist about eight minutes from the end, all was resolved in the last moment. This is what she needed. Something that did what she expected it to do, that didn't let her down. Slimy suspects and cops with good quips. It was all balm to her frayed nerves. That is, until Marlene came stomping in just after the real murderer had been fingered.

"I have the TV now," she said. "I called it."

"What do you mean, *called it*?" Scarlett said. "Called it to who? Is there a TV committee that I don't know about?"

Marlene ignored this. She took the remote control and changed the channel.

"I was watching that!" Scarlett said.

Marlene dropped Scarlett a devastating look over her shoulder.

"Why are *you* home?" she said. "Where's your *guy*? Did he dump you or something?"

There is a limit to everything, and Scarlett had reached it.

"You know what?" she said. "It isn't always going to work. Not everyone, for the rest of your life, is going to care that you used to be sick. You'll have to act normal, like the rest of us. Because if you don't, everyone will just think you're evil and miserable. I'm not even sure they'd be wrong."

Even as she was saying them, Scarlett was regretting the words. They were true, but they landed like a hammer.

Marlene's face, which usually looked slightly contemptuous, begin to sag. At first, Scarlett felt a kind of relief that she'd finally made a point with Marlene. Then Marlene began to cry. Scarlett held her stance for a moment or two. She went over and tried to sit down and put an arm around her sister.

"I'm sorry," she said. "Look, Marlene..."

She got a push off the couch. Then Marlene really began to wail.

Scarlett went back to the Orchid Suite and sat on the bed. Her phone sat there, its screen depressingly blank. No call from Eric.

It took about fifteen minutes for the general alarm to be sounded and the footsteps to come to her door. Those were her mother's. She let herself in after a sharp knock.

"What did you say to Marlene?" she asked. "Did you tell her she was evil?"

Obviously, she already *knew* the answer. Why was she bothering to ask?

"Scarlett, what were you thinking?"

"I was thinking what everyone thinks," Scarlett said. "She's rude. She does things that other people can't get away with. She's eleven. I couldn't act like that at eleven."

"She isn't like you. And you thought the solution was to call her *evil*?"

"It just came out," Scarlett said.

"You know what she's been through."

"That was over four years ago. And what—no one is ever allowed to tell Marlene she's wrong? Other people aren't going to *care* that she was in the hospital once. No one is going to want to deal with her."

There was too much truth here, seething under the surface. It wasn't a fun truth, but it could not be denied. There was little to be done, though. Scarlett was *already* inside. She was *already* stamping brochures. She had practically grounded herself. Her mother didn't even sign off on it with a "I'm disappointed in you, Scarlett," the most meaningless and chilling of parental rejoinders. She just left the room.

Lola knew all the details by the time she arrived home. She let herself into the Orchid Suite quietly, wearing an infuriating expression of placid righteousness.

"Don't," Scarlett said.

"I wasn't," Lola replied, going to the dresser to take off her pink stud earrings. She pulled her hair up into a knot, changed into shortie pajamas, applied moisturizers and toners, and generally did everything but give herself highlights until Scarlett couldn't take it anymore.

"Fine," she said. "I lost it. I told her off. You're going to say that she actually really likes me, aren't you? That she really admires me, and I've just jumped all over her and crushed her."

Lola turned, still rubbing something into her face in a light circular motion.

"No," she said. "I mean, I don't think she really hates you, but she definitely doesn't like you. She probably will when she's like, twenty, but then again, maybe not. Some siblings hate each other for life."

On that note, she settled into her bed to read one of her brochures.

"Spencer's home," she added, crisply flipping a page. "He looks as miserable as you do."

"I don't care."

"Oh, stop it, Scarlett. Hanging out with these theater people has made you dramatic. Go down there, open the door, and sit on him until you've talked this out."

"He's probably locked it."

"So knock."

"What if..."

"Go!" Lola said. "You can't be fighting with all three of us at once. And don't come back until you've fixed it."

She sounded serious enough that Scarlett found herself getting off the bed and walking robotically down the hall toward the Maxwell Suite. Lola had that kind of presence, if she really wanted to use it. That was how she managed to become one of the top salespeople on Bendel's makeup floor before she got herself fired.

Spencer's door was shut, but there was a light on underneath. Scarlett reached up to knock, but then recalled his strange reaction that afternoon. The smug look, the odd laugh...it made her angry and uneasy all over again. She turned and went back to the Orchid Suite room, but the door had been locked.

"That was way too short," Lola called from inside. "I'm serious. Go and talk to him."

This night was unfair, and every door on the fifth floor led to some kind of pitfall. It was only a situation this dire that could make her go down one flight and approach the room at the end of the hall. That door flung open after one knock.

"I was wondering when you'd come and fess up," Mrs.

Amberson said. "When I didn't see you at the cast party..."

"*You* were there?"

"Take a deep breath, O'Hara. All things can be overcome if we remember to breathe. I take it you have some personal issues to sort out?"

"Kind of," Scarlett admitted.

"Then you have done the right thing by coming to me. Meet me in the lobby in five minutes. We're going somewhere fabulous."

Somewhere fabulous turned out to be a restaurant called Raw Deal, where none of the food was cooked above a light steaming and nothing was quite as it seemed. The burgers were made of sesame seeds and millet. The tomato sauce was made of beets. Even the "cola" was some syrupy concoction of tree sap and human misery.

They took one of the sidewalk tables so Mrs. Amberson could smoke, a fact that clearly annoyed the other diners and the staff.

"For the last week," she said, gleefully exhaling a plume in the direction of a particularly peevish looking guy eating a pyramid of lentils, "you have looked like someone about to be sent to the bottom of the Mariana Trench in a second hand Citroën. If you don't tell me what's wrong, I will be forced to investigate, and you don't want that."

The waiter came over, presumably to request that she stop puffing like a dragon at his other tables, but she undercut him with an order for the adzuki dip with blue algae crumbles, punctuated with a "do not cross me or I will set you on fire" smile.

The one thing Scarlett's life was currently missing—and could happily continue to miss—was a deep investigation by Mrs. Amberson. Plus, she had run out of options on her own. It was easier just to tell her.

"I'm sort of...with someone in the cast."

"Ah, the missing verb," she said. "It's like the lost chord. And how are things with Eric going?"

"They're...okay," she admitted. "I guess."

"What do you mean okay? I lock you together in a romantic theater, throw a party, distract your brother while you make your escape....I've practically sent the two of you out to sea in a tiny rowboat. What could possibly be the problem?"

She was, as Scarlett had suspected, already aware of the general situation.

"I don't know what's going on," she said. "With him, with Spencer..."

"Give me the details. And don't be precious. I can't help you unless you give me all the facts."

So, Scarlett told the story. All of it. Mrs. Amberson listened intently. When Scarlett was finished, she snapped her cigarette case open and shut a few times.

"I understand completely," she said. "It all makes complete sense."

"It does?"

"Let's start with Spencer," she said. "He's upset for two reasons, a superficial one and a deeper one. The first I am sure you have already guessed. He's afraid that you might break up, because then he'll have to hate Eric. Working on the show becomes difficult. The deeper reason, the *real* reason, is that he's jealous."

"Jealous of what?" Scarlett asked.

"I watch your brother on stage every day. When he does something, do you know who he looks to? Not me. Not Trevor. Not that poor girl who's been slogging around after him for a week. *You* are his audience, Scarlett. Out of everyone in the room, it's your opinion that matters most. If you laugh, if you are impressed, that counts more than anything I could say. But now you are paying more attention to his partner. Someone else is going to know your secrets first. Someone else will be sharing the inside jokes. And this is very, very annoying."

This all sounded weirdly right.

"He's probably not even aware of where his feelings are coming from," she went on. "But things *have* to change between you sometime. He'll move out. You'll go to college. Someone or something will get in the way. Don't fight the change, just deal with it."

"I'm trying to. But he'll barely talk to me, not like normal."

"We'll move on to Eric," she said. "It all ties in together. They're both actors, and I know actors. That's one subject I've covered in depth. *Believe* me."

She trailed off here and began playing with her lighter and failing. It clicked and spluttered as she tried to light her cigarette. Scarlett watched her, hypnotized, until she finally got it lit and took a long drag.

"An eighteen-year-old actor is a dangerous thing. Especially in New York. They're hungrier than you can possibly imagine. They work very hard to be liked. Eric is no exception."

"He's Southern," Scarlett offered in his defense.

"Being Southern is his gimmick. That's not a bad thing—all

actors have a gimmick. It doesn't change the basic profile. You see, a lot of actors think in order to be appealing, they must seem to be available to anyone and everyone. Their lives are one long flirtation. It's not because they are bad people—it's because they want to work."

"So you're saying that he won't say if we're dating because he's a flirty actor?"

"No. I'm just saying that his being Southern has nothing to do with anything. Using it as an excuse for why he couldn't answer the question about whether or not you were dating was a bit of a brilliant move, though. 'I didn't think people in New York had these discussions.' That's genius."

"It was bad for me to ask, right?" Scarlett said, drooping. "Really bad?"

Mrs. Amberson waved away her smoke.

"Don't worry about that, or his lack of an answer. They *all* dodge the question as long as they can. Welcome to the wonderful world of dating, O'Hara. You need to start thinking strategically. He certainly is. He complimented you on being urban and experienced, all the while sidestepping the issue... not because he doesn't like you, but because this is how the game is played."

Scarlett's head was starting to hurt.

"I thought it was all about having someone you could be really truthful with," she said. "I didn't know there were games."

It sounded so dumb saying that out loud. Mrs. Amberson gave her a look that was infuriatingly affectionate, like she was a very slow but adorable puppy who'd gotten her snout stuck in a shoe.

"You are being truthful," she said. "You're just being very *choosey* about how to present that truth. Life is an art, O'Hara, and we all have to cultivate an image. Don't worry. It's an acquired skill, and you're a sharp girl. But for today, I have a plan to fix all of your problems."

She scooped up some adzuki dip with her finger.

"You are going to run an errand for me. Tomorrow afternoon, about three hours before rehearsal, you are going to take this book down to Eric."

With her other hand, she fished a book called *Viral Theater Tactics in Shakespeare* out of her bag.

"I'll call ahead before your arrival to prepare him. You will wear that dress, so don't get anything on it tonight."

"I wore it today, though," she said, thinking about Lola's experience. "Shouldn't I wear something different?"

"You could wear the same outfit every single day and no guy—who isn't gay—will notice. And there is nothing about that dress not to like. It's a classic. I'd rather have one good outfit than a closet full of half-assed ones."

There was something reassuring in this. Mrs. Amberson was not on the obnoxious dress-snob team.

"Tell him I said that he should read chapter four, not that I have the slightest idea what chapter four is about. Of course, since you came all the way downtown, he'll invite you to stay until rehearsal. You will refuse."

"I will?" Scarlett said.

"Yes. Instead, you are going to wait at that little coffee place on the corner, the one with the red awnings. The lighting there is excellent. Now, I haven't actually read this book, but from what I can tell, it's dull enough to kill a monk. It will drive him out of his apartment. You will be seated, very prettily, in the window, writing. Get that window seat. You will not notice him unless he comes right down and sits with you. Remain intent on your work, as if he was the last thing on your mind."

It was good, Scarlett had to admit. Very good.

"Meanwhile," she went on, "I am going to take your brother down to the theater a bit early to see his ideas for the fight again. I will impress on him, in my subtle way, how sad you've looked the last few days...*except when watching him perform.* Spencer will feel both appreciated and guilty and will want to talk to you. Eric will be intrigued by your firm, independent streak and the sight of you pursuing your own art. Also, you will look good. He will see that he needs to step up his game. If you aren't back on track with both of them by the end of the night, I'll eat a Happy Meal."

From Mrs. Amberson, that was a serious threat.

"There will be one final, perfect touch," she said with a smile. "I will put you on stage to stand in for Hamlet during the fight practice this afternoon. You don't have to do a thing—just stand there and hold still while they work around you. It'll free up Hamlet to run his lines, and it will put you in the forefront of the action."

She snapped her fingers for the check, which the annoyed waiter was more than happy to bring.

"Finish up," she said. "You need to get a full forty winks tonight, and I'll give you Charlie to put over your eyes. He'll help with the swelling."

It took Scarlett a minute to remember that Charlie was a dead ferret full of beads and essential oils—not some guy who hovered over you as you slept and did things to your face.

"What swelling?" Scarlett asked.

"This is another rule in life, O'Hara," she said, throwing down some cash. "Always assume you are a little swollen. Lola understands that rule, I guarantee it. The entire beauty industry is based on that truth."

Mrs. Amberson seemed to be aware of many "truths" floating just under the surface of everyday reality. If she was right, then Scarlett had *never* had any idea what was going on around her.

Which was a scary thought, but it explained a lot.

A PLAN UNFURLS

Scarlett slept surprisingly well for someone with a dead ferret on her face. Charlie had done a good job of blocking out the light from outside. For once this week, she was rested.

Lola, being Lola, did not make a rude comment about the dead ferret. Instead, she picked it up from where it had landed between their beds in the middle of the night, sniffed it, and said, "Lavender. The real stuff. Told you. It makes a difference."

"His name is Charlie," Scarlett explained.

"Whatever his name is, you look much better this morning. A little less puffy."

"I was puffy?" Scarlett said, touching her face. This was disturbing evidence that Mrs. Amberson may have been right.

"It was probably stress from all that stuff with Spencer. Did that go well?"

"Uh...yes?"

"You were down there long enough. I'm glad that's fixed. I couldn't have taken that any longer."

"Me, either," Scarlett said.

Maybe it wasn't entirely a lie if she was going to fix it now, she figured. Then she realized that, no, it was just a lie.

Scarlett followed every instruction to the letter. She put on the black dress, tried to calm down her curls, and applied the red lipstick. She even raided Lola's Drawer of Mysteries for whatever looked useful. Mrs. Amberson called her to let her know that she had spoken to Eric and that he was expecting the book. She packed her computer. All systems were go.

When she arrived at his apartment, it took three tries before Eric answered the door. Instead of buzzing her in, he said he would come down and open the door himself—which was a lot of needless work for a walk-up. He leaned out, blocking the door from locking with his body. He was shoeless, hair unbrushed.

"Thanks for bringing this down," he said. It was friendly, but there was a lack of enthusiasm. "This looks...awful, actually."

This was the place where he was supposed to ask her up, provide shelter from the summer sun. Instead he clutched the book. Now that she had the puffy thing in her head, Scarlett was seeing it everywhere. Eric's face looked odd. He was a bit swollen under the eyes, which were much redder than normal.

"So...see you at rehearsal?" he asked.

Why was she surprised that Mrs. Amberson's plan wasn't clicking from the start?

"Actually," she said, trudging on with it, "I'm just going to be over there. Writing."

She pointed at the coffee shop and slapped at the computer in her bag for good measure.

"Oh. Got it. I'll swing by on my way over, okay?"

Why hadn't Eric, Mr. Southern Manners of 1877, invited her up? There were lots of possible reasons. Maybe it was messy. Maybe he was sick. Maybe there was a Civil War documentary on and his grandmother didn't allow him to watch those with Yankee girls. Whatever the reason, she was down here now and there was no point in going home.

The coffee shop was full, of course. All the good tables in the windows were occupied.

There was a deli just opposite his building. As long as no big trucks came by, she had a good view of his stoop. She opened her computer and settled in to wait with a cup of burned coffee. Yes, it was a *little* stalkerish, but if he hadn't been Captain Mysterious all week, this could have been avoided.

Two hours is a long time to have to wait for someone to come out of his house. She began to understand why the cops on stakeout on *Crime and Punishment* always looked so bored. Her patience and willingness to lower her own standards of appropriate behavior paid off. Twenty minutes before rehearsal, Eric stepped out of the door. He turned toward the coffee shop for just a second, put on his sunglasses, and sat down on the stoop.

"What are you doing?" Scarlett asked herself out loud, very softly, as he continued to sit there for almost five minutes. It finally struck her that maybe he was waiting for her, and she quickly slammed the computer closed and shoved it in her bag.

Just as Scarlett stepped outside, a girl carrying a quilted overnight bag came out of the front door of Eric's building. She was very tiny and coconut-tanned, with a short denim skirt, a stylish tank top, and massive sunglasses. She stopped and spoke to Eric for a moment. Or at Eric. He didn't reply.

A girl was the last thing Scarlett wanted to see.

It was enough to make Scarlett duck down behind a parked car, pretending to fix her shoe. She watched from her crouched position, her heart pounding furiously. The rising nausea that hit when she first saw Coco McBigGlasses subsided when she saw how they interacted with each other. There was a large space between them as they spoke, and Eric kept his arms folded over his chest—not angrily, more like he was just hanging out, maybe giving directions. The girl definitely seemed annoyed about something. She was waving her arms a lot. When she finally finished whatever she was raving on about, she hurried down the street. Eric stayed exactly where he was.

Something had just happened, but Scarlett had no idea what. The girl didn't act like she was there *with* Eric—it looked more like she was stopping to complain about something. Aside from the fact that they came out of the same door a few minutes apart and that they spoke for a moment, there was nothing worrying there.

Scarlett felt like an idiot. She backed up, slipping around the corner, so that Eric wouldn't see her suddenly spring from a crouched position across the street. He had to be on to the shoe trick by now. She really needed a second stealth move. Actually, what she needed was to be less insane.

She waited a minute or two, taking the time to pet a Labrador that had been tied to a stop sign while his owner went into a bakery. The poor dog looked confused by his temporary abandonment, eager for any kind of company or reassurance.

"Waiting is the worst," Scarlett said to the dog. "I know."

The dog wagged his tail in happy understanding.

When Scarlett rounded the corner, Eric was still in his spot, staring up at his window a few floors above. Scarlett shook out her curls and put on her best, "I was just wandering along—I had no idea you were here!" face, which was just her normal face with slightly widened eyes.

"Hi," she said. "I was just walking over."

"Hey," he said. He was extra Southern now. He must have dragged five syllables out of the word. "It's time, isn't it?"

He stirred, like he had forgotten why he was standing outside in the first place, and slowly followed along.

"You seem kind of tired today," Scarlett said.

"Yeah. I didn't sleep too much last night."

And that was it for his end of the conversation for the next four blocks. Scarlett filled in, telling him all about Lola's toilet paper folding and lavender essences and breakfast-redesign schemes. It was impossible to tell if he was listening at all, so she shut up by the final block.

"Stop a second," he said, slowing her down at the corner before the church. He reached for his glasses, as if he was going to take them off, and then decided against it.

"I've just been thinking about your question," he said. "And you're right, we need to figure that out."

This was good. Very good. This made Scarlett love the sun on her skin, and the smell of detergent coming out of the laundry next to them, and the people walking by talking on their phones.

The world *worked*. Everyone in it was happy, really. Maybe that's what he'd been doing in his apartment—he'd been *thinking*. Maybe Mrs. Amberson's plan hadn't worked exactly as she described, but still that little bit of space had really...

"I can't really *be* that right now," he said.

...*what?*

"What?" she said out loud.

A pause. A terrible, terrible pause.

"A boyfriend." More playing with the sunglasses. "And if I can't give you that, I'm not sure we should go on like this."

"If you're worried about Spencer," Scarlett said, scrambling for words, "I've talked to him. He's being a little weird, but it's not you. It's because I didn't tell him."

"You don't understand," he said. "This is my fault. I really don't want to lose you or Spencer as a friend and..."

Scarlett didn't hear the rest. All she knew was that he meant it. She knew it in her bones, her blood, her heart and mind. Eric was dumping her. The smell of detergent burned her nose and the people on their phones were too loud and obnoxious and there was a glare. The ground felt like it was falling away.

She was vaguely aware that they both started walking again in the direction of the church, that a few of the cast members were just a few steps away.

"Excuse me," she said, walking away from Eric and cutting through them.

Inside the church, it was hot enough to bake a pie. Scarlett dropped her bag to the ground with a thud, forgetting her computer was inside, and not really caring when she remembered. The actors buzzed around her, plucking their costumes from the racks. People said hi to her and tried to start conversations, but she couldn't speak. She slipped up to the space behind the stage.

Mrs. Amberson and Trevor were conferring away, and Spencer was circling the stage on the unicycle, trying out some bounces. He was already dressed in his comic suit. All the sights were familiar, but it all felt distant and crazy. She put her head against the wall and tried to breathe deeply.

"All right!" Mrs. Amberson called. "We're going to run Spencer and Eric's fight first just to get the mechanics down. Let's clear some space for them."

Oh, no. The plan was still rolling on to its horrible conclusion.

"Scarlett!" she said. "Scarlett, where are you? We need you to read Hamlet's lines while he gets changed."

She was barely aware of stepping out on the stage and taking the script Paulette was holding out in her direction. Spencer had stopped circling and was staring in her direction, brows furrowed. She turned away from him as much as she could. Eric appeared a moment later, buttoning up his shirt quickly and rolling his sleeves. He didn't look in her direction.

"Okay," Mrs. Amberson said, slipping her a subtle wink. "We're going to work out the mechanics of the fight. The important thing is that you just stay still while they work, okay?"

This was all just noise to Scarlett. She went over and stood in the spot that Mrs. Amberson was pointing to. Eric and Spencer got into position behind her. Spencer was still studying her out of the corner of his eye. He knew something was going on, and that made her panic more.

"And...go!" Trevor said.

Eric immediately grabbed Spencer by the neck to drag him over to her. Spencer rolled out of this, tripping Eric expertly in the process. He landed right below her. Eric was literally at her feet. What was happening? Why were her ears ringing?

"What have you done, my lord, with the dead body?" he asked.

Scarlett's mind faintly registered that she should be looking at the page. The words swam in front of her.

"Compounded it with dust," she read. "Whereto 'tis kin."

Her voice was a squeak.

"A little louder," Mrs. Amberson directed.

"Compounded it with dust," she read again, not really much louder. "Whereto 'tis kin."

Spencer made an escape off to the side, and Eric bounced up from the floor to catch him. They slapped each other around a little on the other side of the stage, giving Scarlett a chance to get her balance. All she had to do was make it a few more minutes...

The smack startled her again.

Spencer was flipped over backward onto his face. Same trick as ever. Everyone in the room broke into laughter, except for her.

"Now, Spencer, get up!" Trevor yelled. "Get over there, turn him around, and hit him."

This part may have been new, not that she cared. Her job was to stand still and let the world spin around her. Then she could go and puke and curl up into a ball and die.

Spencer pulled himself up and strode over as directed.

Scarlett saw him move Eric into position, and Eric responded like a partner in a dance, turning himself so that his body would block the trick. He drew his right arm back dramatically, the comic buildup to the punch. Something unusual passed over Spencer's face—something Scarlett had only seen a handful of times before.

Instead of his fist flying past Eric's face, a move they'd practiced a hundred times, something went wrong. There was a dull noise, not like the sharp fake-punch sound they produced through trickery. Eric staggered, but not a calculated, staged stagger—a real staggering stagger that concluded with him losing his balance and falling to the floor. He landed on his back, hard.

Scarlett decided it was time to go. Immediately.

MISS CALCULATIONS

Every head turned away from the carnage on stage to watch as Scarlett made her wobbling, half-running way out of the darkened room into the blinding sunlight. She allowed her legs to follow their instincts. She rounded the building and headed for the playground. There was a low brick wall on the far side. She ducked behind it and sat on the ground, collapsing her face into her knees.

She was alone for several minutes, except for a few brave pigeons that would not be scared off by a human running at them, arms flapping in the wind. She tried to block everything out—shutting her eyes. But it was all still there. The girl. The look on his face. Eric crumpled on the stage.

She soon became aware that someone was standing nearby, but it didn't seem worth it to look up and see who it was. The person slid down the wall and sat next to her.

"Do you remember when I accidentally set fire to myself?" Spencer asked.

Scarlett pulled her head up just enough to look over at his shoes.

"I saw it on TV, these stunt guys explaining how they do

those scenes where they run out of exploding buildings. I thought I could do it by spraying hairspray over my pants and burning off the fumes. It actually worked for thirty seconds. Looked great. Except that I hadn't worked out the plan for putting myself out. Stop, drop, and roll takes a lot longer than you'd think."

Scarlett remembered this quite well, but couldn't answer because a lump of something had risen in her throat so fast that it gagged her. She tried to force it back down, hold whatever was left of herself and her dignity together.

"I'm not asking for any particular reason," he went on. "Except maybe to see if you noticed how stupid I am. You *pretend* not to see it, but I think you do."

She wanted to say that he wasn't stupid—she took all honors for that. Stupid to think she could date Eric, stupid to follow Mrs. Amberson's advice, stupid not to listen to Spencer in the first place. She wanted to say she was sorry, but all that came out was a noise that almost sounded like a quack.

"That's what I thought," he said, dropping an arm over her shoulders.

Whatever was gripping her throat released it, and a torrent of tears erupted from some unknown reservoir inside. She buried her face in the folds of his jacket and sobbed huge, wheezing sobs that finally scared off the remaining birds. It was like she was draining herself dry.

It felt like they stayed like that a long time, but it was probably only a few minutes, then her tears slowed just as suddenly as they had come. She tried to make her breathing normal, but couldn't. It staggered and fell all over the place, and she started to hiccup. She hadn't felt like this since she was little, when she would run to Spencer when she got hurt or upset. Total regression.

He tipped her chin up to get a look at her face. She felt horrible and genuinely swollen, and the light hurt her eyes. Spencer's jacket was soaked, and something was connecting her nose to the front of his collar. He wiped it away with his sleeve.

"You okay?" he asked.

"I'm fine," she said thickly.

"Yeah...no you're not." He wiped at her face with his hand to try to dry it a bit and unstuck a curl from her cheek. "And I just punched my scene partner in the face."

"I'm sorry..."

"It's not your fault," he said. "This one is all mine. But I'm going to have to go and answer for it."

He stood, and then reached down to help her up.

"It looks like we have company," he said.

Mrs. Amberson was waiting at the other end of the playground, flipping the cigarette case thoughtfully in her palm.

"You should probably go in," she said to Spencer, when they reached her.

Spencer looked to Scarlett, checking on her general condition. It still wasn't great.

"I'm not going back in there," she said. "I'll see you at home."

"Okay..." he said. He didn't seem to want to leave her there or go back inside, but he dragged himself forward.

"The plan," Mrs. Amberson said, when he had walked off, "did not work quite as I anticipated."

Scarlett decided that there was no need to add to this statement. It pretty much covered the situation.

"Think anyone noticed?" she croaked. Her throat was still a mess.

"Oh, don't worry about that. Actors love drama, by definition. You made their day."

"Spencer slipped," Scarlett said dutifully.

"Of course he did. Accidents happen. And this is just a temporary setback, O'Hara...if it's a setback at all. Lovers' quarrels are a natural part of relationships. Making up is always the best part. Now, tell me what happened, and we'll make a plan."

"Please stop helping me," Scarlett said.

"Too soon?" Mrs. Amberson said, undaunted. "Best to take the afternoon off. Here."

She reached into her pocket and pulled out some money for a cab.

"We'll sort it out later, O'Hara," she said, as Scarlett walked to the street. "You'll see!"

Lola the Unstoppable was still at the desk when Scarlett returned, stamping and addressing all the brochures that she had never gotten to the other night.

"Someone left a message for you," she said, holding up a slip of paper. "Probably something for Mrs. Amberson. Are you all right? Your eyes look kind of funny."

"Um...allergies." Scarlett's voice was a bit thick still.

"Are you sure?"

Scarlett nodded and took the note.

"The woman asked you to call right away," Lola said. "Do you even *have* allergies?"

"I'm fine," Scarlett said, walking quickly toward the elevator. "I'll call her. Thanks."

Back in the Orchid Suite, Scarlett dropped the note on her bureau and drew the purple sheers. She could hear her parents yelling about the pigeons ("the flying rats") from the opened window below. She dropped back on her bed and did nothing. She let the heat fall over her and crush her.

A few hours later, the door creaked open and Spencer looked inside. He was carrying a bag.

"I thought you might be here," he said. "I bring presents. Soup dumplings from Joe's Shanghai. Yes, I am actually that good."

Soup dumplings were, arguably, Scarlett's favorite food. They were dumplings full of the most delicious soup in the world, plus a little meatball.

"I'm not really hungry," she said. "You can eat them."

"Come on," he said, holding out the bag. "I went all the way down there. And you're telling me you won't even eat one?"

Scarlett accepted the bag and pulled out the container of steaming-hot dumplings. She stared at the little globlike forms inside—forms that would usually have made her indescribably hungry. They did nothing now except repulse her slightly. Spencer flopped down next to her.

"How is he?" she asked, unable to even say Eric's name.

"Bruised," he said. "But fine. I was kind of hoping that if I screwed up that big I'd at least have given him a black eye, but I guess it's good that I didn't. I didn't hit him *that* hard.

267

He just wasn't expecting it. If he'd had a chance to react, things would have ended differently."

"Are you in trouble?"

Spencer shook his head.

"He obviously wanted to drop it. Someone got him some ice, he made a joke, I made a joke. We waited half an hour and did the fight again. Eat."

Scarlett tried nibbling at the thin dough for Spencer's sake, but gave up on the effort and set the soup back down.

"Why did you do it?" she asked.

"I know you like soup," he replied.

"You know what I mean."

Spencer took the container for himself and very deliberately avoided her stare.

"All I know," he said, "is that Amy came by in the afternoon to work with me and was going on and on about how sad you looked. For about an hour."

Right. The brilliant plan at work again.

"Then you came in with Eric. I've never seen that look on your face before. We were on stage, things were going fast, someone was telling me to hit him. My brain just decided to go all literal. I sort of watched myself do it. I saw the spot where my fist was supposed to turn, and it just didn't turn."

He shoved a dumpling in his mouth, not taking the time to create the vent on top that was so critical in the eating process. He jerked back when he felt the burn and opened his mouth to let out the steam. Scarlett had the feeling that that was self-punishment.

"You knew about the other girl," she said. "Didn't you?"

He looked at her as he waved his hand in front of his mouth frantically. He showed no surprise hearing that there was another girl.

"I didn't *know*," he said, when he had gotten it under control. "I guessed."

"How?"

He sighed.

"Whenever anyone asked him if he was seeing anyone, he would always give cagey answers, at least around me. Once you said that it was his idea not to say anything...it all fell into place. There's only one reason he would do that."

"Why didn't you tell me?" she asked.

"There was nothing to tell. I never saw her. I told you I had a bad feeling. That was all it was."

"Well," she said, sniffing. "You were right."

Scarlett was hit by a wave of exhaustion—a welcome chance to block it all out.

"I just want to sleep," Scarlett said. "And never go back."

She rolled over on her stomach. Spencer scrunched her curls until she settled herself—another throwback to when she was little. She heard him take the bag of soup away, heard him shut the door. What she couldn't possibly have heard was his arm brushing the bureau as he left, causing a small slip of paper to flutter to the ground. It landed just under the bureau, where it could hardly be seen.

THE IMPORTANCE OF TOWELS

"Let's talk about towels," Lola said, coming into the Orchid Suite late the next morning.

Scarlett looked up over the top of her blanket blearily.

"What time is it?"

"Eleven. Spencer told me to let you keep sleeping. You must have been really sick. Do you feel any better?"

Scarlett had to make an effort to collect her thoughts. She'd been sleeping for something like fourteen hours. Her mouth was dry, her head hurt, and she was starving. Oh, and Eric had still dumped her.

"Not really," she said.

"I'll bring you up something to eat," Lola said. "Unless you feel like you can get up."

"No," Scarlett said, sick of being in her bed. "I'll get up. I need a shower."

"Towels," Lola repeated, indicating that it was the word of the day and needed to be used as frequently as possible. "That's what sets certain hotels apart. Really nice towels, and lots of them. As many as you like. I think towels are one of the big reasons people like hotels at all. You can use them and drop

270

them on the floor...."

That was about how Scarlett felt. Used. Dropped on the floor. And she was really starting to miss Chip. She never had to deal with these kinds of wake-up calls before.

"...and someone comes along and picks them up and gives you new ones. Towels are nurturing. Towels go against bare skin. Now, lots of hotels provide piles of thin, scratchy towels. But when you use a good towel, a really thick, soft, amazing towel, you feel cared for. You remember the towels. And their cousin...the bathrobe."

Scarlett picked up her shower basket and stared.

"Why are you talking about towels?" she finally asked.

Lola held up a photo from some high-end catalog. It showed some woman getting out of a tub the size of an SUV and wrapping herself in a massive blanketlike towel.

"Egyptian cotton," Lola said. "These are pretty expensive, but once you feel them..."

"We have towels."

"We have terrible towels from some bargain supply place."

"They're monogrammed."

"They scratch! I've been trying to explain this to Mom and Dad. People are not going to come back if the towels scratch."

"There are a lot of reasons people won't come back," Scarlett said. "Like, birds in the rooms and nonfunctional toilets. Do you really believe that expensive towels are going to solve our problems?"

"I'm just trying to come up with a few practical solutions," Lola said.

"A bunch of towels we can't afford for guests who aren't

here...that's not really a solution."

Lola looked genuinely saddened by Scarlett's lack of support for her towel idea. It wouldn't work...but Lola was the only one trying to help the hotel. Scarlett would have faked some more enthusiasm, but it wasn't in her.

"Spencer told me to tell you that he'll be back around six," Lola said, carefully refolding her picture. "And it's family dinner night tonight. Mom and Dad are out getting some pipes or something. There's a leak in the kitchen. I have to get back down to the desk."

"Hey," Scarlett said, as the guilt sank in. "I'll take the desk for a while. I mean, I'm here."

The front desk of the Hopewell was not a good place to distract yourself. It was, however, a great place to really let the loneliness and pain sink in. Lola had gone off to try to find the towels of her dreams at a lower price, her parents were still buying pipes, and Marlene was off at her friend's apartment. Even their three guests were out.

Scarlett was the most alone person in the city of New York—a city that never let you be alone. She tried to distract herself by reading e-mails from her friends, but it only made them seem farther away and their lives so much better than hers. She tried not to replay every single moment of what happened the day before...that didn't work. Then she really tried to avoid watching Eric's commercial online.

Seven viewings later, she was openly weeping at the desk. This was probably the only good thing about no one being around.

Unable to take it anymore, she hung the sign and headed out down the street to buy herself an iced coffee. She was just locking the door, when she heard someone speak.

"It's not Tara," the voice said. "It's Lola, right?"

"Scarlett," Scarlett corrected whoever it was. She gave her eyes a quick rub, just in case they were still dripping, then turned to find herself facing a woman with very short silver hair.

"Oh. I must have read it wrong. Nice name, though."

Donna Spendler looked very different with a crew cut.

"Going out?" she asked.

"Just to get a coffee," Scarlett said. There was the throat thing again. The clamp was on her—but this time, it was all panic.

"I'd like a coffee myself. Do you mind if I come down with you?"

It wasn't like she could refuse, so the two walked together. Donna seemed strangely at ease as they went together. She even paid for Scarlett's coffee before Scarlett could stop her.

"I left a message for you yesterday," she began, when they sat with their drinks. "You may not have gotten it."

"Sorry," Scarlett said.

"I'll bet you're wondering how I got here."

This was precisely what Scarlett was wondering. Her brain was working feverishly on this problem and getting nowhere.

"It took a while before I knew something was wrong," she said. "I was so pleased to get a television show that I let some oddities slip by. But when I didn't hear anything about the script, when my agent couldn't confirm what was going on with any of the trades...sometimes those things are normal.

273

But then she really started looking, and no one had heard anything about *The Heart of the Empire*. *The Heart of the Empire* really did not seem to exist. And I started to think. Paul. I kept thinking he looked very familiar. I started to think very hard about where I had seen him before. Then I remembered. It was a commercial."

The famous commercial. Scarlett felt her eyes roll back into her head in realization. Mrs. Amberson probably didn't know that his face was already familiar—she had been in Thailand when it was shown.

"It wasn't hard to trace his name online. He posts his resume. From there, I was able to find his agent, find out what he was working on. Do you know that someone in that cast keeps a blog about what's going on with the show, complete with pictures? Imagine my surprise when I saw his assistant in there as well. I looked up your brother, and lo and behold, both of you are pictured on the Web site for this hotel. The Internet is an amazing thing."

The picture with the braces glistening in the sunlight. Apparently, she still looked like that.

"Now," Donna went on, ripping open a packet of sweetener, "I had to ask myself, why did the cast of *Hamlet* at a little theater downtown want to set me up like that? You see, that stunt ended up costing me a big part in a show. And I can't help but feel that maybe that was the goal."

Scarlett looked past the tips of Donna's clipped locks, out of the window to the street.

"I figured the explanation behind this had to be pretty interesting," Donna said. "So, Scarlett, would you care to enlighten me?"

"I don't know," she said.

"You don't know what? Why it was set up? Who did it? Because it wasn't you or your brother or his friends who planned this."

Scarlett sucked hard on her straw. What was she supposed to say?

Donna took out a leather case, which she snapped open. She wrote down her number on a piece of paper inside, and ripped it off.

"You should know," she said, "that I work both with theater people and the tourist industry. It's easy to get a bad reputation in the theater world, and it's also easy for a hotel to get the wrong kind of publicity. I am taking this very seriously, Scarlett. Don't think for one second that the fact that I'm not screaming and yelling means that I'm not angry. Whoever it was can contact me here. They should make it soon."

Donna got up and left, leaving her coffee untouched. Scarlett put her head in her hands and allowed herself to panic. Spencer was under threat. The show was under threat. The hotel...

And Spencer didn't even know what he had done.

"Oh," she said to herself. "This is so not good."

A COZY DINNER

There was a sickly smell gassing up the lobby, where Scarlett was pacing between the desk and the door, occasionally pressing her face into the diamond-cut glass to get a wobbly view of what was going on outside. She got the sinking feeling that the odor was homemade pizza. That acrid smell was the crust burning—the tangy, bitter smell was cheese being turned to rubber.

Both Spencer and Mrs. Amberson had sent her messages saying that they were on their way back from the move-in to the parking garage, the play's final home. Mrs. Amberson arrived first in her cab.

"The cab wouldn't take your brother's bike," she explained, as she pulled out her cigarette case. "He's coming on the subway. You look better than I expected. You have good, fighting stock in you, O'Hara. I was also thinking about getting you an appointment with this wonderful girl, Katiya…"

"Donna came over," Scarlett said.

Those three words didn't quite have the chilling effect that Scarlett had hoped. It took Mrs. Amberson two matches to get herself lit, but otherwise, she didn't look disturbed.

"Came over where?"

"Here!"

"And how was her haircut?" she asked, a wry smile slipping on to her face. "Was it very, very fetching?"

"Did you just hear me? She was here."

"You're repeating yourself, O'Hara. How did she get here?"

"She figured it out. Not about you. She recognized Eric, then worked back to Spencer and me."

"Well, well," she said. "Donna is a little smarter than I remember. I hope you were nice to her. Did you rub her head for luck? Did it feel like a squirrel?"

"She *also* said that she could cause trouble for Spencer and Eric, and that she might say things about the hotel."

Mrs. Amberson gazed at Scarlett for a moment.

"She doesn't have the nerve," she said dismissively. "Or the brains."

"Are you sure? She found us."

"A little luck, that's all."

"Don't you think you should maybe talk to her?" Scarlett asked. "She left her number."

Scarlett produced it, and Mrs. Amberson visibly bristled.

"Listen to me, Scarlett," she said. "She angry, so she's putting on a little show, pretending she has clout. Someone like Billy... now he can make or break a career. But not Donna Spendler. Ignore her."

"But..."

"What could she possibly do to Spencer? What could she *possibly* do to this hotel? In two days, this show is going to be performed in front of over fifty influential people from the

New York theater community. *That's* what we have to pay attention to. I'm going to go freshen up before dinner."

Marlene came out of the elevator as Mrs. Amberson was going up. She hadn't spoken to Scarlett since the fight the other night, but her stance was no longer combative. Or, it wasn't as combative as normal. There was a grudging respect behind it, like she now accepted Scarlett as a fellow warrior.

"We have to set the table," she said. "Mom said."

The burning smell was much worse in the dining room. Scarlett and Marlene exchanged a look of mutual disgust as they worked. They were almost getting along until a familiar black car pulled up in front of the building.

"He's back!" Marlene yelled, rushing for the door.

"Oh, God," Scarlett said.

Chip was getting out with a freakishly tall arrangement of white and pink orchids when Spencer came skidding along on his bike.

"Oh, God," Scarlett said again, almost dropping the plates in her rush to get outside.

Chip and Spencer were staring at each other like two cats who haven't quite worked out if they're going to claw each other apart or groom each other to death. Spencer was almost twitching in his desire to say something. Marlene, meanwhile, was swarming around Chip in unfettered delight, openly flirting and batting her eyelashes.

The arrangement he was carrying, aside from being three feet tall, was delicate and vaguely Asian, in a square vase wrapped in strips of bamboo. It looked very, very expensive.

"Those are pretty," Scarlett said, stepping between the

steely-gazed Spencer and Marlene and her dance of love.

"Oh." He looked down at the flowers as if he had forgotten he was holding them. "Yeah. I tried. Lo likes white, and this pink color seemed good. I was just going to leave them. I should just leave them...."

There was a look on his face that she recognized—a hopeful, pained look.

"No," she said. "You can come in."

Spencer coughed. A tiny, polite cough.

"You should," Marlene said, tugging on his sleeve.

It was clear that Chip had planned to leave his flowers at the desk unnoticed, and instead, three separate Martins had accosted him on the street.

"It's okay," he said, passing Scarlett the flowers. "And if she doesn't want them, you can keep them."

There was so much sadness in his voice. Stupid Chip, with his bottomless bank account and his Number Ninety-eight status and his repulsive friends.

"Hello, Chip," Spencer finally said. His voice was completely normal, but the delay was oddly menacing.

Marlene continued to protest, asking him to come in, requesting a ride in his car, on his boat...

"Come on, Marlene," Scarlett said, trying to pull her back while balancing the huge flowers. This did not improve Scarlett–Marlene relations, and when Chip eventually left, she stormed inside.

"It's nice to see him," Spencer said, watching the car disappear around the corner. "Really. I miss him."

"I felt bad for him," Scarlett said.

"He can go home and suck on a credit card."

Scarlett looked at the flowers. Chip had chosen them with care—they really were perfect for Lola.

"Sorry," Spencer said, putting his hand on her shoulder. "I forgot. I guess you would feel bad for him now. Special circumstances."

He did a quick up-and-down check of her overall demeanor and expression and didn't look completely satisfied with the result. Spencer must have assumed that her pale and stricken expression was still the aftereffects of the day before. It was—but it was also having Donna Spendler on their doorstep.

"You never punched Chip," she said.

"Yeah," he said. "I kind of wish I discovered my violent streak earlier."

He locked up his bike, and they went inside. Scarlett set the flowers down on the desk. Lola came down the stairs a moment later and reeled at the sight. She kept a radius of several feet around them, like they might reach out for her.

"Chip brought them," Scarlett explained.

"Why didn't you get me?"

"He didn't really want to stay."

Lola looked to Spencer accusingly.

"I did nothing," he said, holding up his hands. "Besides, why would you *want* to see him? You broke up with him. Don't you want me to keep him away?"

"That's not the point," Lola said.

"It's not?"

"Just...forget it."

She stormed into the dining room, leaving Spencer to shake his head in bafflement.

"Someone's in a bad mood," he said. "Always at me."

The elevator opened, and Mrs. Amberson joined them. She had changed into a rare pair of jeans and a formfitting tank top.

"These are lovely," she said, flicking a petal as she walked by. Scarlett watched with revulsion as Spencer's gaze followed her along.

There was a palpable tension around the dining room table, not entirely caused by the blackened pizza. Lola was still miffed over some imagined offense. Marlene was annoyed in general because of Chip. Scarlett was sick for several different reasons. Mrs. Amberson was fidgeting in her seat.

"You know," she said, "I would just kill for a drink. I'm not sure if that's possible, but..."

"We don't have a bar license," Scarlett's dad said. "But you're our family guest for dinner. I'll just make you whatever you'd like."

"A double whiskey would be lovely," she said with her most toothpastey smile. "It's a bit heavy for summer, but it's made with whole grains, and that's what counts. It's a celebration today, after all. The show is about to open! Just two more days!"

"Is the show going well?" her mom asked, chopping ineffectually at the pizza with a butcher's knife. "Can we expect some tickets?"

"Of course!" Mrs. Amberson said. "Of course! Best seats in the house for all of you! Spencer does a wonderful job. He's absolutely a star."

Scarlett's father returned from the kitchen with a bottle of whiskey and a glass of ice. Mrs. Amberson dumped the ice into her water and poured herself what looked like a serious amount of straight alcohol, which she downed with alarming speed.

Spencer kicked Scarlett under the table, but she couldn't watch. This didn't bode well.

"You must have been thirsty," her dad said, trying not to look at the empty glass.

"Oh, just one of those days!" she said. "But, yes. Spencer is quite a performer. How do *you* feel about it, Spencer?"

"Like I'm on top of the world," he said, watching her closely. "Like that guy from *Titanic*. But less dead."

She laughed a truly silverware-rumbling laugh that made all six Martins lean back in their chairs.

"Mind if I have another?" she asked, plucking the rejected ice cubes back out of the water. "Just a small one. Little chaser."

Another whiskey slid to its death. Scarlett was officially terrified. The Donna news had evidently sunk in.

"I knew a wonderful young actor once," Mrs. Amberson said, setting down the glass. "God, it was a while ago. He was a musical-theater performer. His family was Italian. They run a restaurant in Queens, as a matter of fact. That's where I learned about good pizza."

She smiled at the untouched slab of carbonized dairy and wheat product on her plate.

"He could dance," she went on, "but he was really a singer. You could feel that when he was performing—he didn't just want other people to see him and clap for him, he really wanted people to be entertained. And they were. That's what the best actors are like. I think you've got that, Spencer. Cheers to good actors."

She raised her half-empty glass.

"Does your friend still perform?" Scarlett's mom asked.

"Oh, yes," Mrs. Amberson said. "He's quite successful. Haven't seen him in years, though. He lives in Hollywood."

"That sounds promising."

Mrs. Amberson stood, slightly unsteadily.

"If you'll excuse me," she said. "Thank you for the lovely meal, but I have to be off. Spencer...no late night tonight! We head out at eight in the morning, on the dot!"

Mrs. Amberson's behavior shortened the dinner a bit. As everyone scattered and Spencer and Scarlett gathered the dishes, she took his arm.

"I'm coming with you tomorrow," she said.

"Scarlett," he said. "Are you sure that's a good idea?"

Whatever had happened with Eric, whatever she felt... something much bigger was going on now. Something he didn't know about. Something he wouldn't have even wanted to know about.

"I am coming with you," she repeated.

SOMETHING IS ROTTEN IN DENMARK

The parking garage was a multistoried one, a winding concrete mess, overlooking an East Village street. The stage was being set up on the second level for the first part of the show, then the audience would be moved up to the open air on the third level for the big final act. Every part of the garage was being used, so there was commotion and equipment everywhere. The whole cast had been hard at work for hours.

Scarlett made it a point to stick close to Spencer, or it could have been Spencer making a point to stick by her. It was difficult to tell. There was a magnetic connection going on no matter what, probably in their mutual interest to avoid more heartbreak and scenes of violence. At the moment, all she could see of him were his feet. The rest of him was underneath the half-assembled stage with a drill, tightening a support. She sat next to him, supporting a light so he could see what he was doing. From here, she had a perfect view of Eric across the way. He was lifting lights out of the back of a van. He was wearing one of his tighter T-shirts.

She dug her fingers into her leg as hard as she could.

"Ow."

That wasn't her. That was Spencer. She had let the light droop, and now the drill had gone silent.

"You okay?" she said, peering fearfully into the void.

Before she found out what damage she had just caused to her brother, Mrs. Amberson swooped down on her with a handful of twenties.

"O'Hara," she said. "Go downstairs to that pizza place on the corner and have some food and drinks sent up. There's a health food store across the way, so you can pick me up a carrot juice. I'll get this."

She took the flashlight and assumed Scarlett's place, bending low to peer at Spencer in the dark little space under the stage.

"Has anyone ever told you how well-articulated your knees are, Spencer?" she asked. "I know several dance teachers who would love to get their hands on them."

Scarlett decided to avoid the stairs, as they had a pungent odor, so she wound her way down the two stories through the parking area. She didn't notice that she was being followed until she was almost at the street.

"Hey," Eric said, jogging up behind her. Even in the shadows of the parking garage, the greenish bruise that ran along his cheekbone was still perfectly clear.

Just standing across from him—it was different now. It was the most painful, messed up, exciting, and disturbing place in the entire world. It was an insult to some part of her, the part in the past that had been so happy.

"How's the...?" She pointed to the mark.

"It's fine," he said, running his hand along the bruise. "Accidents, you know? Luckily, Spence and I wear white

285

makeup. Can't even see it."

"Oh. Good."

No. This wasn't awkward *at all*.

"I wanted to talk to you," he said. "I thought we should. Sorry to chase you...I just wanted to do it in private."

"Talk about what?" she asked, warily.

He took a long, deep breath.

"You saw Sarah come out of my apartment," he said.

So Coco McBigGlasses had a name.

"Sarah was my girlfriend from home," he said. "When you saw me, I had just broken up with her."

"You had a *girlfriend*?" Scarlett managed to ask. "Even when we..."

She waved her hand to signify the kissing, all the moments spread out over the course of a week. That's what happened when you had no definition. Your life was reduced to floppy hand gestures.

"This isn't easy for me to admit," he said. "I just want you to know the whole story. Do you want to hear it?"

It was a very good question. He sat down on the cement barrier, and invited her to do the same. She stood.

"In my town," he said, "a lot of people settle down right out of high school. Something about that always scared me, that people got stuck doing that one thing for the rest of their lives, in that one town. I wanted to move to New York. I wanted to meet lots of people. Once I moved, I realized I couldn't go back to that. Sarah's great, but she was ready to... well, not get married right away, but stay together forever. That wasn't what I wanted."

"So why didn't you break up with her before?" Scarlett asked. "Before me?"

"I knew I wanted to do it," he said. "But we've...we had been dating for two years. I couldn't break up with her over the phone, or in a note. I had to do it in person. I owed it to her. Believe it or not, I was trying to be decent."

"Decent?" she repeated.

"It made sense to me at the time," he said. "I was going to do it when I went home to visit, after the show closed. Which is a while from now. So I kissed you. I thought if I didn't make a move, you'd meet someone else."

Ordinarily, that would have had Scarlett in hysterics, but she wasn't in a laughing mood. The familiar pang was kicking in. Eric wrapped his hands around the back of his head and gave a long, sad sigh.

"I thought I knew what I was doing until Sarah surprised me the other night. She drove all the way up from North Carolina. I had no idea she was coming. She just showed up at my door at one in the morning, exhausted. When you saw me the next day, we had just started the talk. It went kind of badly."

It made Scarlett queasy to think that he had had a girlfriend all along—a tiny, tan, perky girlfriend—a girl who had been around for *two years*. But he had wanted to do the right thing. He had gone about it a little clumsily, but the effort was there. And he had broken up with her under emotional duress. The mouse of hope was chewing its way through the baseboard of "you don't stand a chance."

"Don't think I don't realize how this all makes me sound," he said, his voice getting soft and drawly again. "And I don't

287

blame Spencer for what he did. He's your brother. I would have wanted to do the same thing. I swear I was trying to do right by everyone, but I hurt two people in the process. A punch in the face is understandable. And I like to think the bruise makes me look more rugged."

He laughed a little and poked the bruise hard with his finger.

"So," Scarlett said, "doesn't that make things okay between us now? I mean, if you're broken up?"

Eric got up and started to pace, digging his hands deep in his pockets.

"I don't know what I'm doing, Scarlett," he said. "I've been so overwhelmed since I moved here. I start NYU in a few weeks. When school starts, I'm going to be busy all the time, meeting lots of people. It might just be the same thing all over again. I hurt Sarah. What if I hurt you? I like you too much to get this wrong."

"I don't understand," Scarlett said.

"Me, neither. That's the problem."

They were both so wrapped up in Eric's confusion that neither of them noticed that someone had walked up behind them.

"Excuse me," a voice said.

Scarlett knew she knew the voice, but the wires in her head didn't send the information quickly enough, and she didn't care enough to turn away from Eric and look.

"The garage is closed," Eric said, not looking over either. "Sorry."

"I really need to speak to whoever is in charge."

Out of the corner of her eye, Scarlett caught the glint of very short, very silver hair.

COMBUSTION

Having met her old friends "Tara" and "Paul" by the entrance, Donna Spendler didn't need much more confirmation that she was in the right place. She strode inside the garage and up the ramp, with Scarlett and Eric trailing a few paces behind.

"That's the woman from the audition," Eric said quietly. "Why is she here, and why does she look so mad?"

"You really don't want to know," Scarlett said, hurrying to catch up.

Donna stopped short when she saw Mrs. Amberson leaning against the outside wall, smoking and issuing orders about the placement of the stage.

"I'm starting to think we need to come about five feet forward," she said. "That way we can have an even flow of energy around the space. Circular motion, like we're creating a whirlpool of drama."

"Amy?" Donna said. "It's been a long time. I *love* your facelift. I've heard you can get great deals on them overseas."

This was enough to get the attention of at least half the *Hamlet* crew. Mrs. Amberson didn't so much as flinch.

"Hello, Donna," she said stiffly. "I didn't realize you could come out in daylight."

Pleasantries thus exchanged, the two settled into an uncomfortable, grimacing silence. Spencer rolled out from under the stage, where he had been attaching a brace for one of the unicycle ramps.

"What a small world," Donna said, giving him a nod of greeting.

"It certainly is," Mrs. Amberson replied.

Everyone was aware of what was going on now, and all focus was on Donna and Mrs. Amberson.

"Why don't we go get a coffee?" Donna said. "We need to talk."

Mrs. Amberson didn't stop smiling, but her eyes had gone hard and fixed. She squared off in that superhero stance that Scarlett had first seen her in.

"I'm afraid we're a little busy right now," she said. "Maybe some other time. Tell you what. I'll *call you*."

She meant those last two words to sting, for whatever reason.

"I have some unfortunate news," Donna said. "In a few hours, this will all be shut down. I came down here to tell you that you should get your things out while you can."

"What are you talking about?" Trevor said, stepping forward.

"Peddle it elsewhere, dear friend," Mrs. Amberson said, puffing slowly on her cigarette. "We have full permission from the owner."

"The owner didn't look into the zoning laws carefully enough. You can't perform here. It violates several city ordinances."

"People have before," Trevor said insistently. "We're the third show in this place."

"They would have been booted out if the shows had made the radar at the right places."

"No," Trevor said. "No. The city *can't* kick us out twice."

Mrs. Amberson dropped her cigarette, jabbed it out with her toe, and stepped forward to where Donna was standing. She looked quite menacing.

"If you want to pick a fight, pick it with me," she said. "I'll settle this with you in private. Leave them out of it. They didn't do anything."

"This isn't me," Donna replied. "There's nothing I can do about this. You should have been more careful. A lot more careful. But we should talk, Amy. Give me a call when you're finished up here. You already have my number."

With that, she was gone, her shoes clacking in the echoey garage.

"What just happened?" Trevor asked. "Is this for real?"

Mrs. Amberson grappled for another cigarette.

"Listen," she said, fumbling with her lighter. "I think we're going to have to get creative. In twenty-four hours, we have a crowd of reviewers, agents, and other creative types coming to see you do *Hamlet* in this fantastic new production. And they *will* see a show."

Silence from the group. Just the echoes of their shuffles, and the shriek of an ambulance stuck in traffic out on the street. Mrs. Amberson's spell, which had held the cast in its thrall for weeks, was visibly weakening. Half the cast looked angry. Half looked down.

"There is nowhere," Trevor said. "Maybe we can find somewhere in a few weeks, but by then..."

"What about the rehearsal space?" someone asked.

"Another group already moved in there," Eric said.

Scarlett turned to see how Spencer was, but he had rolled back under the stage to block it all out.

"I found a place for you before," Mrs. Amberson said. "It's just a matter of..."

"We blocked this space," Trevor said, his voice rising with emotion. "We advertised for this space. We don't have the time or the money to move it now. We have lights coming, props..."

The reality of the situation settled on the group. Scarlett saw them all sagging. Stephanie started to cry softly. For the first time since Scarlett had known her, Mrs. Amberson looked a bit cornered. She turned and walked lightly to the other side of the garage, out of sight. Scarlett followed her. She was leaning against a concrete bumper letting the cigarette burn away between her fingers.

"It's possible that I didn't think this through," she said.

Coming from Mrs. Amberson, this was the equivalent of a grand confession of blame.

"They have to do the show tomorrow," she said. "Some of those people I got to come are very hard to pin down. It's in their best interest to do this show. But I don't think they feel like listening to me right now, do you?"

Mrs. Amberson smiled, but it wasn't a toothpaste commercial smile. It was a wry, soft one.

"What do I know?" she said, almost to herself. "I seem to have really done it this time."

292

"Maybe she was lying," Scarlett said.

"Oh, I don't think she was. I think she was being deadly serious. No, I think this is really Waterloo, O'Hara. And it's my fault."

Scarlett wasn't about to say, "No, it isn't." Because it *was* her fault. Sort of. Maybe not about the zoning issue, but bringing Donna into it.

"What do we do?" Scarlett asked.

"Well, I think I've done enough, don't you?" Mrs. Amberson opened and shut her cigarette case a few times. "I think the best thing would be for me to go back to the hotel and get my things together."

"You're leaving?" Scarlett couldn't keep her voice under control. "You're leaving *now*?"

"Every actress should know when to make a good exit. And I think you'll be better off."

She thought this over for just a moment, gave Scarlett one last smile, and walked off, down the ramp, away from the broken remains of the show.

ACT IV

In 1931, at the height of Prohibition, Lily "Honey" Vauxhall and Murray "Jinx" Rule produced a homemade gin so high in quality that it was even deemed fit to serve in the prestigious 21 Club.

Honey and Jinx produced their wares out of two adjoining rooms in the elegant Hopewell Hotel on the Upper East Side. Guests were scarce during the Great Depression, and high-quality gin even more so. The hotel's owner, Charlie Martin, never openly professed any knowledge of the goings-on. He did, however, install a "laundry chute" leading from a room called the Diamond Suite down to the basement. Laundry chutes are not typically installed in guest rooms—or, even more strangely, only one guest room, with no openings on any other floor. Nor can it be explained why the chute was outfitted with a pulley mechanism, much like the kind you would use to lower bottles of gin down to waiting hands many floors below.

Martin could hardly be blamed for going along with

the scheme. It was a simple move of survival, and, some would say, a public service.

Operations came to an end in 1933, putting Honey and Jinx out of business and returning the Hopewell Hotel to law-abiding status. The quiet little hotel has never again been host to any "Jinx," high or otherwise....

— "A ROOM WITH A BREW" FROM *ILLEGAL NEW YORK*

DESPERATE TIMES

"Well," Spencer said later that day, having returned from schlepping all of Mrs. Amberson's bags to The St. Regis in a cab, "what now? You have no job. I have no job. Wanna play Jenga?"

Scarlett didn't reply. She was flat-out on her bed, staring at the yellowing ceiling. Spencer was on the floor next to her, doing the same.

"Oh, right," Spencer continued into the silence. "We don't have Jenga. Wanna just keep pulling out your dresser drawers until it falls apart? Same thing!"

"I can't believe this," Scarlett said.

"I know. *Everyone* has Jenga."

"Why did she leave?"

"Maybe because all of our stuff falls apart when you touch it. Like Jenga."

Scarlett rolled to the side of the bed.

"If you say Jenga again, I'm going to tell Mom and Dad about that time you said you were going away for the weekend to learn about opera singing, but you really went to that party in the Green Mountains to try to hit on that girl, Anika.

Didn't you end up sleeping in a car all weekend because she wouldn't let you in?"

Spencer had been through this many times, but was prepared to oblige.

"Her *boyfriend* wouldn't let me in. Big difference."

"Oh, that's right," Scarlett said. "He threw you into the lake. Was the water cold?"

"I seem to remember it was a bit on the brisk side. It was January. In Vermont. I guess I was just lucky that the layer of ice was so thin."

"That *is* lucky."

"Yeah. I remember feeling lucky when I swam out and walked a quarter of a mile through the dark woods to the house, soaking wet."

"They let you in then, right?" Scarlett asked.

"Only because I would have frozen to death if they hadn't. Anika told me to go in one of the bathrooms and take off my clothes, and that she'd put them in the dryer. She said she'd bring something for me to put on in the meantime. I must have gone nuts from the cold, because I can't believe I made such a classic mistake."

"She didn't bring you any clothes?" Scarlett prompted.

"Surprisingly...no. At least, not mine, or anything like mine. Someone finally brought me these girly pajamas—pink ones, with kisses all over them. They came up to my knee and I couldn't get the top on, but it was something. It kind of sucked going home in them."

"I love those pajamas," Scarlett said.

"Well, I always like to get you something when I go away.

297

But want to know the best part? That girl who gave me the pajamas? Or gave *you* the pajamas?"

"I know, I know. She asked you out that Monday when you got back to school."

This story was one of their favorites during times of stress. It had entertained them both during several long nights at the hospital. It always provided a few moments of comfort. They let it linger for a moment in the stifling air.

"You know what?" Spencer said dryly. "I'm starting to think Mrs. Amberson and that woman knew each other. What do you think?"

Before Scarlett was squarely shoved into the position of having to reveal all or lie her face off again, the door opened and Lola came in.

"I have some bad news," she said.

"What?" Spencer replied. "Not today. Not when everything's been going so well."

Lola, of course, had no idea of the trauma of the morning. She stepped over Spencer to sit on the bed.

"We're empty," she said.

"Empty?" Spencer sat up on that one. "I thought we had those three guys coming in from Tokyo?"

"They canceled earlier this morning. That travel agency doesn't like us anymore. I think that guy in the Sterling Suite three weeks ago complained about the toilet."

"At least I don't have to deal with *that* today," Spencer mumbled. "Not that I don't love doing that job."

Lola slumped onto her bed. More than anyone else, she had been trying to keep things going. She had folded the toilet paper and researched the towels and gone without sleep. It looked like she took this as a personal failure.

"It's not your fault, Lo," Spencer said. "And it'll be okay. Some idiot will find us and check in. Someone always does."

Lola shook her head.

"This is bad, Spencer," she said. "Really bad. I'm not sure if we've ever been *completely* empty before."

"We're empty," Scarlett repeated.

The wheels in her head, which had been ground to a halt by the many obstructions life had thrown her way that day, started to click back into motion. The plan came in a rush, a chain of ideas loosely linked together. All of the fallen fruit of the summer gathered into one basket.

"Stay here," she said to them, shoving herself from the bed and stepping over Spencer.

"Where are you going?" Lola asked.

"Just don't go anywhere," she said again, as she grabbed her bag and phone. "I'll be back in an hour or two."

The St. Regis was one of the major grande dame hotels of New York, with a massive white and gold lobby bursting with uniformed staff and hung with massive chandeliers that were actually clean and operational. When she arrived at the plush, cream-colored room, Mrs. Amberson was splayed out on her bed. All visible parts of her were covered in something sticky and brown and wrapped in plastic, the rest was covered by a plush robe. Her chipmunky hair had been wound in a pink turban, and a woman in a long-sleeved tunic and flowing yoga pants was jamming her thumb into her right ear.

"Scarlett!" she said. "Don't mind Katiya...my God, Katiya, I think you just resolved all the problems from one of my former lives....She came over at a moment's notice, bless her, to unblock one of my chakras. Help yourself from the minibar, and boil some water in that kettle and make me a nice, hot cup of rosehips tea, will you? Bags are on the side table."

She was trying to act like nothing had happened that morning, just hours before—like the show hadn't exploded or she hadn't moved out. But Scarlett could hear the tension running underneath the sudden chakra crisis. She filled the little coffeepot from a bottle of spring water and took a soda from the minibar.

"Ginger wrap," Mrs. Amberson explained, pointing her chin at her wrapped body. "I do love ginger, but it..."

"Stings," Scarlett said. "I know."

Katiya got up on the bed, stepping onto the thick pillows, and straddled Mrs. Amberson's reclining figure like a triumphant warlord.

"Do you want your chakras done as well? You seem off-kilter."

Scarlett watched a smiling Katiya grind her elbow into the top of Mrs. Amberson's head.

"I'm good," she said. "Can we talk?"

Scarlett looked at Katiya meaningfully. Katiya didn't notice this. She had closed her eyes and started vibrating her lower jaw in a silent chatter.

"Of course," Mrs. Amberson said. She reached up and tugged on Katiya's long sleeve. "Katiya? Katiya, darling? I hate to break your meditation...I think I'm done for today. I'll unwrap and bathe myself, thank you. Same time on Friday?"

Katiya smiled, but didn't speak. She swayed a bit, then raised her hands high before collapsing, bowing to both Mrs. Amberson and Scarlett.

"She's just taken a temporary vow of silence and is only communicating through interpretive dance until the next lunar cycle," Mrs. Amberson explained after Katiya had slipped out of the room. "Trust me, it's actually a relief that she's not talking. I'm not sure I could get through another one of her analyses of my aura without killing her. Sweet girl, though. Magic hands. Come sit over here. I can't move."

Scarlett came over to the foot of the endless white bed and sank into a deep, high-quality mattress. It was amazing what other hotels offered.

"Why did you leave?" Scarlett asked.

"I told you, O'Hara. I never overstay my welcome. Now, I need to shower off these toxins. They're just flooding from my pores. Unwrap me, will you?"

She extended one plastic-wrapped arm to be helped up, but Scarlett did not budge.

"We need to figure out where to do the show," Scarlett said.

"I'm serious, Scarlett. The toxins will get back into the opened pores. I really need a hand out of this bed."

She continued extending her hand for help. It took a minute before she realized it wasn't forthcoming.

"Don't you think I've already caused enough problems?" she said, sinking back into the pillows. "With the show, you and Eric, your brother. And there is nowhere for the show to go in the next twenty-four hours. A week, two weeks, maybe..."

"Not a week or two," Scarlett said. "We're doing the show when we said we would. But the only way that's going to happen is if you and Donna get to the bottom of whatever has been bothering you for the last thirty years or however long its been."

"It's not that simple."

There was a knock on the door.

"Actually," Scarlett said, "it kind of is."

THE FINAL BATTLE

"That is a lovely, lovely look, Amy," Donna said. "It's so nice to see you twice in one day."

Mrs. Amberson was frozen, somewhat literally, in horror.

"Well, O'Hara," she said darkly, "this, I did not expect. I may have taught you a little too well."

"Yes, Amy." Donna took a seat on one of the blue French-style chairs opposite the bed. "I'm sure you deserve all the credit."

The pot hissed, signaling that the hot water was ready. Scarlett made two cups of the tea, handed one to Donna, and brought the other to Mrs. Amberson. They didn't speak; they just stared. Donna, with her cropped head and Mrs. Amberson, wrapped tight in plastic, unable to flee—together at last.

"Why has it been so long, Amy?" she asked.

"I've lived abroad for some time," Mrs. Amberson replied.

"You never called. You never wrote. It's been years and years. And now, this."

"And now, this," Mrs. Amberson said.

"Until the two of you settle your problem, other people are going to keep getting run over," Scarlett said. "What is so bad that you have to keep sabotaging each other?"

"I didn't sabotage anyone," Donna said.

There was a loud snort from the bed.

"All right, O'Hara. You want the story? I'll tell you the story. Have a seat."

Scarlett sat at the bottom of the bed, between the two, in case she had to get up and separate them.

"I'll begin, if that is acceptable to you, Donna," Mrs. Amberson said snidely.

"However you like. I'm dying to hear what you have to say."

"I'm sure you are. Our story begins a number of years ago, a fabulous time in New York. I had been living in the city for a year, auditioning, doing odd jobs. I had lost my apartment and was desperate for a new place to live when I met the woman who sits in front of me now."

"We met at an audition for the musical *Annie*," Donna said. "We were both trying out for the part of Grace Farrell, Daddy Warbucks's secretary."

"Which neither of us got," Mrs. Amberson cut in. "At the same audition, I met an actor named Rick, who was trying out for the part of Rooster. I had never met anyone so talented, so funny, so naturally able to entertain. This was someone you just knew, instinctively, was a star. The three of us went out for a bite to eat afterward, and two things came out of it—I found a place to live, and I also met the *love of my life*."

"My roommate had just moved out to go on tour," Donna explained. "Amy came at the perfect time."

"That was a happy time," Mrs. Amberson went on. "Rick and I were so in love, and I had a wonderful new friend and a snug home on Seventy-seventh Street. The apartment was small, but we didn't care. I had never gotten along with anyone so well. All three of us became great friends, going to auditions together. Everyone commented on what a good group we made, what amazing timing and rapport we had. And then, one day, the show came along...."

Scarlett had to swing her head back and forth to keep up, but so far, their story was exactly the same.

"It was a bunch of Hollywood types," Donna said. "They were trying to make a new late-night show. Something very sharp, very hip. They wanted ten players—ten of the sharpest, funniest, most versatile that New York had to offer. Rick, Amy, and I were all selected to go in for the first audition, which was three hundred people."

"We all made it through nine rounds, down to the last twenty," Mrs. Amberson said. "The producers seemed to love the chemistry among the three of us, and we were all sure, in our gut, that we had made it together into the group that was being sent to California. There, the final ten were going to be chosen. They said they were going to make their calls over the course of a week. That was a Saturday."

This is where they both stopped, showdown-style.

"Would you like to continue, Donna?" Mrs. Amberson asked. "I'm sure you remember what happened next."

"Of course I do," Donna said, unperturbed. "Rick got his call on Monday night. I still remember the three of us sitting around the kitchen table, knowing that it was happening. We were going to go off to California together and be stars. And then you and I waited. And waited. And waited."

"This was before cell phones, O'Hara," Mrs. Amberson

explained. "Or even answering machines, really. To make sure we didn't miss the call, one of us was in the apartment at *all times*. When we heard nothing by Wednesday, I was feeling horrible and sick, and Rick went out and brought home this."

She pointed stiffly in the direction of the cigarette case.

"Remember how I told you someone knew it was right for me, like he'd read my mind? Of all the objects in an entire city, Rick knew this was the one I wanted. I remember being so amazed, so in love, and my hope came back."

"That?" Donna said. "You..."

"I will take over from this point, thank you." Mrs. Amberson had gained total composure, and almost seemed glad to be telling her story. "Donna got her call on Thursday afternoon. There was one more day. I waited, never left the house, but the call never came. Three days later, in the bitter cold, they went off to California for the final round. My boyfriend and my best friend. I remember going with them in the cab to the airport in the snow, crying as the plane took off. I was so happy for them, and so heartbroken at the same time."

"We got to California," Donna jumped in, "and called Amy right away. We called her whenever anything happened. Over the next week, we were put through endless improvisations, interviews, and test screenings. They tried us in all the possible combinations. For me, it didn't work without Amy there."

"Oh, spare me..."

"Rick performed well," Donna forged on, "but I didn't. At the time, though, I didn't really know what the problem was."

"Lack of talent, I think," Mrs. Amberson said. "I was so proud of Rick. I was bursting. I planned to make my own move out to California to be with him and try to start my career there. But in the meantime, as luck would have it, I got a call offering me another part. On Broadway. Not a lead, but a good, solid part. Actors need to take work when they can get it, so I accepted. I told Rick I would be out to LA as soon as I could."

"Wait," Scarlett said. "*Neither* of you got the part on the show you wanted. Only Rick got in. What was the problem?"

"Thank you for asking, O'Hara. Weeks passed. I figured Donna would come home. But she said she liked the warm weather—it was horrible in New York that winter—and that she would be back in a few weeks. Rick and his new cast bonded, developed their characters, enjoyed themselves in LA. He called all the time to tell me he missed me. And then one day, two weeks before the big premiere, Rick called me one night, all tears, saying how sorry he was. He and Donna had decided that they liked the new climate, and each other."

"I was told you had long been on the rocks," Donna said.

"On the rocks! Did we *look* on the rocks?"

"So this is about Rick?" Scarlett asked. "This is about a guy?"

Donna was nodding, but Mrs. Amberson uttered a grave, "No."

"No?" Donna said.

"No," Mrs. Amberson said. "I found out the truth."

"What truth?"

"Evil deeds," Mrs. Amberson said. "They'll always haunt you. Three years later I was having lunch with a mutual friend, someone else who was connected with that show."

"The show never aired," Donna explained to Scarlett. "Some producer changed his mind, and the whole thing was pulled at the last moment."

"That's correct," Mrs. Amberson said, annoyed at the interruption. "My friend said to me, 'You were smart to turn that show down. It was a disaster.' Naturally, I had no idea what he was talking about. He said I had gotten the call and that the casting director had spoken to me."

Donna almost dropped her tea.

"You see, I *got the part*, Scarlett," Mrs. Amberson said, forcibly enough to cause a visible crack in her crust under the plastic. "They called me to tell me I made the last cut. They called me the next Gilda Radner on the phone, but *some woman* in *my apartment* pretending to be me said I wasn't interested because live television was too scary!"

"You think *I* did that?" Donna said. "This is the first I've ever heard of this! This certainly explains your actions. There's only one problem."

"The only problem I'm seeing right now is that I'm entirely wrapped in plastic and can't come over there and feel your peach fuzz."

Scarlett was worried for a moment that Mrs. Amberson would get up and throw her clay-encrusted figure on top of Donna. She struggled to move, but Katiya had wound her too tight.

"I never took any phone call," Donna said, standing up. "If you had gotten the part, I would have told you, Amy. You were my best friend, my partner. I couldn't get through the last audition without you. I couldn't keep up with Rick, so he played to the other actors."

"Don't try to deny it," Mrs. Amberson said. "The person on the phone was female, Donna. Who else could it have been? The three of us were the only ones in that apartment."

Donna fell silent. Mrs. Amberson gloated triumphantly.

"Can't get out of it, can you?" she said.

Donna didn't look like she was paying any attention. She drummed her nails on the arm of the chair.

"This is starting to make sense," she finally said.

"Oh, is it?"

"There *was* someone else, Amy," Donna said. "One time, when you were out and Rick was doing his phone shift—I came home unexpectedly and found another girl in our apartment, sitting at the table with Rick. Alice. The redhead from the audition. Do you remember her?"

It was hard to read Mrs. Amberson's expression, but she nodded slightly.

"He said she had just come by for moral support, and she left right away. But it gave me a strange feeling, like I'd caught him doing something, but I had no idea what."

"If this really happened, why didn't you tell me?" Mrs. Amberson said skeptically.

"There was nothing to tell. I didn't want to make you suspicious about nothing. All I had was a funny feeling and nothing to back it up. Then when Alice left, I remember that Rick said to me that he wanted to get you something special, to celebrate what he thought was going to be a big week. I suggested that case...."

She pointed at the red cigarette case.

"You did?" Mrs. Amberson was clearly shocked now. "How did you...?"

309

"You babbled about it all night when we were coming home from some party. You were a little drunk. I remember you said how much you liked it, and how you wanted to buy it when your big break came. He told me not to tell you that I suggested it. You believed in all that mystical stuff. He said you would take it as a good omen if it looked like he had read your mind. He seemed so concerned for you."

It was Scarlett's turn to fill in the silence that followed.

"Alice played you on the phone," she said. "Rick was lying to you the whole time."

"It makes so much sense," Donna said, nodding. "There were only ten spots on that cast. Rick told me later, when we weren't getting along so well, that he was never afraid that I'd get one of those ten places. He never thought I was good enough, but he was definitely concerned about *you*. He took you out of the running, Amy. *He* took your spot, not me."

Mrs. Amberson was still trying to process this rewriting of the last half of her life.

"But," Scarlett said, "at least it never aired, right? He didn't make it, either."

"Oh, he made it," Donna said. "That show never aired, but he started making the Hollywood rounds. That's when he realized he didn't need me anymore. I can't turn on the television without seeing his smug face. He eventually married two or three of his costars."

Mrs. Amberson creaked to life, cracking as she pulled herself up to her knees.

"That *bastard*!" she screamed. "That absolute bastard! Donna!"

310

Donna swept in and embraced Mrs. Amberson, mud and all. Scarlett let them have a few minutes of weeping and drama while she ate some chocolates from the minibar.

"So now," Donna said, when the tears had stopped for a moment, "you understand where I come into this. You conned me out of a job. You had someone cut off all my hair. Yes, I tried to find you. I wanted to know what kind of a complete psycho would do this to me. Wouldn't you?"

Yes, Scarlett thought to herself. *She would*. She felt too bad to even look over. She shoved more chocolate in her mouth.

"So you shut the show down," Mrs. Amberson said.

"No!" Donna replied. "I never meant for that to happen. I work for the New York tourist commission part-time, in the theater section. I have lots of connections. I was just calling around to get more information, to find out more about who was doing this to me. It turns out that the owner of that garage had been cited before. He rents that place out all the time for things it's not allowed to be used for, because of zoning or fire regulations or something. I accidentally tipped off the wrong people. I came down there to try to give you some warning, but you stormed off."

"The show," Scarlett said, glad that they had finally made it to the relevant issue. "We really need to take care of that now, and you guys can talk all you want when it's done."

"There's nothing I can do," Donna said. "That's well out of my hands. I'm sorry."

"O'Hara," Mrs. Amberson said, her face a muddy mess. "As much as it pains me to say this, I just don't think we're going to find a..."

FAMILY BONDING

A plan this bold, this ridiculous, required a total rewriting of the rules. This is why Scarlett walked past the Orchid Suite door and went down the hall to the Jazz Suite, where Marlene was engrossed in some show about a high school where everybody sang all their feelings to one another. She dropped down on the couch next to her.

"Listen," she said, "want to come down the hall and be in a secret conference with Lola, Spencer, and I?"

Marlene gave her a suspicious look.

"What?" she asked.

"Do you want to come down and talk with us?" Scarlett said plainly. "We're planning something, and we need you."

This direct approach confused Marlene, and she sat silent for a moment, chewing a cuticle.

"What is it?" she finally asked.

"Spencer's show is in trouble," Scarlett said, in a breathtaking show of honesty. "So we have to do the show at the hotel. And if Mom and Dad find out about this, they will have us killed, first individually, and then as a group. I'm asking you to help us pull this off."

"What will you give me?"

"I don't have anything to give you. I'm just asking you to do it because we need you."

Marlene ground her jaw a little before replying.

"You never ask me to do stuff with you," she said, still clearly not believing that there wasn't some catch.

"I know. But I want to change that, starting now. You can come with me, or you can go tell on us, whatever you want. The choice is yours. The door is unlocked."

Marlene made no move except to turn back to the television. Scarlett's stomach lurched, and she got up and went back to her room. Either Marlene was going to be lured in, or she had just destroyed the whole idea, and possibly Spencer's life.

Not that he looked too worried. Neither of them did.

Spencer and Lola were sitting on the floor of the Orchid Suite. Scarlett's clothes were everywhere, and Lola's dresser drawers were pulled out. The dresser itself was leaning frighteningly to the left.

"It's the *anti*Jenga," Spencer explained. "You add things until it falls over."

"We need to talk about the show," Scarlett said.

"I told Lola. She knows."

"I know," Lola said, carefully shoving a handful of Scarlett's underwear into the middle drawer. "That's why dresser Jenga seemed okay. Today's the day when things fall apart."

"I never thought I'd be able to get her to do it!" Spencer said. His worry had made him giddy. "Oh, I can so top that. Watch..."

Spencer reached for Scarlett's pajamas, but she snatched them out of his hand.

"You," she said, pointing at him, "on my bed, now. Over there. And you..."

That was to Lola.

"...get on yours. I need you to listen."

Like Mrs. Amberson, they were both so shocked at Scarlett's sudden change in demeanor that they did as she said.

"This show is going to happen," she said. "It's ready. There are over fifty agents, writers, and producers coming to see it. All it needs is a place to exist for a few hours. Now, let me explain the whole thing before you interrupt. Our dining room fits a hundred people. Not well, but it does..."

Spencer raised his hand, like you would in class, but she ignored it.

"We can use half the room for seating, and half for performance," she went on, thinking it through as she spoke. "You can have the entire rest of the hotel for a backstage. It's empty, for a start."

Spencer shook his hand impatiently.

"We can put the stage and the platforms on the far wall, under the windows. And with the sliding doors open between there and the lobby, there's plenty of room for you to ride your unicycles around."

Spencer couldn't hold his thought in any longer.

"You may be right. We could probably fit. And it is nice. But—and I don't think you'll argue this point—if I said to Mom and Dad, can I bring home the entire cast of *Hamlet* and maybe do the show right here, tonight, with fighting and unicycles riding around on our nice, shiny floors..."

"They aren't that shiny."

314

"...they would look at me and laugh. Not a funny ha-ha laugh, either. It would be one of those laughs that you make when you're really sad."

"They'll never allow it," Lola said.

"Of course not," Scarlett said. "We don't tell them."

Spencer and Lola looked at each other.

"We did this already," he said. "In the basement? Remember how it didn't work? Remember how we got caught? I think if we did it in the lobby, right in front of them, they might notice even more quickly."

"They aren't going to be here," Scarlett said, quickly grabbing the side of Lola's dresser as it suddenly realized that it was horribly off-balance.

"Where are they going to be?" Lola asked. "They never go anywhere."

"They're going to be on vacation," Scarlett said, shoving one of her sneakers under the short leg.

Spencer was intrigued by this point.

"Vacation?" he said. "Where did you have in mind? Florida? The Alps? Grand Canyon?"

"Nope."

"Okay," he said. "I'll bite. Where?"

She turned to Lola with a toothpastey smile all of her own.

"Remember how you owe me?" she asked.

The door to the Orchid Suite creaked open, and Marlene poked her head in.

"Oh, Mar..." Lola said. "Now isn't..."

"I invited her," Scarlett said.

Marlene proudly took a seat next to Lola. Spencer tried

not to look alarmed by this turn of events, and failed miserably.

"This is a big favor," Scarlett said. "And it involves both you, Lola, and you, Marlene. We need to get Mom and Dad out for a solid twelve hours or more. And the only way I can think to do that is to put them in or on something that they can't get back from. Like a boat..."

"Chip has a boat," Marlene said, catching on immediately. "He said he would take me on it."

"The good ship Chipster," Spencer said.

"You're not serious," Lola replied.

"You wouldn't have to go," Scarlett said.

"Well, why else would he take Marlene? And Mom and Dad for that matter?"

"She's got a point," Spencer said. "But you love boats, Lo!"

"I actually hate boats. They make me ill."

"Love, hate..." Spencer said. "Interconnected emotions."

"And you haven't puked on a boat since you were twelve," Scarlett added. "It was on the Circle Line."

"I remember," Lola said grimly.

"Chip has a nice boat. Fancy boat," Spencer went on. "And he did promise Marlene a ride."

"This is my *ex*-boyfriend we're talking about," she said.

"I know," Scarlett said. "It's asking a lot. I'm not asking you to get back together with him..."

"She's *definitely* not asking that..." Spencer cut in.

"This is just asking him to take a little boat ride," Scarlett finished.

"You mean you want me to use him."

"Stop it," Spencer said. "You're making me love you more."

"Look," Lola said, squaring off to Spencer, "just because I broke up with him doesn't mean you can still be mean."

"Mean? When have I ever been mean?"

"You were *always* mean to him. Do you know how scared he was of coming here?"

Spencer looked like he was going to swoon with joy on hearing this, but Lola had lost her earlier playfulness.

"I'm serious, Spencer," Lola said. "It hurt me. It really did. All those things you said about him. The two of you always thought it was funny, but it wasn't. I would never have said anything like that about someone you were dating, and you brought home some crazy ones."

Obviously, Lola had been holding this in for a while, and it stunned all three of them when it came flooding out. It certainly shocked Scarlett, who was still in the middle of delivering her amazing plan. Marlene loyally squeezed in next to Lola and wrapped her arms around her waist.

"I think half the reason I broke up with him was because you guys hated him so much," Lola said, sniffing a little. "Especially you, Spence. You never gave Chip a chance. I'll bet if Scarlett went out with someone you didn't like, you wouldn't pick on him."

Spencer looked down at his hands quickly.

"Don't be so sure," he said. "I think you'd be surprised."

"I liked Chip," Marlene said.

"I know you did, Mar. He liked you, too."

Spencer looked to Scarlett nervously. He swung over to the side of the bed to face Lola.

"I'm sorry," he said. "I didn't like him, but I never meant

317

to make you feel bad. I didn't think you were paying any attention."

"Not paying attention?" she asked. "How could I *not* pay attention?"

"Because you think I'm an idiot," he said, as if this was completely self-evident. "Seriously. I had no idea you cared at all about what I was saying."

Lola was shaking her head, unable to comprehend what she was hearing.

"Spencer," she said, "you're my *older brother.*"

This simple statement landed on Spencer like a pile of lumber. Plus, all three of his younger sisters were staring at him.

"Oh," he said.

He reached his hand over, but Lola preempted him and moved over to Scarlett's bed, wrapping him in a hug.

"Why would you listen to me?" he asked, as he hugged her back.

Scarlett put her hands over her eyes. This was the second major emotional catharsis she had caused that afternoon—and all she was trying to do was get people to get themselves together enough to put on a show she wasn't even in.

"Guys..." she said.

But Lola had earned her cry time. Marlene, moved by Lola's distress, came over and joined the group, attaching herself to both Lola and Spencer. Spencer glanced up at Scarlett helplessly from over the human pile that had formed around him.

Scarlett began to pace. She accidentally knocked the sneaker out from under Lola's leaning dresser, and it shifted swiftly.

By the time she had it propped up again, Lola had regained control and was sitting up.

"So," Lola said, wiping her eyes, "if you need help, I'll do it. I'll talk to Chip."

"Okay," Scarlett said, feeling more positive, "this is how it works. You guys set up the boat trip—make it long and make it far. The show takes a full three hours, plus at least an hour to clean up."

"Longer than that," Spencer said. "If we put up the stage, we're talking two hours minimum."

"Okay. So the show starts at seven, it's over at ten. We need at least until midnight."

"The ride to the boat basin takes about twenty minutes," Lola said. "We can drag our heels getting off and getting to the car, I guess."

"If you have to, make Chip say the boat stalled or something," Scarlett said. "Keep it out there as long as you can."

Lola sagged a bit. Spencer gave her a cheerful squeeze around the shoulders to hold her up.

"The part with Mom and Dad," Scarlett said. "That's up to you, Marlene. We need them both to go. We'll tell them it's like a mini vacation we set up for them, and that it really matters to you."

"A mini vacation with Lola's ex," Spencer said. "Cozy. We're going to need to do better than that."

"I can get Mom and Dad to come," Marlene said firmly. "What time are we supposed to go?"

"Ten in the morning," Scarlett said, calculating based on her many hours of observation. "That gives us nine hours to

319

get everybody in, and you guys can practice at least once. Does that sound possible, Spencer?"

"The whole thing sounds nuts, but nine hours—yeah, we could set up, reblock it, run it once. It won't be smooth, but it's possible."

"Okay," Scarlett said. "The first part is up to you, Lola."

Lola rose unsteadily.

"I'll do this," she said, "but..."

This was to Spencer.

"No remarks about Chip. Ever."

"I promise," he said seriously. "No remarks about Chip, ever again. For life."

Lola took her phone from the tipsy dresser and went out into the hall. Marlene followed to watch.

"I don't know what just happened," Spencer said. "I had no idea I upset her so much. *You* haven't been listening to anything I say, right?"

"Of course not," Scarlett replied. "I know way too much about you. Besides, I don't want you to punch me."

He shook his fist at her, then turned it on himself, knocking himself backward onto the bed.

"I'm going along with this, because the only other option is to do nothing at all," he said from his flopped position. "But it's never going to work."

"It *could* work. And you were the one complaining that you never threw a party at home. Now's your big chance."

"True," he said. "Might as well go out with a bang."

Lola's call was amazingly brief.

"It was almost like he was waiting by the phone," she said.

"He'll do it. He'll take us out on the boat whenever we like, for as long as we like. He'll get some food brought on. We'll have a picnic up the Hudson. Honestly, he picked up so fast, it barely rang once...."

This obviously stressed her out. She sat on the bed and twisted her hands together.

"All right," Scarlett said. "It's you now, Marlene. You have to convince Mom and Dad that you all need a family day out. Spencer and I won't be going, so don't stress the family togetherness thing too much."

"This is easy," Marlene said, cracking her knuckles.

Her confidence made Scarlett a little alarmed—but she was on board.

"I'll go down with her," Lola said. "To confirm the details."

The two of them left—Marlene strutted, glad to be in the middle of it all, and Lola looked like part of the defeated army.

"Are we leaving my future with Marlene?" Spencer asked.

"Yes," Scarlett replied. "We are."

"I really want to see this now," he said. "It's like getting to find out how you're going to die."

THE PLAYERS ARRIVE

At ten the next morning, Scarlett waved off Lola, Marlene, and their parents...who had reluctantly accepted the offer of a day off. They were obviously wondering why Lola was willing to go on a day-long boat ride with her ex, but Marlene's extremely skillful nagging did the trick. Plus, the prospect of a day in the sun and a catered picnic up the Hudson was appealing.

"You're sure you don't want to go?" her dad asked, as they got into the cab.

"Positive," Scarlett said. "I'm just going to hang out. I have those school passes to the art museum. Spencer and I might go over later."

Spencer had pretended to go to work that morning. In reality, he had long ago taken the day off. He was over at Trevor's, helping to pack the props and stage components into a van.

Mrs. Amberson had been lingering down the block in a cab of her own. She pulled up as soon as the Martin family cab drove away.

"O'Hara," she cried, stepping out. She was dressed in her

dancer clothes again, and carried a small suitcase. "What a gorgeous day for a subterfuge. Though, it does look like it might rain a bit later. Perfect for Denmark! I was up all last night talking to Donna—*so* much to catch up on. Visits to other old friends to plan."

"You mean Rick."

"I do," Mrs. Amberson said. "You're always very quick with these things, O'Hara. But that is not a matter for today. Today, we do a show!"

At ten-thirty, they all began to arrive. Paulette and Leroy came first, squabbling about one of Hamlet's cues. They dribbled in over the next half hour, filling the lobby with their many bags of costumes and supplies. Eric was one of the last to arrive, having come with the group in the van with most of the stage components and props. Scarlett herded them into the dining room, where Mrs. Amberson had taken position near the windows.

"Right!" She clapped her hands loudly. "We don't have a lot of time, so this is how it's going to go. Scarlett is in charge."

Scarlett looked down to see fifteen faces looking up at her, ready to take direction. Fifteen actors and theater people, when she herself had no real experience, no real idea what she was doing. Which meant that the only choice was just to start talking.

"It'll be easiest to use the second floor for your changing rooms, because it's closer. There are two good rooms there— the Metro and Sterling Suites..."

"Do *not* use the bathroom in the Sterling Suite," Spencer said. "Seriously. Don't even *look* at it."

"You have two ways of getting down, either the elevator, which is really slow, or the back stairs. For your backstage, to keep your swords and stuff, the kitchen is over here."

She led the group over and pushed open the door, revealing the cavernous space and its many antique appliances.

"We can take all of these tables to the basement, and the chairs are for the audience, obviously. So, I guess the first thing is to clear this room."

They didn't move.

"You heard her!" Mrs. Amberson said. "Let's get these tables out of here."

It took all day, even with everyone working at once.

First the carrying of all the tables—out of the dining room, through the lobby, down the steps. Then the van was unloaded, and all of the contents spread around. There was just so much. The stage was made of a dozen or so small platforms, each one only a few feet square, plus the supports that held them together. It took ten people to assemble. In the meantime, Scarlett carried all the bags and costume pieces up to the second floor and set up one room for girls, the other for guys. Scarlett kept passing Mrs. Amberson in the hall. She was ducking in and out of the various guest rooms and spiriting away objects.

By the time Scarlett got downstairs, the actors were in a full rehearsal, reblocking all their moves. She tried to watch as much as she could, but there was so much to do. She brought up the rain and snow mats that they usually put down in the winter to protect the lobby floor. These would provide a path for the unicycles to ride on. There were at least a dozen calls to answer about the where and when of the performance, fragile objects to move out of the way. The actors kept popping out needing hammers and water glasses and pieces of string... so Scarlett had barely noticed the time going by until an arrangement of flowers as big as her leg turned up. A half hour later, a truck rolled up, and two caterers stepped out, carrying crates of champagne and glasses.

"Social lubricant," Mrs. Amberson said, waving them in. "There are few problems in this world that a case of decent bubbly can't fix."

Scarlett tried not to give in to her nerves as Mrs. Amberson ordered them back to the kitchen with a seemingly never-ending amount of booze and ice.

"We're only having fifty people," she said. "Isn't this a lot?"

"I always figure on a bottle a person," Mrs. Amberson said. "Plus a little extra. And I invited a few more, just some people I thought of at the last minute. Don't worry. That room can *easily* seat a hundred..."

"Seventy-five," Scarlett corrected her. "With the stage."

"Close enough. Time for you to change, O'Hara. Put that nice black dress on. You're a host tonight. Make it snappy. You have twenty minutes."

As Scarlett went to the elevator, she heard Mrs. Amberson cheerfully barking out commands to the caterers.

"You can set the bar up here—and you have one basic instruction for tonight. *Refill.* I bought this stuff, and I want to see it used. No half-pours..."

She headed up with the general crush of people going to the second floor, stopping in to make sure they had everything they needed. Everyone was doing their makeup, so the mirrors were all full to capacity.

The fifth floor seemed comparatively silent. Scarlett dressed quickly, taking just a moment to get into the dress, apply her lipstick, and give her curls a fruitless shake. When she emerged, she heard voices coming from Spencer's room. Spencer emerged, wiping makeup from his fingertips. He was completely transformed—full white on the face and black lining around his eyes. He held up a warning finger.

"This is silent-movie makeup," he clarified. "Not mime. We had to apply more heavily because the light is different downstairs."

"Sure," she said. "Whatever you say."

Eric emerged a moment later. He had the same makeup on. The white only brought out the beautiful shape of his face, and his eyes looked darker. Scarlett felt the familiar lump rise in her throat, that ache that his beauty caused her. She swallowed it down hard.

"I'm going to go down to get things ready," she said, ducking past him. "See you there. Good luck."

Back downstairs, Scarlett was astonished to see that the front desk had been converted into a full bar, complete with an ice sculpture of a book as the centerpiece. It was already dripping a bit onto the parqueted floor. Bottles of champagne were lined up and ready to go, along with a small pyramid of glasses.

"Okay," Mrs. Amberson said. "I'm going to go gather the troops. It's your watch now. The guest list is behind the desk. When they've all arrived, or at quarter to seven, come and get us in my room."

She repeated her demand about no half-pours, then vanished, leaving Scarlett to fend for herself.

The guests started arriving a full half hour in advance. They were normal looking enough people, casually dressed. Most of them were happy to accept a glass of champagne and mill around, making phone calls or talking to one another. At quarter of, Scarlett went back upstairs to the Empire Suite. The entire cast was stuffed in there, squashed into every possible nook, with Mrs. Amberson on her normal perch in a black dressing gown and looking newly showered. Eric sat at the moon dressing table. The were all holding hands in a big lumpy circle and doing some kind of actor chant to get themselves ready.

"They're here," she said.

Mrs. Amberson nodded and dropped her cigarette, possibly on one of the arriving luminaries.

"All right," she said. "Spencer and Eric. Take your unicycles and get down there and buzz around the crowd. Entertain a little."

It was an odd little elevator ride, with Scarlett crushed between her brother in an oversized suit and a unicycle, and her former not-boyfriend in an oversized suit and unicycle... all riding downstairs together to entertain almost a hundred people who shouldn't have even been there. The elevator, in a typically uncooperative move, decided to go extra slow, and even stalled a bit between the third and fourth floors.

Spencer brought it to a halt on the second floor.

"Could you get out here and walk down?" he said. "We're going to make a big entrance out of here, so we need to make sure no one is in front of the doors, or we might, you know, kill them with unicycles."

Scarlett ran the last flight and got downstairs just in time to see the elevator door come open. Eric emerged first. He wobbled uncertainly through the guests. This was a fake out, Scarlett knew. He was completely steady on it. The guests laughed and moved out of his way. Spencer shot out a moment later, cutting a quick path through the crowd. He made a beeline right for the closed doors of the dining room. Scarlett watched in horror when he didn't slow down. He took them at full speed, knocking himself backward off the unicycle, doing a backflip through the assembled guests. They fell silent until he sprang up and pretended to be embarrassed. They exploded into applause and laughter.

Scarlett realized she'd been holding her breath. That was a new trick, and it looked amazingly real. Eric wheeled up next to her, lingering a moment by her side. He leaned in close—close enough that she could feel his breath on the side of her neck.

"Your brother is a show-off," he said in a low voice.

This was followed by a wink, then he was back in the crowd, wrangling them, making conversation.

The elevator door opened again. Half the cast had crammed into it, and they processed out. The other half came down the back steps. They all went into the kitchen in a strict formation, greeting the guests in character as they passed. The last person to appear was Mrs. Amberson. She wore a slinky black dress with a minor explosion of fresh violets on her shoulder.

"Ladies and gentlemen," she said. "Welcome to our show."

The doors of the dining room snapped open by unseen hands. Inside, all was shadow and flickering candlelight.

"Please take your seats," she said, pointing the way. "Anywhere you like. The show is about to begin."

Mrs. Amberson hooked her arm into Scarlett's and pulled her along.

"It's your show, O'Hara," she said. "Come and watch."

MEANWHILE, IN DENMARK . . .

It wasn't the dining room anymore. It had been completely transformed.

The chairs had been formed into curved rows facing the windows, which had been draped in familiar-looking silver and rose cloth. It took Scarlett a moment to work out the fact that what she was looking at was the bedding from the Empire Suite.

All of the normal overhead lights were off, except for the crystal chandler, which had been draped as well, to dim it. Her purple window sheers were much easier to recognize. The effect was amazing. They hung all the way to the tops of the surrounding chairs, suspended like a regal ghost. Some clip-on lights had been attached at strategic points to chairs, poles, curtains, and wall sconces. At least three dozen unprotected candles were placed around in the room in a blatant violation of the fire code. The smell of candles, extinguished matches, and the sweet stickiness of the champagne filled the air.

Outside, there was a flash and a loud crack of lightning, as if nature itself was getting in on the act. Rain pounded the window.

And then it began—the stylish *Hamlet*, old-movie style. There were the guards walking the perimeter, waiting for the ghost of the dead king. There was Hamlet, the angry college student home for his father's funeral and his mother's wedding, storming through the room in the suit that Scarlett had helped make. As all the adults conspired against him, he flirted with and tormented his girlfriend, Ophelia. His ridiculous friends on the unicycles came riding in, adding both comedy and a weird touch of menace. Spencer and Eric both spoke their lines well.

Scarlett began to lose track of time. She forgot that her parents were out on Chip's boat. It was Demark inside...a strange, gleaming Denmark, full of murder and conspiracy. She was startled when the lights went out, and a cast member with one of those movie clapper-things came out and announced a "cut." The audience broke into applause, and the doors were opened. Intermission was underway.

"For the love of God, keep them drinking," Mrs. Amberson said quietly. Her voice was happy, though.

Scarlett slipped out of the crowd and into the kitchen, where she found Eric and Spencer collapsed on the floor, drinking some water.

"How's it going?" she asked, trying not to look at Eric, or even really direct the question toward him. His presence was making her too crazy and queasy. "You scared me with that door trick."

"Yeah," Spencer said. "I just thought of that on the spot. I'm kind of glad it worked. Otherwise, I guess I'd be in the hospital or something. How do they seem?"

From the lobby, Scarlett could hear Mrs. Amberson's low, smoky voice.

"Well," she was saying. "They didn't actually use it in the show. But I'll tell you what it was later. It's not really for mixed company..."

"Happy," Scarlett said. "Entertained. I think Mrs. Amberson is telling her *Chorus Line* story for the five hundredth time."

"We should go back," Eric said, getting up. "Do some more party tricks."

"I guess you're right." Spencer drained the last of his water. They picked up their cycles. As they walked out, Eric brushed against Scarlett ever so lightly. If it was anyone else, she would have thought it was an accident. But one thing she had learned living with Spencer and knowing the tricks—those little moves never were.

"Don't think about it," she said to herself quietly. "Do. Not. Think. About. It."

When she stepped out, Mrs. Amberson immediately latched on to her and started introducing her around. She had clearly had a few glasses of champagne herself. Spencer and Eric decided to entertain the crowd with a fight this time, starting with a casual bump, like the one she'd just received. This escalated into slapping, and soon, the crowd had given them room to have a full-on smackfest. It was just a taste of what was coming later.

As an afterthought, Scarlett pulled out her phone and checked it. Three calls had come in—all from Lola. But there were no messages. She tried calling her back, but there was no answer. There was something a bit disturbing about this.

"Everyone!" Mrs. Amberson called. "Please get your drinks refilled and take your seats again. Take a whole bottle in if you like! We're about to start!"

Spencer staggered over in Scarlett's direction, landing hard against the wall, close enough that she could clearly see him strike it with his hand and cushion himself against the blow.

"What's the matter?" he mumbled under his breath. "Why are you staring at your phone like that?"

She clicked it shut.

"It's nothing," she said.

"Seriously?"

"Seriously. It's all good."

He had no time to reply, because Eric grabbed him by the collar in an unexpected bit of extra comedy and threw him into the dining room. Then he shut one of the doors and stepped in front, out of view of the people in the room. He stayed there just a moment too long looking at Scarlett, until Mrs. Amberson swept past.

"Coming, O'Hara?" she said.

"I think I should..." She looked at her phone again. "I think I should stay out here."

"Are you sure?"

"I'm sure."

She waved Eric inside, and slid the doors closed herself.

For the next hour, Scarlett sat at the desk, listening to the action and staring at her phone. She missed the big fight, but it was clear that the audience enjoyed it immensely. They were just burying Ophelia when Lola called again.

"Where have you been?" Lola asked. "I was trying to call you earlier...."

"In the show. What's wrong?"

"We're on our way home," she said cheerfully, at normal volume. Someone else was obviously there. "Yeah, probably about a half an hour."

Scarlett felt her heart tremble.

"Half an hour!" she hissed.

"Right!" Lola went on, using the same clear, chipper tone. "About a half an hour! It's been a great day! But it's raining! And we have to come in!"

"The show's still going on," Scarlett said. "Lola, do something."

"Right..." Lola said, still faking her way along. "Yeah...I don't know..."

"There are almost a hundred people here, Lola. There's an ice sculpture on the front desk, which is now a bar."

Dead air on Lola's end for a moment.

"I see what you mean," she said. She was still doing the happy voice, but there was a clear strain to it now. "I'll see what I can do. Okay! See you soon! Clean up that big party you've been having!"

There was a pained fake laugh, and she hung up.

"Okay," she said, glancing around quickly and settling on the caterers, who were slouched on some chairs in the corner. "I kind of need you guys to go. Now. As quick as you can."

"I'll take us fifteen minutes to bring the van around and find a place to park," one of them said.

"Fifteen. Whatever. Just fast."

They stared at her, a little slack-jawed. Scarlett wondered if she should just ask the caterers to beat her to death with the big, melting ice book. What did Mrs. Amberson do at times like this? Offer to pay people. Seem confident.

"Look, if you can do it, I'll make sure you get an extra... fifty bucks each."

This seemed to change the situation entirely. Suddenly, they were moving.

"What about this champagne?" the other one asked. "That lady bought it all."

"Uh...right. Fourth floor, Empire Suite. Door's open. And can you take these flowers up there, too?"

There was no time to be delicate. Scarlett threw herself at anything she could possibly move. She dragged the mats from the floor and threw them down the basement steps. When the final round of applause rang out and the cast had left the stage and made their way into the kitchen, she grabbed Mrs. Amberson while she was still in her seat, pulling her away from whatever conversation she had started.

"O'Hara," she hissed. "What are you...?"

"You need to get these people out of here, now," Scarlett said. "They're on their way home."

Mrs. Amberson clicked her teeth together once.

"Everyone!" she said, standing on a chair. "Due to the usual constraints of this performance space, I have to ask you to make your way out now. However, may I suggest that we reconvene at The St. Regis bar?"

These words had little effect. The group was busy chatting amongst one another. Scarlett had to resort to pulling up all the unoccupied chairs and stacking them, just to give them the idea that they really did have to go. It took fifteen minutes for the two of them to get everyone out of that room, but some still lingered in the lobby. Scarlett closed the dining room doors and looked at the scene in front of her. A stage, curtains and blankets and candles, ramps...There was no way it could all be hidden.

Some of the cast members began to creep out, not knowing that anything was amiss. Scarlett ran to the kitchen to find Spencer. He was sitting on the table, talking to Stephanie in a very flirty manner. He had wiped half his makeup off, roughly.

"I need you," Scarlett said, physically yanking him down.

"What?" he said, when Scarlett got him into a corner of the dining room. "What's wrong?"

"They're coming."

"They aren't supposed to be here for two hours!"

"It's raining," Scarlett said. "They are *on their way*."

"Like, now?"

"We may have ten minutes."

Spencer wheeled around and looked at the stage, the ramps, the piles of props.

"We can't move any of this in ten minutes," he said.

"I know. Just...get everyone in here and tell them what's going on. *Don't* let them go upstairs."

Mrs. Amberson had done a fairly good job of expediting the evacuation of the last of the guests. She had not resorted to physical violence, but she was pressing the last three lingerers out with a decided firmness. Scarlett was left alone in the lobby for a moment, her head swirling. There was a small trail of water where the melting ice book had been dragged away. There were obvious skid marks on the floor from where the unicycles had gone off the mats. She grabbed a champagne glass that was hiding under one of the chairs and a champagne bottle that must have just been set down. What else was lurking around? There was evidence everywhere.

"I have them all," Spencer said, coming in from the dining room. "Now what?"

"Now we...get them out?"

"And hope Mom and Dad just ignore the set?" he asked.

"First things first! First we get the cast away from here, and we..."

Scarlett had no idea what came after that. She spun around, as if the answer was hiding behind the front desk. There was no answer there, but there was another champagne glass. She shoved it into the file cabinet.

"I don't think we have to worry," Spencer said, while she was doing this.

"What? Why?"

"Because Chip's Mercedes just pulled up. And everyone is getting out. I believe the phrase 'game over' applies."

Scarlett wasn't giving up just yet, though. She flung herself at the dining room door.

"Everybody!" she screamed. "Turn off the lights, keep quiet, and don't move!"

She slammed the doors shut and threw herself against them just as her parents came into the lobby.

"Hi," she said, brushing the curls back from her eyes. "Nice ride?"

THE GREATEST SHOW THAT NEVER WAS

Lola was much paler than usual, and Scarlett got the impression that she had thrown up more than once during her day. She looked around at the deserted lobby warily.

"It was fine until it started to rain," her dad said.

Spencer came over and joined Scarlett in her door-leaning.

"You came home in your costume," her mom said, taking in the sight of his baggy, shortened suit. "And half your makeup."

"Oh, yeah," he said. "Long day, so I thought...thought I'd just come home. You get a better seat on the subway this way."

He reached up and rubbed some of the white makeup off his face with his fingers, as if he didn't have a care in the world.

Spencer held no real surprises for them. They had, after all, also seen him arrive home from the "opera singing weekend" in high school with none of his own clothes, wearing only a tiny pair of pink girl's pajamas. They nodded and busied themselves at the desk, sifting through the mail, checking the computer and phone for messages. When they were both bent over the desk, Spencer jerked his thumb toward the dining room door and mouthed the words, "They're still in there." Lola looked staggered and bit her lower lip.

"Why is the desk so sticky?" her dad asked, retracting the elbow he'd set on it.

"That was me," Scarlett said. "I...spilled a Coke. Sorry. Have to clean it up."

A noise came from the dining room. It could have been anything. A piece of the stage giving out. A sword hitting a wall. A unicycle falling over. And just under it, a tiny, tiny laugh. Spencer reacted almost as quickly as it happened, breaking into a massive coughing fit that drew even more attention.

"Ugh," he said, banging on his chest. "God, so many smokers in the cast. I think, I think I have secondhand smoke disease."

Again, their parents stared at him for a moment, and decided to dismiss it as Spencer doing something a bit odd, probably to cover up something he had personally done that they really didn't want to know about.

"I put some mousetraps down in the kitchen earlier," her dad said, walking to the door. "I'm going to check them, then I'm going to bed."

Spencer and Scarlett unconsciously moved closer together to guard the way. There was nothing to be done to stop him. And then...Marlene spoke.

"There's something in my room," she said. "I think it's a mouse, too. You have to come there first."

"There's one in your room? Why didn't you tell me before?"

"Don't worry about these," Spencer said. "I'll get them. I'm in the mood to kill something tonight, anyway. Why don't you guys go to bed? You look beat."

"Yeah," her mother said with a yawn. "They'll be there in the morning."

The three of them went to the elevator, leaving Scarlett, Lola, and Spencer behind. When the coast was clear, they opened the doors and released the cast.

It had been decided to keep as few people in the hotel as possible, to reduce the risk of being heard and getting caught. Only Eric and Trevor remained behind. While Lola and Scarlett carefully restored the Metro and Sterling Suites to order, Spencer, Eric, and Trevor worked all night taking apart the stage. They formed a human chain at four-thirty, passing all the pieces of the now-dissembled set down the line to the illegally-parked van. All the bedding and curtains that had been taken down were replaced in their respective rooms.

By a little after five, Scarlett was feeling like a zombie, making her way up and down the basement stairs in the endless cycle of moving tables. She had mostly been partnered with Trevor in the carrying sequence, but this time, she turned to face Eric.

"Hey," he said. He sounded as tired as she felt.

"Hi."

They'd been working side by side for almost eighteen hours, so the greeting was technically pointless. Eric sat on the edge of one of the remaining tables and rubbed at the traces of

340

white makeup around his jawline. His bruise was barely visible in the dim light.

"I feel like we were talking just a minute ago," he said. "I was trying to explain myself, and then everything blew up around us. Nothing ever goes normally around here, does it?"

"I guess it depends on what you think normal is," Scarlett said, not looking up. Looking up would be a disaster. She pretended to have an unnatural and absorbing interest in the containers of chemical de-icer on the ground by their feet. When you really put your mind to it, you could get interested in anything. You could almost like chemical de-icer.

It was a good thing, too, because it was only through the power of de-icer that she could withstand the next sentence.

"All I want to do is kiss you," he said in a low voice. "It's taking all I've got not to do it."

Scarlett could almost hear a circuit in her brain sizzling its way to extinction.

"So why don't you?" she asked.

"Because I don't know if you want me to. Do you?"

More than anything. Almost anything.

"Do you really think you'll dump me when you get to NYU?" she asked.

"Right now, no. But I don't know who I'll be then, once I'm there, once it all starts. Does that make sense? Am I the worst person in the world?"

There was probably some stupid self-help book out there that said this particularly brand of honesty was healthy and wonderful, and if Scarlett ever found that book, she was prepared to rip out those pages and eat them.

"I kind of hate that you tell the truth," she said, her voice cracking a little.

"Me, too."

"Eric?" Spencer called from the top of the steps. "You down there? You and Trevor need to get the van out of here."

"Got it," Eric said over his shoulder.

"I guess you'd better go," she said, coughing and getting her voice back to normal. "We should take this table up."

"I guess."

He made no move to kiss her. They each stood their ground on opposite sides of the table, staring at each other.

"It has to be up to you," he said in a low voice.

There were footsteps pounding down the basement stairs, and Spencer appeared. He regarded them both slightly suspiciously, but clearly had other things on his mind.

"The cops are coming down the street," he said to Eric. "The van is about to get ticketed. You have the keys. I'll get the table."

"Right," Eric said. "See you guys later."

It was probably better that it ended so abruptly, because Scarlett had no idea what to think. Spencer had to pry the table from Scarlett's grip.

"Do I even want to know?" he asked.

This is where the witty reply would have gone if she'd had one, but she didn't.

THE THING IN THE BOX

Scarlett woke to a clap of thunder. Outside of her bare window (the sheers had been brought up but not rehung), the sky had gone green. Lola was awake and standing at her bureau unstrapping something unfamiliar from her wrist.

"What's that?" Scarlett asked sleepily.

"Nothing," Lola said, shoving her hand into the Drawer of Mysteries, obscuring whatever it was. She moved something around and pushed the drawer closed firmly—so firmly that Scarlett was worried for a moment that whatever the thing was, it was alive and wanted out.

"I was wondering if you'd ever wake up," Lola said. "It's almost one in the afternoon."

Scarlett reached her arms over her head and stretched, then leaned over to look outside. The clouds were heavy and low. Naked Lady was bending over low to drag her potted tomato plants to safety, giving Scarlett a very clear view of her posterior assets.

"She's got to be doing that on purpose," Scarlett said under her breath. "No one bends like that."

Out of the corner of her eye, Scarlett saw Lola open the

drawer again. Whatever she had in there, it was causing her intense interest. She almost seemed afraid of it.

"What's wrong?" Lola asked. "I thought you'd be thrilled today. You don't look happy."

"Has your life ever been...complicated?" Scarlett asked.

Lola quickly applied some facial toner, then sat down on the foot of Scarlett's bed.

"Talk to me," she said. "Is this about Eric?"

"Is it that obvious?" Scarlett asked.

"Kind of. I saw the way he was looking at you, both the night he came for dinner and last night. I figured you'd tell me when you were ready. So what's the story?"

"I don't know," Scarlett said.

"Did you kiss him?"

"Yeah."

"More than once?"

Scarlett nodded.

"Is that what Spencer was being so weird about a few days ago?"

"Sort of," Scarlett said. "Spencer kind of...punched him."

"Spencer *punched* him? Our brother? Punched Eric?"

"Yup."

"Oh, my God," Lola said. "What did Eric do to you?"

"Nothing. I was upset, and Spencer just...it was kind of an accident. Sort of. Like I said, it's complicated."

"It sounds complicated," Lola said sympathetically.

"Eric seemed to like me, then he broke up with me because he was breaking up with his girlfriend...that's when Spencer punched him...and now he wants me back...except he's not

344

sure if he does. He's afraid that we're going to start dating, and then he'll meet someone when he starts NYU and hurt me. So he told me it's up to me whether or not we go out. Got anything in your magic drawer for that?"

The words came out in such a rush that Scarlett ran out of breath.

"I wish I did," Lola said, giving Scarlett's hand a squeeze. "On the good side, it sounds like he's being honest, and we like honesty. He's saying he doesn't really know himself right now."

"But shouldn't he just *know*? I know I like him. Why is this so hard?"

"Look, you saw Spencer in high school. He had loads of girlfriends, and they were always crazy and passionate, and then they would split up in a week. It doesn't always happen fast. Sometimes, you have to give yourself a chance to get to know someone, to figure out what you really want."

It was very much Lola's style to use Spencer as an example, pointing out things he had done wrong in the past, but she said it without any judgment in her voice. In fact, Scarlett got the feeling that she wasn't really talking about Spencer, or her, or Eric anymore. She was talking about Chip.

"What do you think you're going to do?" Lola asked softly.

There was a sharp knock, and once again, Spencer broke in just as this question was floating in the air. It was like he knew on some level that she needed rescuing from her own deep confusion. He had worked a full shift on no sleep, after a very long day, and it was showing in his face. Despite the comment she had just made about his past relationships,

Lola gave him a look of respect as he yanked off his sopping T-shirt. Evidently, the punching thing had made a good impression.

"Any news?" he asked. "Anything online? Why aren't you looking this up?"

Scarlett pulled the computer over from her bedside stand while Spencer wrung his shirt out into their wicker wastebasket.

"Nothing, nothing...wait...Something titled 'Hotel Elsinore.' It says..."

She skimmed down the part that explained the strange circumstances of the play in the hotel, blah, blah...

"Here we go. 'Eric Hall and Spencer Martin performed some of the best physical comedy I've seen on stage in years. Martin, in particular, is spectacularly gifted in everything from combat to clown, with razor-sharp timing. He is certain to be an actor to watch.' That's good!"

"Spectacularly gifted," Spencer said, pulling his damp shirt back on. "Razor-sharp timing? Actor to watch? Was that *The New York Times*? *The Village Voice*?"

"It was some guy named Ed," Scarlett said.

"Ed?" Spencer repeated.

"On a blog called Treading the Boards with Ed Mordes."

Spencer came over and took the computer to read the article for himself. Lola started messing around inside her special drawer again. She stared at something inside of it very intently, and then closed it.

"I think it's great, whoever he is," she said, turning around. "It's a great review. I'm going to take a bath—I've been cleaning all morning. Let me know if you find anything else."

When she had taken her robe and gone next door and started running water, Scarlett got up and quietly slid the drawer open.

"What are you doing?" Spencer asked.

Scarlett *shh*-ed him and pointed at the wall. Spencer nodded in understanding of the fact that Lola could hear them—but still looked puzzled by her actions. Scarlett carefully pushed aside the pack of fabulous wipes and some mysterious tubes of cream. She knew what she was looking for the moment she laid eyes on it. It was a dark red box marked "Cartier." She removed it carefully from the drawer and brought it over to Spencer.

Inside the box was a white-gold watch with a single diamond on the face.

"Holy..." Spencer said under his breath as he took the box. "This thing even smells expensive. This is probably a few grand worth of watch."

"She's not wearing it," Scarlett said.

"But she took it. She accepted it. I have a bad feeling that Number Ninety-eight is going to..."

Scarlett elbowed him.

"What?" he asked.

"You're not allowed to call him that anymore," she said, taking the watch and carefully replacing it in the drawer.

"In front of Lola."

"He saved you yesterday," Scarlett said. "You have to be nice to him now. We both have to try. We have to practice."

"But..."

"You made Lola *cry*," Scarlett said, dropping her voice even lower. "Remember?"

Spencer looked like he felt a little betrayed by this remark, and then held up his hands, admitting his shame.

"Okay," he said. "Okay. I will be nice about the watch that Chip spent many thousands of dollars on to impress my sister, who he isn't even dating right now. And should she decide to date him again, I will never call him Ninety-eight or ask him whether his major is Letters or Numbers."

"Thank you," said a voice from the doorway.

Lola stepped around Scarlett, removed some product that she had forgotten to bring to the bathroom, and pushed the Drawer of Mysteries closed. She didn't appear to care too much that Scarlett and Spencer had been going through her things.

"And no," she said, "I haven't made up my mind yet about what to do about Chip or the watch. It is worth about eight thousand dollars—I know you'll just look it up online later. But I did just see Dad on his way down to their room, and they want to talk to you about the plans for tomorrow night. You know, when you give them tickets to a show and perform *Hamlet* for them, and they can see that you have an acting job?"

"This is where I take a long, long nap," Spencer said. "And in my happy, happy dreams, this problem goes away. And those Dutch twins who love tall and weedy New York actors come and offer to help me *prepare* for my role. And we all put on the fuzzy squirrel outfits and get big bags of nuts...I'm revealing too much about my internal life, aren't I? It's weird between us now, isn't it?"

He yawned hugely.

"I'll call Mrs. Amberson," Scarlett said. "She's supposed to be doing all the follow-up."

"This is the good part about being this tired," he said. "You stop fearing for your life. This is it, beloved sisters of mine. This is the day that it really all gets decided or it all falls apart. So do me a favor..."

He got up and left the Orchid Suite with a slow, dragging walk.

"...don't wake me up. I have a bad feeling those Dutch twins are the only fans I'll ever have."

THE GIRL IN THE MOON

Mrs. Amberson had left a voice mail for Scarlett while she was asleep.

"Please tell your parents I will be coming along to family dinner night, as usual," she said. "They very kindly extended me an invitation. I have some very exciting news."

Scarlett's multiple attempts at calling back to get this news were unsuccessful. Mrs. Amberson was simply not answering.

By five, she had to go rouse Spencer, who was deeply asleep fully dressed in his wet clothes. For some profoundly disturbing reason, he shouted the word "peanuts" when Scarlett finally shook him back to consciousness.

"Anything?" he asked, rubbing his eyes.

"Mrs. Amberson is coming over," Scarlett reported. "*Something* happened, but she won't say what."

Spencer shook his head hard to get the blood flowing and blinked at her a few times. There were still tiny specs of white makeup around his ears that he hadn't gotten off—the last evidence of the show that probably was no more.

"No matter what happens tonight," he said, "even if I walk out of dinner as a culinary student and not an actor...I owe you.

I want to tell you this now, because I have a bad feeling that I'm not going to be the best person to be around for a few weeks. I won't forget what you did. And we had fun, right?"

He smiled, but it sounded like he was conceding defeat in his mind.

Downstairs, two pans of the lasagna of death had been roasted into existence. The rolls and salad had been purchased premade, so they were edible. A cab rolled up and Mrs. Amberson stepped out, wearing her brown karate ensemble. Scarlett met her on the sidewalk.

"I love these early dinners," she said. "So serene, and good for the digestion. We should always eat this early."

"What's going on?" Scarlett asked. "Have any agents contacted you? Have you heard anything about where to move the show?"

"All will be revealed," she said, in an irritatingly sly way.

She took out her cigarette case and opened it. It contained no cigarettes. Instead, it was full of long toothpicklike objects.

"Bamboo soaked in tea-tree oil," she explained, popping one in her mouth and chewing on it ferociously. "I've given up smoking. My acupuncturist says these are very soothing."

She looked like she was about to gnaw it up and eat it, which probably wasn't the idea. She swanned along inside, leaving Scarlett to follow. She greeted the Martins effusively, even Marlene, as if she hadn't seen them in decades.

"Funny thing," she said, sniffing the air. "Quitting smoking has left me ravenous. I can't wait for dinner."

Much to Scarlett's amazement, Mrs. Amberson took a huge helping of the scary lasagna, a chunk of bread, two scoops of

351

salad, and she even accepted a large glass of the instant iced tea. She dug right in, eating and making small talk for a full half hour, rambling on about anything and everything but the show.

"I've been doing a little research," she said, setting down her fork in triumph. She had cleaned two plates. She removed a book called *J. Allen Raumenberg: Design for an Age* from her bag. "The man who designed this hotel...do you know what he went on to do afterward?"

"Did he invent Jenga?" Spencer offered.

Mrs. Amberson clearly had no idea what Spencer was talking about, but smiled like she did.

"No. He went on to make things like this."

She held the book out, story-time style, showing fabulous black-and-white pictures of stage and movie sets.

"J. Allen Raumenberg was one of the greatest set designers of the golden age of Hollywood and Broadway. Your home was essentially a test run for a dozen different sets. Here, do you see?"

She flipped a few pages and held up a photo from a film called *Midnight Journey*. It could have been a picture of the Empire Suite, except you could see the Chrysler Building through the window.

"You see," she said, "I chose this hotel for two reasons. One, I wanted the lovely family atmosphere that was promised, and certainly delivered. The second was that I wanted New York glamour—real New York glamour. The kind you can't just manufacture somewhere. I was so sad to leave...but I've developed terrible allergies. I'm sure Scarlett has told you.

Absolutely terrible. I had to move to a place with a centralized air conditioning system with air filters. Hence the quitting of the smoking."

This, Scarlett felt, probably had a lot more to do with the origins of the cigarette case, and not this imaginary illness.

"We're very excited to see the show tomorrow," her father said, finally bringing the dreaded topic to the fore. "We've been waiting for weeks. Sounds like it's going to be great."

Spencer physically braced himself, then looked his parents and Mrs. Amberson right in the face, ready to take the bullet that was coming.

"Yes," she said. "About that….A very funny thing happened. I ran into an old friend of mine, a very good friend named Donna. It was thanks to Scarlett that we got together, actually."

Spencer shot her a look of confusion. This was going in an odd direction.

"Donna works for the tourist commission, for Broadway really, helping advertise the arts to tourists. I was telling her how your hotel is sadly empty much of the time. She had the most *remarkable* idea. It turns out there are loads of amateur theatrical groups who want a taste of real New York action, up close and personal with the performers. She deals with them all the time. 'What if,' she asked me, 'what if there was a way to bring a show *into* a hotel? Let people see the process really up close? Spend time with the actors, see the preparation.' An extraordinary proposition, really."

There was a desperate, scary silence, which Mrs. Amberson moved quickly to fill.

"I couldn't follow how that could possibly work either, but

she pointed out to me that I, as the director of a theater company, could potentially join forces with you, bringing the production of *Hamlet* here."

"Here?" her mom said. "But I thought this show was a very successful company, in a theater...well, some kind of theater downtown."

"Oh, yes," Mrs. Amberson said. "It is. That's what I told her. I said, 'Donna, it's a nice idea, but we're about to have a massive success on our hands right where we are.' But she kept talking and managed to convince me that this just might work out. Why, I imagine that with a little rearrangement, we could perform in this room with no trouble at all!"

"But..." Scarlett's mom said.

"Then I got to thinking," Mrs. Amberson went on, skating over the interruption. "With the personal service you provide here, you'd really be able to give these people the trips they've been dreaming of! Large hotels are so impersonal. But here, they could get advice on the hottest shows to see—aside from *Hamlet*—right from the in-house actors."

"And shopping," Lola cut in. "People love to come here to shop. I could show them where to go. I could even take them around."

"A personal shopping guide!" Mrs. Amberson said, clapping her hands. "A stroke of absolute genius!"

"It's an interesting idea your friend had," Scarlett's dad said, trying to be polite, "but I'm not sure it would draw more people here."

"It's like you're reading my mind," Mrs. Amberson replied. "I said, 'Donna, it sounds good, but can you actually get groups to come up and do this?' And you know what? She typed some things into her computer, made a few phone calls...well, let's see."

She produced a thick swath of papers from her voluminous bag.

"A group from Florida," she said, glancing through them. "They'd be interested in coming for a week. A Japanese tour operator is interested for three days. A small company from England, four days. Another from France. A community group from Ohio. All of these people are looking to book soon, before the rates go up in the fall. There's probably enough here to fill this whole place for a month, if you were, you know, interested."

She pushed the pages over, all innocence. Scarlett's dad reached over for them, wide-eyed.

"I had another thought," Mrs. Amberson said, allowing a triumphant smile to sneak onto her face. "My sudden attack of allergies could probably be remedied by one of those portable air filters. So if you were interested in doing this, I could come back and take my old room, if it's available. In any case, purely for your information."

She concluded this performance by taking a huge bite out of a roll. The others didn't know it, but Scarlett could read her expressions now. This one said, "I'm so good, I'm going to eat this baked good made with bleached flour."

There was a long pause during which Scarlett felt that many things about both their immediate and long-term futures were probably being decided.

"Mrs. Amberson," Scarlett's mom said, "would you mind giving us a minute?"

"Not at all! I'm used to taking smoking breaks, anyway. The habit is still there, even though the cigarettes are gone. I was just about to excuse myself for a moment."

Scarlett's mom snapped into action the moment she was gone.

"Lola, I need you to check all the rooms and storage closets, make sure there's nothing we need to order. Marlene, you're going to do the dishes tonight while your dad and I call all these people."

Marlene looked up in surprise. Frankly, so did everyone else. Marlene *never* got asked to do anything. She opened her mouth, possibly to object, then closed it decisively.

"Come on, Mar," her dad said, getting up. "I'll show you how to do the first few. We'll get a system going."

Lola got up as well to start her round of the hotel. This left Scarlett and Spencer.

"Why do I have the strangest feeling that there is something you all want to tell us?" their mother said.

"Tell you?" Spencer asked, looking to Scarlett and shrugging. "I don't think so..."

"Not me," Scarlett added, trying to plaster on an innocent expression.

More troubling silence, then she lost control of the serious expression she had been trying so hard to hold.

"You two help Mrs. Amberson get her things and move her back in. Oh, and, Spencer..."

She reached into her pocket and produced a card.

"Someone came by and left this for you. He said he saw you here last night. I won't even *pretend* to know what that means."

Spencer took the card and read it, then quickly passed it to Scarlett. It read: TOM HICKMAN, COMMERCIAL CASTING. Along the bottom, there was a line added in pen that said, "Call tomorrow re: washing machine commercial."

A few hours later, Mrs. Amberson sat on her perch in the Empire Suite, twitching like a bug. She had chewed up a dozen tea-tree sticks while waiting for Spencer to carry up all her bags from the lobby. She seemed to have acquired some more things during her stay at The St. Regis.

Spencer collapsed onto the bed next to Scarlett after the last bag.

"I've been thinking," Mrs. Amberson said, pulling out another stick. "You're going to need an agent. You don't have one, do you? Commercial or straight?"

"No," Spencer said. "I could never get one before. No one would talk to me. I was way too unemployed. I'm still unemployed. It's just an audition."

"It's more than that," she said. "They've seen you. This is a callback, at the very least. I have a good feeling about this."

Even exhausted, Spencer was crackling with energy from all the news.

"You know," Mrs. Amberson said, "at a big agency, you just get lost in the shuffle. They spend all their time on stars and big-money clients. What you need is an agent with a small list, dedicated to building your career. Someone who wants to nurture you to the top, *make* you a big client."

"Do you know someone like that?" Spencer asked.

There was a light in Mrs. Amberson's eyes that Scarlett

immediately recognized.

"I believe I do," she said. "Someone with years of experience in the theater world, who knows their way around a contract, someone with nerves of steel and total dedication. Someone who is just starting to build a list of new clients."

"Who is it?" Spencer said. "Can you put me in touch, maybe give me a recommendation?"

Mrs. Amberson smiled her slowest, most toothpaste-commercial ready smile.

"There's some money on my writing desk," she said. "Do me a favor and run to the corner deli and get me a pack of licorice? I have such a craving for it. I'll make a call or two while you're gone. And pick up one of those organic protein smoothies they make. That's for you. Make sure to drink it. They're delicious."

After Spencer sprinted from the room, Mrs. Amberson looked to Scarlett.

"One of the first goals will be to put ten pounds on him," she said. "Muscle mass. Also, I wonder if that girl Stephanie is ever going to stop being so annoyingly professional and finally ask him out. That is a situation to watch over the next few weeks, O'Hara. I'm sure there's something we can do about that....I like my clients to be happy and fulfilled. Keeps them out of the tabloids."

"You're not an agent," Scarlett said. "You don't have clients."

"I'm not an agent *yet*. But I will be as soon as I call one of my lawyer friends and have her draft me up a contract for your brother to sign. I'm perfect for this, Scarlett. Molding people. Forming relationships. Lunching. What do you think

I should call it? I was thinking AA for Amberson Agency—but that acronym is taken. But hey, most actors have belonged to the original AA, they might just want to join the new one as well. I could get a gorgeous monogram made. The cards and stationary will be exquisite. A double A, linked together and overlapping. Oh, that'll look like an M, won't it? Maybe I'll just do back-to-back *A*'s, then."

As usual, Mrs. Amberson's priorities were well in order.

"I'll need an assistant, of course," she went on. "Someone reliable. Someone *invested*."

"I start school in a few weeks," Scarlett said warily. "There's so much to do and..."

"Then it's perfect! You couldn't find a better after school job than this. What is there to lose?"

A lot, actually. Like her sanity.

"We'll have to go to shows, premiers, gala events! Who else is going to pay you to be entertained? Starbucks? I don't think so. Maybe we'll need to do a few teeny-tiny phone meetings during the day, but that's easily manageable. It won't be disruptive at all!"

Scarlett felt a familiar thrumming in her head. Working for Mrs. Amberson in the summer was one thing, but during school was an entirely different matter. There would be no time for a job like this, a job which was clearly the path of doom, destruction, woe, failed classes, possible imprisonment...

"I'll pay you a commission," Mrs. Amberson said, giving Scarlett a sly look. "If this business is a success, which it will be, you could end up making your entire college tuition. And what will you be working for? Success for your brother!

Happiness for your family! Think about *that*, O'Hara. In the meantime, I know wonderful people in the design department at the Manhattan Theater Club. We can get a whole new set built. This starts *now*."

"What, now, now?"

"There is only one now, O'Hara," she said, springing from her perch. "Oh, that was good! Quote me on that. Where is your notebook? We are so behind on work on my book, you realize that don't you? Anyway, I'll be down the hall."

She grabbed her purse and flew out the door.

Scarlett took a long look at herself in the moon mirror. Puffy curls. Check. Chipped nail polish. Check. Improbable new job. Check. And somewhere out there, a guy who may or may not have been her boyfriend.

"The elevator is here, O'Hara!" Mrs. Amberson screamed from the end of the hall. "I'm holding the door! Do you think William Morris spent all his time sitting around in hotel rooms? Are you coming?"

"Do you hear that?" Scarlett asked her reflection. "That's the sound of your future. Is that really what you want?"

The reflection just grinned in reply. Apparently, that *is* what it wanted.

"Coming!" she called.

Now was now, and there was a show to do.

360